Lake Shore
SPLENDOR

A REDEMPTION SHORES NOVEL

JENNIFER RODEWALD

Copyright © 2023 Jennifer Rodewald.

Lake Shore Splendor

Print ISBN: 979-8-9874510-4-5

All rights reserved. No part of this publication may be reproduced, distributed, or transmitted in any form or by any means, including photocopying, recording, or other electronic or mechanical methods, without the prior written permission of the publisher, except in the case of brief quotations embodied in critical reviews and certain other noncommercial uses permitted by copyright law. For permission requests, write to the publisher, addressed "Attention: Permissions Coordinator," at the address below.

Any references to events, real people, or real places are used fictitiously. Names, characters, and places are products of the author's imagination, and any similarities to real events are purely accidental.

Front cover images from Shutterstock. Design by Jennifer Rodewald.

First printing edition 2023.

Rooted Publishing

McCook, NE 69001

Email: jen@authorjenrodewald.com

https://authorjenrodewald.com/

All Scripture quotations taken from the Holy Bible, New International Version®, NIV®. Copyright ©1973, 1978, 1984, 2011 by Biblica, Inc. Used by permission of Zondervan. All rights reserved worldwide. www.zondervan.com The "NIV" and "New International Version" are trademarks registered in the United States Patent and Trademark Office by Biblica, Inc.

Scripture quotations marked (NLT) are taken from the *Holy Bible*, New Living Translation, copyright ©1996, 2004, 2015 by Tyndale House Foundation. Used by permission of Tyndale House Publishers, Carol Stream, Illinois 60188. All rights reserved.

CONTENTS

1. One — 1
2. Two — 8
3. Three — 13
4. Four — 21
5. Five — 29
6. Six — 40
7. Seven — 48
8. Eight — 57
9. Nine — 72
10. Ten — 80
11. Eleven — 90
12. Twelve — 99

13.	Thirteen	112
14.	Fourteen	124
15.	Fifteen	130
16.	Sixteen	136
17.	Seventeen	148
18.	Eighteen	160
19.	Nineteen	170
20.	Twenty	179
21.	Twenty-One	185
22.	Twenty-Two	191
23.	Twenty-Three	200
24.	Twenty-Four	211
25.	Twenty-Five	225
26.	Twenty-Six	233
27.	Twenty-Seven	237
28.	Twenty-Eight	247
29.	THE END	254

One

Fall brought all kinds of wonderful things to Luna, Montana. Vibrant yellows on the aspens, creating a landfall of brilliant gold against the rise of the Rocky Mountains. Frigid mornings that made Hazel's breath magical white puffs against the backdrop of deep-green pines. And the warm aroma of caramel apple pie in Janie's Café.

It was the last on that list that Hazel enjoyed the moment she pushed through the door and strode into her best friend's establishment. After a week of not being in town and not seeing Janie, and double that space of time of not seeing Bennett, she had been ready for a good visit and satisfying comfort food.

Janie smiled warmly. "Hey, girl. Glad to see you can still find your way down the mountain."

Hazel shrugged. "It's easier now. Much as I hate to admit it, Hunter's truck does make the trip less of a... well, trip."

Janie snorted. "Ah. The stubbornness of a Wallace. Glad to see it *can* be tamed."

"Huh." Hazel accepted the warm mug, wrapping her chilled fingers around the white ceramic and inhaling the bold richness of Janie's coffee. Actually, it wasn't Janie's old brand of coffee. Her friend had switched to Bennett's favorite brand.

Goodness, but that man was a convincing force.

"Some things are worth bending on," Hazel muttered, more to herself than to Janie, her thoughts still tangled around Bennett. Some things, yes. They were worth compromising.

But what about the *one* thing that had wedged between her and the man who had wrangled her heart?

"So you're good with Hunter's lodge now?"

Jarred back to the conversation, Hazel jerked her gaze from the black depths of her coffee. Janie pressed her lips together, making her expression all anxious. Sitting across from her at the polished blue-stained pinewood bar, Hazel considered carefully. Her mind raced through the seismic shifts that had reshaped her world in the last year. Almost a year before, Bennett Crofton had crashed into her world, and nothing had been the same since. Now? Now her brother had come home to stay, and he was going to build a monster of a cabin and call it a hunting lodge—the Lake Shore Splendor.

Was she good with that?

After a pause, she released a slow breath and nodded. "I don't know that *good* is the right word. But I see what Hunter was saying—that he needs to find a life here. And I know Bennett is right—I should be grateful that Hunter is back. And I am. And I'm grateful that Hunter wants to include me, even if I don't love the idea of a big lodge filled with strangers just on the other side of the ridge."

"But you're in?" Her blue eyes dancing, Janie pressed her palms against the counter and leaned in. "You're going to do the guided hunts?"

Hazel shrugged. Interesting that Janie seemed to know all sorts of details about Hunter's hopes for the lodge. How much time, exactly, had those two spent together in the past few weeks? And was Janie eager for Hazel to be excited about this? Or was there something else stirring her interest?

Sheesh. Hazel had never been good at understanding other people. Why should she start unwinding the complexities now? Take care of herself. That was what she should focus on. That had forever been her focus before. Should everything change now?

"It's what I've always done." She summoned a smile as she thought of Hunter's enthusiasm for her to be a part of his plans. That meant something. No. That didn't just mean something.

It meant a whole heaping mountain of somethings.

Emotion welled up from the depths of her smothered heart as she thought back to what Bennett had said when he'd urged her to reconcile with her brother. *He loves you, Zel . . . Hunter only wanted to take care of you.* Hazel had been dumbfounded and deeply moved to discover that Bennett had been right. And Hunter was still trying to take care of her.

This time she understood. She was listening. And she saw Hunter for who he'd been all along—her big brother trying to do best by her, even when she was too angry and nearsighted to understand.

She was loved. The idea of it—the deep stirring of her soul at that revelation—nearly stole her breath. Loved not only by the brother she thought had rejected her and abandoned her, but by a really *good* man who wanted only good things for her.

So though she didn't love the idea of the Splendor, Hazel was determined to try, to support Hunter this time around. Because for all their rocky past, she loved that dumb brother of hers. As she thought on him—about the way Hunter had taken her around the footprint of that eight-thousand-square-foot mountain monstrosity, then showed her where the carriage house would be and the new barn and corrals—a grin pulled on the corners of her mouth.

"Ah, she even smiles about the future." Janie giggled. "Look at you, Zel! You're *excited* about this."

"I am not." Her full smile—the one she couldn't tame—told on her.

Take care of herself, and that was all? Yeah right. Everything had changed, and Hazel knew she could never go back to her narrow world. While that felt terrifying, it also felt strangely right. Like she was made for more than the lake and her dogs.

"I'm happy Hunter is home. That he's got a plan and he's going to stay." There, Hazel fixed a serious, inspecting expression as she searched her friend's face. "What about you?"

Janie tried to play dumb. "What about me? I have my own life and business. Which means I have no part of what is happening up at Elk Lake."

"You know what I meant." Hazel tipped her head. "What about you and *Hunter*."

"Pshh." Janie waved her hand. "Let's get something straight here. There's no *me and Hunter*. There won't be a *me and Hunter*."

"You think not?"

"I know not. He and I are too far gone to go back. He's moved on. I've moved on. End of story."

Hazel raised her eyebrows. "That's not what I saw."

Frowning, Janie glared for a moment, then gave Hazel her back as she straightened glasses on the wall shelf. As if that tidy line of shimmering dinnerware needed it. "As much as you've been avoiding Hunter this summer, you haven't seen anything."

That was true. Hazel hadn't observed her brother and Janie together. But she had seen the both of them on their own. She'd witnessed their separate reactions whenever the other had been mentioned. And she knew for a fact Hunter was about as close to over Janie Truitt as the earth was to the sun. By Janie's rumpled reaction now, and in previous times concerning Hunter, Hazel would bet that Janie's heart, though broken, still beat for Hunter.

ONE 5

They could go back. And Hazel was all for that. At one point in time, Hunter and Janie had been happy together. Hazel believed they could be again. If only Janie would get past the resentment.

Ironic that Hazel would think that of her friend. Wasn't that what Bennett had been telling her since January—to get past her resentment and reconcile with her one and only living relative?

Goodness, but these hills made for some granite souls. But even granite could crack.

At that thought, the recollection of Bennett's sort-of proposal brushed through her mind. Again. She quivered with a sensation that both thrilled and made her cower. The fact that he loved her and wanted a lifetime with her was still wonderfully unbelievable. And also disturbingly unbelievable.

Like the immovable mountain woman she was, Hazel clung to the fear. Even though she felt it tearing them apart.

Blinking against the surge of messy emotion, Hazel pushed away from the pine bar and stood. She no longer felt like teasing her friend about Hunter. Relationships were complicated, and she didn't have any business poking her nose in Janie's. Not when she knew it stirred havoc in her friend's heart.

"I was going to take a trek tomorrow and see if there are still some wild raspberries. Do you want some?" It'd be unlikely, as frost had hit most of the high country. But still worth a look.

Janie turned back with a grateful smile. "You know I do."

Hazel nodded and pivoted for the door right as the entry bell jingled. In strode a tall man, younger—in his mid to late twenties, Hazel would guess—medium build, and rusty-brown eyes shaded by a Game and Parks cap.

"Good afternoon." The man spoke without a smile, but his expression seemed pleasant enough.

Another good-looking stranger... Last time Hazel had seen one of those in Janie's Café, her world had slid sideways.

She nearly shook her head and laughed out loud. But then she glanced back at Janie.

There stood her friend, dish towel in one hand, clean glass in the other, motionless and gooey eyed.

"Hi," Janie breathed.

No! Hazel's heart plummeted. She looked back at the handsome guy moving deeper into the café. Toward Janie.

Ruining everything.

Janie regained her business self, though her smile was certainly *not* what she flashed toward Jeremy Yates or old Jasper. "Hi," she repeated. "Welcome to Luna. What can I get you?"

"I hear that you make a pie that could make a man believe he's found heaven. Have any?"

"Sure do. Apple or pecan?"

"Apple."

"Ice cream? It's homemade."

"Absolutely."

"You got it." Janie winked.

Hazel's stomach knotted, and panic stamped in her veins. She headed for the exit pronto, before she had to witness any more of this . . . this *flirting*.

But then the man turned and addressed her before she could escape. "Are you from around here?"

"Yep." Was that a hint of southern drawl in his deep voice? Heaven help them.

"Then you're the hunting guide, right?"

"How did you know that?"

He nodded toward her. "The hat. The woman at the general store said you usually wear a headband or an Australian cowboy hat."

Hazel swallowed against the swell of dislike she had for this man she hadn't even met yet. "Oh." She put her hand on the door, ready to push through it.

"I'm Grady Briggs."

She didn't care. "Welcome to Luna, Grady." No. He was *not* welcome. Not if he was going to make Janie all mushy eyed. And . . . *winking?!* Ridiculous.

"Thanks." He stepped toward her. "I'm a new Game and Parks ranger, working the back side of Yellowstone."

"That's a little way from Luna."

He shrugged. "A bit of a drive, maybe forty-five minutes."

"When the weather is good." He couldn't possibly be intending to live in Luna, could he? Didn't park rangers have federal accommodations or something?

"I'm also working a grant for a study in the backcountry. Mostly the BLM land by Luna. That's your way, isn't it?"

Great. Just dandy. Hazel knew she scowled, and she didn't care to fix it. She also knew it was rude not to answer, but Bennett had once labeled her the badger lady for a reason.

Janie came back from the kitchen, carrying a plate of apple pie à la mode. Was that an unusually large slice? That was certainly a hefty scoop of cinnamon ice cream. Maybe even two?

Hazel gave Janie the squinty eyes.

Janie ignored her, putting a sugary grin toward the guy standing there about ready to wreck everything. "Here you go, fresh baked this morning, and my homemade cinnamon ice cream."

"Perfect." Grady-the-plan-ruiner moved to a barstool and sat. "I've heard good things."

Janie set the plate on the counter in front of him. "Have you?"

"Sure. The Game and Parks guys know all the good spots—especially on remote assignments." Grady put a forkful of warm pie and melting ice cream into his mouth.

"Glad to know I made the list."

After a short groan—*ugh!*—he leaned against the counter on a forearm. "You've made an impressive leap to the top of the list."

That was it. Hazel couldn't handle hearing any more *friendly* banter. She pushed through the door and nearly stomped across the boardwalk.

Hunter better figure out what he wanted real quick. Because Janie was flirting her way right out of his life.

Hazel was pretty sure her brother would be devastated.

Two

Arms crossed, Bennett leaned hard against the thick scrolled-iron railing on the balcony overlooking the pool. The crystal-blue water, disrupted by Gemma and her friends playing in it, however, was not in his line of view.

Bennett stared at his dad, eyes bulging, lips pressed hard. The past few weeks had not been what he'd hoped for. It'd not been the reconciliation that Hunter and Hazel had found. Instead, this visit had been all superficial, *look what I've accumulated, aren't you impressed with me* stuff. No, Bennett wasn't any more impressed with this man than he'd been when he wasn't speaking to him.

And this? This was . . .

Chip—Dad!—shook his head and chuckled. The sound was all condescension. "Don't gape at me like that, son."

"How should I gape at such a request?"

Dad leaned back against his thickly padded deck chair, an ankle crossed over one knee. His leather loafer bounced with the movement of his foot. "It's not forever. A semester, maybe. Perhaps the school year. Nathan needs a new scene before he gets involved with any more bad influences. And Gemma will adjust. She's easygoing that way. All sunshine, that girl. Just like her old man . . ." A smile that Bennett felt certain he'd used himself on several occasions smoothed over his dad's face. The one that sealed the deal more often than not. "Anyway, they're not trouble. Give them a pool or some kind of tech, and you basically never hear from them."

"Nice, Dad." Bennett straightened, pulling his weight off the railing, and glanced down at his younger half sister. Gemma favored their shared father—she had his ruddy coloring and a pair of adorable dimples that could likely gain her about anything she wished. She dolphin dove beneath the water, swimming after her dark-haired friend as they played a game of water tag. Her happy world was teetering, and the poor eleven-year-old girl didn't even know it.

Bennett shook his head. "There aren't a whole lot of private pools in Montana." He turned to pin a scowl on his dad, only to find the man had stood and now wore a pleading expression.

"Look, Ben."

"Bennett." Bennett held a stern expression on his dad.

"Son." Dad exhaled a long, dramatic sigh. "The truth is that Mindi and I probably are not going to make it. I've accepted it, but she wants this one last try. Figure after this long, I owe her that. This couple's retreat is . . ."

Bennett shook his head. A rising holy temper drummed in the depths of his soul. Honestly, he didn't care about his father's four-month-long intensive couple's whatever in Europe—except that was so Dad. Throw some money at a problem and hope it stuck.

If it didn't . . . eh. Oh well. Move on. Leave a wife . . . She'll get over it. Abandon some kids . . . they'd be fine with a padded bank account.

Who needed an actual dad?

How had this man claimed to follow Christ and had even pastored a church for seven years? The confounding mystery of that antagonized Bennett exceedingly. But at the moment the more pressing and exasperating puzzle was why his dad had thought Bennet would want to take on guardianship of his half siblings while Chip and his likely-soon-to-be ex-wife took off for four months. Or longer.

And here Bennett had stupidly thought that when Dad had asked him to come and try again, he had actually meant what Bennett had meant—to be reconciled.

Bennett blew out a hard breath. "Dad, you can't do this to them."

Chip frowned. After a quick glance toward the pool, he shook his head. "They don't know about Mindi and me right now." He shrugged. "Who knows? Maybe they'll never have to know."

How could this man be so disgustingly cavalier about this? "They'll know something's wrong if you send them to live with me in Montana."

Another shrug. "Either way they'll not be staying. The other option is a boarding school in New England."

"What?"

"Chicago isn't what it used to be, and Nathan, as I've already alluded to, has been finding trouble. He just needs different people around him . . . Anyway, the point is, either way they're going somewhere."

"Dad." Bennett huffed out the title with pure exasperation.

Chip stepped next to Bennett and covered his shoulder with one hand. Bennett had to discipline away the reaction to sidestep out of the man's touch. Resentment bubbled up from the deep storage of years' worth of anger. He flinched at the strength of the surging reaction.

And then he let his gaze rest on the copper-haired girl laughing in the water below. Hazel's face drifted through his mind. She would have been about the same age as Gemma when she'd lost her parents.

At least Hazel had had her brother to see her through.

Bennett swallowed. His chest ached. He had to clear emotion from his throat before he could speak. "I need to pray about this."

The hand on his shoulder squeezed. "Sure. Sleep on it, why don't you?" Then Chip clapped his back. "The guest house comfortable enough for you?"

With a glance over his shoulder, bypassing his dad's impassive face, Bennett looked through the glass French door that led into the guest suite above the pool house—his quarters for the past few weeks. It was nothing short of luxury. Something Bennett would have put in one of his more high-end resorts.

The tech industry certainly paid well. Much better than the church gig. Couldn't hurt that Mindi was an accountant in a highly prized firm used by the beyond-wealthy people of the Northern Shore.

"It's fine, Dad." It took work not to allow the sharp edge of his irritation to cut through his tone.

"Good." Dad turned, strode toward the padded deck chair, and stopped to snag his Eagle Rare Bourbon. Pausing, he raised his glass. "Can I get you one?"

"Nine is a little early for me." Bennett couldn't school the frown that pressed on his mouth. "Thanks."

"Suit yourself." Dad turned back toward the spiral stairs and descended as if he hadn't a care in the world.

"Dad!" Gemma's call broke through the splashing and giggles of the three girls in the pool. "Watch this!"

"Of course, princess." Dad's smooth reply rippled with adoration.

Bennett's stomach burned.

Gemma dove into the water and performed a handstand, her manicured toes pointing straight up to the clear blue late-September sky. Then she pulled them in as she executed a perfect flip-turn and sprang to the surface.

Chip clapped. "I give it a ten, baby doll."

Her smile stretched. "Thanks, Daddy."

"When you girls are done, I've ordered some of those yummy cinnamon crispies you like."

A round of squeals ensued from all three girls, loud enough to wake the perpetually sullen Nathan, who had not emerged from his bedroom before one in the afternoon since Bennett had been there. Likely because he stayed up until the wee hours of the morning playing on the new iPhone Dad had gifted him with as a back-to-school conciliatory prize.

How could Chip be this stupid?

He was buying them off. Just as he'd attempted to do with Bennett. And it was revolting.

Bennett wanted no part in aiding his dad's continued trek into the great abyss of self-indulgence. But those kids . . .

At least when Chip had abandoned Bennett, Bennett had still had his faithful mother. Nathan and Gemma?

From what Bennett could see, Mindi wasn't much like his mom. Starting with the fact that she was willing to dump her teenage kids off on a stepson she barely knew. No, not starting there. Starting with the fact that over a dozen years before, with zero qualms, she'd been sleeping with a man who was married to someone else.

Nathan and Gemma would get washed out to sea in this churning storm of selfish living, and they would have no one to show them what real love and faithfulness looked like.

That possibility broke Bennett's heart.

Three

At the sound of his truck's approach, Hunter straightened from the card table he'd unfolded and set up. Hazel was back.

He shot a grin toward Evan Kerst, the man who had also been leaning over the table, where the blueprints had been unrolled and held down by rocks. "That'll be my sister."

"Good. I'm looking forward to meeting her."

Hunter's smile slipped, and he shot a silent, urgent plea that Hazel would be in a good mood. Was that how prayer worked, or was it irreverent to do it that way before the God who was King of kings?

He hoped God would understand the situation—and he'd ask John about the rules of prayer later.

The engine cut, and then the sound of a door squeaking open and slapping shut rippled through the forest. Several birds' wings rumbled the calm as they left their safe perches, annoyed by the intrusive disturbance. The churling of an offended marmot carried on the thin mountain air. Hunter watched the mild chaos happening at the tops of the pines and then moved his gaze to the path that would deliver Hazel from the end of the road to his camp.

There she was, her hair twisted in a braid that draped over her shoulder and head topped with Pops's leather hat. She wore a long-sleeve plaid shirt—likely one that Janie had gifted her at some point—and bootcut jeans. Typical Hazel apparel.

"There you are." Hunter strode to meet her, then walked beside her as they made their way to the table. "This is Evan, our head contractor."

Hazel shot Hunter a quizzical glance, but Evan held out his hand to shake hers, stalling whatever was about to spill from her lips. Hunter couldn't be sure, but that might be a good thing. Hazel had said she'd support him on this business venture, but he knew she didn't love it. And if something had provoked her in town—which, by the way her brows had been folded into a scowl, was possible—his little sister might not be her aimable self. After all, that version of Hazel wasn't well practiced.

"It's nice to meet you." Evan's handshake and demeanor were professional. "Shall we get started?"

"Started?" Hazel's questioning look once again found Hunter.

"Right. Evan wants to solidify the details before we break ground."

"You haven't started yet?" Now her brows lifted.

Something soft unfolded in Hunter's chest at his sister's shocked response. "Of course not. We waited for you."

"You—why?"

"We're in this together, right?"

Hazel blinked, then turned to the table. Her mouth pressed firm, but Hunter was 90 percent sure the emotion she worked to suppress wasn't anger. This was new for them—being on the same side. Well, not new, exactly. But it'd been a long time. He wanted to hug her, to let her know he still wanted her to be his partner in this, that this thing was for both their good. But knowing Hazel, she'd not appreciate that. So Hunter plunged ahead with business.

"The footprint is marked off with stakes." Hunter pointed to the section of meadow he'd cleared and measured off. "I'm sure you'll want to redo that, because who knows if my measurements are accurate, but the general outline is there."

"It's a good place to begin." Evan peeled the top layer of blueprints from the stack on the table and moved toward the footprint Hunter had marked off. "Let's make sure we have the same vision. If everything falls into place, we can break ground before it freezes solid. Framing will be done before Thanksgiving, cross our fingers."

They went over the details. Where the front door would be. How the covered porch would face both the lake and the falls, and how the elevation of it would lend itself to a perfect view. The pitch of the roof. The location of the rock chimney. Where the carriage house would sit, and the views that would be offered for the owner in the quarters above. Evan considered all the angles, and he and Hunter discussed everything the project would entail.

And Hazel remained present but quiet.

After nearly two hours, Evan was satisfied they shared a common vision. With a handshake for both Hunter and Hazel, and a start date just around the corner, he bid them a good afternoon. Hunter walked him to his four-wheel drive.

When Hunter came back, he found Hazel standing in the middle of what would be the great room, her gaze glued to the minor lake.

"Can you see it?" Hunter gestured, as if painting the image of his vision for her.

"No." Her tone sounded flat. "But I've never been a visionary."

"Are you still upset about it?" His enthusiasm took a nosedive.

"No." Hazel turned to look up at him. "No, it's just overwhelming to think of such a change. But I'm not mad."

Hunter blew out a relieved breath. But then he shook his head. "Something's wrong." His sister didn't wear her heart out where everyone could read it—though she could be dramatic at times. But he knew her well enough to know when something poked at her.

"I . . . I'm surprised you waited for me. I wasn't needed, you know."

Hunter stepped closer. "Zel, when I said I wanted you with me on this, I really meant it. This is a whole new life for both of us—and it's a little scary. I get that. It scares me too. The last thing I want is for you to feel excluded. Or that I'm stealing your inheritance or life. In fact, I was thinking about the cabin. We can work on that too. Fix it up. Make it bigger. Or update it. Make it something you and Bennett would really love."

Hazel crossed her arms. "What is that supposed to mean?"

"The cabin hasn't been touched in, like, thirty years. It just means we could—"

"Bennett doesn't live there."

"Ah." Hunter rocked back on his heels. His thoughts moved to the texts he and Bennett had recently exchanged.

Hunter: *Hear you're going to be out of town?*

Bennett: *Yeah. I was going to call you about that. I have a project going up here. Should be fine, but if I need some eyes on it, could you be the guy?*

Hunter: *Of course. Don't know what I could do, but I can make it up to Bozeman if you need me to. Going back to Chicago?*

Bennett: *Yes. Visiting my dad. And my mom.*

Hunter: *Are you okay?*

Bennett: *Sure. Just need to go back for a week or two.*

Hunter: *Hazel told me about your conversation . . . I mean are you okay?*

Bennett: *Oh. If you want the truth, I don't know. Would you be okay if you proposed and the woman said no?*

Hunter: *No. Not really. Kind of been there, actually. Not okay at all.*

Bennett: *Well, that's where we are. Not sure where to go from here.*

Hunter: *I get that.*

Hunter: *Bennett? Don't give up on her.*

Bennett: *I told you, I love her. I don't think giving up is an option. I just don't know what to do. I'm mad and frustrated. But I know why she said no. Like I said, I just don't know where we go from here. Step back? Don't know how. Pretend it didn't happen? Not possible. Move on? To what? It's a no-win.*

No-win was exactly what it was. Objectively, Bennett was handling the situation way better than Hunter had handled his. After all, Hunter had evaded the woman who'd rejected him for as long as possible, and he had labeled her *vampire* in his phone contacts when she became unavoidable again.

Man, women could sure bring out the worst in men.

As Hunter refocused on Hazel, he felt his own frustration rise on Bennett's behalf. Hazel had her reasons, that Hunter knew, but she was going to lose something really good if she couldn't get past them. "Still being a fool, hmm?"

Her frown darkened. "Do you intentionally find the single thing that will provoke me the most?"

"No. I find the thing I think will be best for you, and for some undefined reason, you dig in your heels against it like I'm suggesting you become an actress or something. Bennett is good for you, and he only *wants* good for you. You're being a fool."

"How do you know what will be best for me? I'm a grown woman, and I've lived on my own for seven years."

"You've been lonely for seven years."

"I was not."

"So lonely that you thought it was a good idea to lie to a man who had lost his memory, making him believe that he'd married you."

"That was *not* because I was lonely."

Hunter raised his eyebrows, holding an unflinching challenge on her face until she looked away.

"How is it going to feel if he gets tired of waiting for you to come to your senses?" Hunter pressed. "How would it feel to see him with someone else?"

Hazel sucked in a breath. She recovered in the next heartbeat though. "That will just prove my point. People change. They let you down. Why make promises no one can live up to?"

"Self-fulfilling prophecy?"

Hazel huffed, rolling her fists at her sides. "We were fine. Happy. Why can't things just stay the way they are?"

Though compassion moved in his chest for his exasperated sister, Hunter shook his head. "Zel, he's a man, not one of your dogs you can train to sit and stay and wait until you throw him a treat or scratch him behind the ear. Bennett wants a future, and somewhat shockingly, he wants it with you. You're not being fair. And worse, you're being really foolish. I know you don't want to lose him."

She visibly swallowed. Then with hands planted on her hips, she turned to square up with him. She tipped her chin up so he could see the mossy tint of her eyes beneath the brim of her hat. "How about you worry about your own life."

"What is that supposed to mean?"

"Some guy came into town today."

Hunter stared at her.

"A good-looking guy. Late twenties. He came into the café for pie and was full of compliments." Hazel raised both eyebrows. "Apparently, he's moving to town. Janie about swooned."

Hunter's stomach clenched hard. Janie . . . *swooned*?

"Winked. Flirted. Gave him a double scoop of ice cream on his pie. And could *not* stop smiling."

Flirted? His Janie had flirted with another man? One who was moving to Luna? Hunter's lungs clamped, and his pulse shifted into overdrive. He stood there dumbfounded. Nauseous.

Rattled clear to his toes.

Some other guy had been the recipient of Janie Truitt's (should have long since been Wallace) sweet smile. Had her blue eyes danced with warmth? Had she nibbled on the side of her bottom lip in that mesmerizing, half-smiling way?

Dear heaven and earth! Hunter might be having a heart attack with the way his chest tightened.

A look of warning, and maybe laced with a touch of spiteful satisfaction, filled Hazel's blazing golden-green eyes. "You have your own problems to deal with, Hunt." She strode toward the path that would take her over the ridge and back to her cabin. "Leave Bennett's and mine alone."

Hunter watched his sister disappear into the pines, and then he turned to stare absently at the falls.

Janie.

His Janie.

She couldn't fall for someone else.

Janie swam in heady giddiness. Even several minutes after Grady Briggs had touched the brim of his cap, given her a shy half grin that revealed white teeth and a dimpled chin, and thanked her for the pie. And coffee. And the two refills of said coffee.

Goodness, but that man was *handsome*. And he'd come to her café specifically to taste her pie. He'd sat there specifically to talk with her.

Probably.

Most men didn't linger over three cups of black coffee because they had nothing else to do. There were smartphones, after all. Games to play. Google to search. They didn't just hang out in a mostly empty café for over an hour just to pass the time.

Did they?

Then again, this was Luna, and the man was new. Maybe he just had time to kill before a meeting or something.

I'm looking forward to some more pie, Janie Truitt.

Her heart fluttered as she leaned one elbow against the counter, propping her chin against her palm. Ignoring the supper prep that was calling to her from the kitchen, she watched Grady stride toward the Game and Parks truck parked across the road in front of the Pantry, his athletic form filling out those green pants and that gray button-down in a way that could make any girl gawk with appreciation. And Janie was sure appreciating. She sighed, a girly, swoony sound as she indulged in the last thing Grady had said before he'd walked out of her shop.

"Just as soon as possible."
Uh, yes please! And make it quick.

That was flirting, right? Her pathetically lonely heart hadn't made it something it wasn't, had it?

Surely not.

Time would tell. But Janie willed Grady Briggs to find a place to rent in Luna for the next few months while he traveled to Yellowstone for his ranger gig and conducted his study on the western spotted skunk. (Ew. But if that had that sort of man hanging around Luna . . .) More, she hoped he would make himself a regular at her counter.

She'd need to work on her own flirting game. Her history had given her limited experience at that. And she'd have to work to be better at banishing Hunter's brown eyes, all warm and intense, from poking from her memory at the most inconvenient moments. But those were doable.

So what if she hadn't flirted in years, nor accomplished the latter item since Hunter had gone and come back home. She was a smart woman. Mountain bred and as tough as the alpine winter. She could do it.

With the help of a handsome, dark-haired man and his slow, melt-her-like-butter-on-hot-biscuits smile, Janie would finally leave whatever lingering feelings she had for Hunter Wallace in the past.

That was long overdue.

Four

Bennett dropped onto the overstuffed chair in his mom's living room, noting absently that the flower upholstery—a cottage-style from the early 2000s—was badly faded and the seat cushion poked at his backside. Had she owned it since before the divorce? Sheesh, that was a long time. It was time Mom had something new. He'd take her shopping—though she'd protest—before he headed back to Montana.

But old furniture wasn't the pressing item weighing on his mind right then. Leaning forward, he ran his fingers through his freshly cut hair, then folded his hands to use them to prop up his chin.

"The visit has been long, huh?" Mom passed one of the two mugs she carried to him and then turned to move to the matching faded couch. She cozied into the corner and tucked her feet up close beside her. "Talk to me, Bennett."

Bennett blew the steam across the top of the spiced tea Mom had given him and then sighed. "He wants me to take the kids."

Having just sipped her tea, Mom coughed. "Your dad wants you to take your siblings?"

Nodding, Bennett met Mom's shocked expression. "Unbelievable, right?"

She blinked twice before answering. "For how long?"

"Four months. Maybe the whole school year." Bennett shook his head, still dazed by his father's cavalier request. "He didn't know."

"School has already started, hasn't it?"

"Yep." Bennett leaned back, slouching against the uncomfortable chair. And that summed up the man who had procreated him. Nothing had more significance than whatever Chip wanted at the moment. "Doesn't seem to matter. He and Mindi are going to Europe. It's planned. They're leaving. That's the end of it." Bennett paused, considering carefully how much he should tell his mom about her ex-husband's senseless life. Maybe not too much. Mom had reached a place of release where Dad was concerned. She didn't need anything to re-root resentment.

Of course, this conversation would likely do exactly that without Bennett's mentioning that Dad was ready to end his second marriage and seemed to have no qualms about doing so.

Mom shifted her stare to the window above Bennett's shoulder, likely watching the birds that chattered at the feeder in her flower bed. "What will you do?"

"I don't know." Bennett set the mug on the table beside the worn chair and leaned his elbows against his knees. "At first I thought *no way*. But . . ." Was he truly considering this? Who was he to take on two teenage kids? He had zero experience in parenting at any level, and he was barely getting his life together in a way that he could respect for himself. Not to mention Hazel. What would she think?

What on earth was *he* thinking?

"But Nathan and Gemma might need you," Mom said softly.

That was what he was thinking. Bennett met her gentle gaze. "Do you think so?" Maybe he wasn't being arrogantly foolish.

She nodded. "Who else do they have?"

Rubbing his forehead, Bennett allowed her words to penetrate deep. It was like a confirmation of the impression of God's leading—one that terrified Bennett.

"They need to see a godly man, Bennett."

"I'm hardly a poster boy for that." His heart sank into his gut. If he'd not chosen a life of resentment and wild abandon, maybe he'd be a better candidate. But he couldn't change the years he'd spent living exactly like the man who was piling frustration on him now.

"You are not who you were a year ago."

Could Mom read his mind?

"I see God's work in your life," she continued.

Mom's high praise filled in equal parts gratitude and guilt. If she knew how he'd been failing—living in the flesh, especially with his physical relationship with Hazel—earlier that year, she wouldn't say that. Truth was, he'd messed up everything with Hazel, and it hadn't taken him long to do it.

Weak!

He couldn't help but wonder if he hadn't slept with her, would she'd see him as a more honorable man now? One she would feel safe marrying?

Instead she saw him as live-in-boyfriend material. One not trustworthy with a promise of a lifetime. A ripple of ache ran through his chest as he replayed her rejection on the dock.

"I'm not the kind of girl who marries." The way her eyes had burned as she'd stared at him and their argument that had followed . . . It was all still as fresh as the crisp Montana air. But not nearly as pleasant.

The thing was, he'd done this. He'd set them up for failure the moment he'd caved to his physical passion. How could Hazel believe he'd honestly become a better man when he had chosen desire for the moment rather than faithfulness to his convictions?

Just like Chip.

It made him want to cry. To tear his clothes and sit in ashes. Literally. Because now he suddenly understood why remorse provoked that sort of response. It came powerfully, from the depths of his soul, a physical outpouring of how he felt deep inside.

Wretched. Dirty. Broken.

God, cleanse this filthy life.

God had promised He would do that. But He wasn't obligated to remove the natural consequences of Bennett's willful indulgences. Even so, Bennett's repeated prayer over the past weeks had been exactly for that. *Please set us right...*

"I see you, Bennett." Mom spoke tenderly into his remorse.

Though his eyes burned, he dragged his gaze from his feet and dared to meet his mother's.

Only compassion stared back at him. "I know that you've stumbled—I don't need to know the details. But I also see your remorse. Godly people don't live perfect lives—even though they strive for it. What they do is repent. Whatever it is, however you've stumbled, you are sorry, and I know it. That is a far cry from the stubborn, arrogant man who lived only for himself just a short while ago." She leaned forward. "You are changed, son. Don't let the old man intrude on this decision. Don't let guilt lead you away from a holy calling. If God is asking you to take in your siblings, then do it. No matter what you've done in the past."

Bennett swallowed the hard lump in his throat as a single tear escaped the corner of his eye. The events of the past several weeks—and his own failures that had triggered the cascade of them—had his emotions bowed to the snapping point.

"Bennett?" Concern saturated Mom's tone. "Is there something more?"

So much more... "Hazel doesn't want to get married." And there it was. His wounded heart on display. He peeked toward her across the room, the heat of humility and heartache washing over his face.

"Oh, Bennett." Mom left the couch, crossed the small area rug, and lowered to her knees at his side. One hand cradled the back of his head, and he dropped it to her shoulder. "I didn't know you'd proposed."

He shook his head and then lifted it. "It was an impulsive thing, and I shouldn't have done it. But now it's out there, and she said no, and I don't know where that puts us."

"You didn't break up?"

"No. I don't want that, and neither does she. She's scared of marriage—thinks it's a trap."

"I can understand that, especially if the only example she's witnessed wasn't good."

Mom was pretty good at reading between the lines, and she was dead on with that assumption. A grandfather who had died as a drunk and a grandmother who had worked hard to hide it—that had been Hazel's experience. Even Bennett couldn't blame her for being afraid.

"Do all marriages fail, Mom?"

Mom rubbed his arm and then turned to press her back against the stone of her small fireplace. "Sometimes it sure seems like it, doesn't it?"

A space of silence settled. Bennett scrubbed a hand down his face and dropped back against the awful cushion of that long-expired chair. "Weak men."

"What's that?"

"Weak men. That's the problem. We are weak when we're supposed to be strong. We choose selfishness over sacrifice. Pleasure over faithfulness." Bennett bounced his rolled fist on the faded upholstery, every sentence a self-indictment.

Mom stilled his hand with her palm. "It's not just men. A good marriage takes two. And maybe you don't remember, but there was a time your dad was selfless and honorable."

Bennett *did* remember. The memories were faded and wispy, but they were there—and they actually frustrated and defeated him even more. Chip was radically different now from the dad Bennett had had as a child. "What happened?"

Tipping her head back, Mom sighed. "He became disillusioned. First with the church. Then with God. And I'm sorry to say that I wasn't a very kind or patient wife when he walked through the darkest parts of that struggle. I wanted him to just snap out of it." Mom sat forward again, her shoulders rounding. "You know that Stephen Curtis Chapman song 'Go There with You'?"

While Bennett knew of the musical artist, he couldn't recall a single song the man had sung. "Not really."

"That's okay." She fiddled with her fingers, rolling her lips together. "It's a hard one for me to hear. Because it cuts conviction deep, even after all these years. I wasn't that kind of spouse to your dad."

Bennett watched for several heartbeats while his mom wrestled with regret. "Mom. That doesn't excuse an affair. Certainly doesn't account for his deconstructed faith—a sacred thing between him and God. And it didn't give him the right to leave us." He knew these things for sure, because he had his own failings before God. Things he couldn't pin on his dad, even though he'd tried exactly that for most of his adult life.

One of the things that had become clear as he'd regained his memory last year—and saw his life for what it really had been—was that he was accountable before God for his life. Sans all excuses, legitimate or otherwise, Bennett was responsible for every selfish act. Every rebellious moment.

It had been an awful revelation. But it had led to a glorious path of redemption. This conversation with his mom was proof of it, because a year ago, such a thing would not have happened.

"No. It doesn't excuse him." Mom lifted her eyes to his face and searched him with a pleading look. "But I wasn't perfect either. That's what I'm trying to say here. A good marriage takes two—and even a good marriage will have struggles, because it's going to involve two imperfect people."

FOUR

"What's the secret, do you think?"

Mom shrugged. "I'm not sure. From the few successes that I've witnessed, I'd say, they devoted themselves to putting each other first. To be the other's greatest advocate. Determined to fight for each other more than with each other. And most of all, they share a common love for the Lord."

Despair hung on Bennett. Hazel didn't share his growing love for God. Was this relationship doomed from all sides? Did he need to walk away?

His immediate response was to slap that thought away. He did not *want* to walk away. But doing whatever he wanted, regardless of God's input, was how Chip had lived. And how Bennett had wasted more than ten years of his life. It wasn't who he wanted to be now. So instead Bennett forced the disquieting query toward his heart so that he could lift it before God in prayer later. Right alongside this issue of his siblings. Which brought him back to where this conversation had started.

"You think I should say yes to Dad?"

"I think you should follow where God leads on that."

"Even if I know I'm not qualified and have no idea where to even begin with a pair of teenagers who are not likely to be excited about moving to Montana?"

"Even then." Mom rose from the floor, stretched her back, then started toward that awful couch. "Maybe I should go with you."

Her offhand comment, certainly made tongue-in-cheek, caused Bennett to freeze and hope at the same time. "Would you?"

She turned, her expression caught. "I was kidding. Mostly."

"I want you to though. It would make things easier."

"Not sure about that. I barely know them. Anyway, how would that even work?"

"We could figure it out." Bennett pushed off the chair. "Seriously, Mom. You'd like Montana. You'd get to know Hazel better. And meet José and his wife, Rosalina, and Janie and Mama B and Hunter . . ." All the people in Bennett's life who had marked him for the better over the past year.

"I—" Mom shook her head.

"Luna could use a nurse practitioner. They don't have anything, really. A school nurse at the county coop school twenty minutes down the highway. Nearest doctor is forty-five minutes away at the critical-access hospital in Big Sky."

"You don't live in Luna."

That was true. But . . . but a whole new plan exploded in Bennett's mind. He hadn't intended to stay in the house he was in in Bozeman—it was a fix and flip. And it wouldn't work with two kids anyway. Being closer to Hazel was always his goal. And now with his involvement with Hunter's lodge, the move made even more sense.

"Mom. It could be your next chapter."

"It's been a while since I've started a new chapter."

"Right." Bennett clapped his hands and rubbed them together. "It's time."

"Then you'll say yes to the kids?"

"On the condition that you come too." He glanced back at the chair, still feeling the hard lumps that had balled against his back and seat. "And you leave this awful furniture behind."

Mom laughed. Bennett took that as a yes. And he felt a fresh burst of excitement—the first he'd had in weeks.

Five

Hunter stared out the windshield of his truck, his eyes fixed on the broad window set in the middle of the log structure that was Janie's Café. Two days ago he would have had anticipation buzzing through his veins, and he would barely have had the engine shut off before leaving his vehicle to head through that jingling front door. Two days ago all he would have thought about was seeing those blue eyes—even if they were piercing and likely mad at him.

Two days ago he hadn't felt the panic triggered by the knowledge that another man had flirted with the woman who refused to budge from his mind. And she'd flirted back.

Snowflakes drifted lazily from the light-gray sky, dusting the chilly late-September ground. Usually Hunter liked the first snow. How could one not smile at white flakes lazily drifting against the backdrop of the deep-purple layers of majestic peaks? It was quintessential Montana. And that first dusting felt clean and fresh and wasn't yet a problem when it came to the simple tasks of daily living.

That late-September day, however, Hunter didn't pay attention to the dancing flakes. He couldn't see anything, really. Not the layers of indigo and plum mountains at the west end of the dirt road Luna called Main. Not the remaining vestiges of bright-yellow aspen leaves rustling in the cold westerly breeze. Not the crisp flag flying on the pole in front of the Elk County Sherriff's building. Not Mama B waving at him from the boardwalk in front of Luna Pantry.

He just felt . . .

Desperate.

I'm gonna lose her all over again. He didn't even have her. How could he lose someone he didn't have?

But the thought circled back even louder. *I'm gonna lose her . . .*

"You just going to sit there?" Hazel's sharp tone drilled into his chaotic mind.

"Huh?"

"I'm getting a cinnamon roll before I grab supplies. Guess you can sit and stew all you want." She popped out of the passenger seat, smacking the door shut behind her.

The hollow sound made Hunter startle. Sheesh, he was some kind of mess that morning. Two sleepless nights could do that to a guy. That, and the sight of a green Game and Parks truck parked on the other side of Luna Pantry—something that had registered in his mind. The intruder who was trying to steal Janie was still in town.

Hunter's gut clenched. And then resolve locked into place.

If it was to be a battle, then let it begin. He was not one to back down, and Hunter was not about to let Janie just go ahead and fall in love with some other guy. They had too much history together.

They had too much future together.

He slid out of his truck, put iron into his back and shoulders, and shut the door. Pausing, he checked his reflection in the window. Sandy-brown hair groomed, but not overly so—not like he was *trying* too hard. Full beard trimmed, teeth cleaned, and breath minty fresh. And he'd used the cologne with spiced bergamot that Janie had liked. Good to go.

Crossing the dirt road, Hunter let his attention zone in on that green truck. Hazel hadn't said anything about what the Game and Parks guy looked like—other than he was good looking. Good looking in what way? Bookish good looking? Burly good looking? Preppy good looking? He'd not asked, and even if he hadn't been too dumbstruck to push for details, he didn't think he could trust Hazel's evaluation. Up until last fall, Hunter hadn't known Hazel to know or care how a man looked. She'd been infinitely more interested in the gun he carried and if he could shoot straight.

How on earth had she ended up in love with Bennett Crofton, a man who didn't even *like* guns, let alone know how to shoot one?

The greatest mystery in Elk County.

But not what Hunter was stewing on.

He shifted his gaze just in time to stop himself from catching his boot on the boardwalk leading to Janie's Café. That'd be impressive, stumbling into her establishment like a drunken fool. Man, he needed to pull it together. Tugging his camo jacket straight, Hunter drew in a breath of crisp air and forced his mind toward something useful. Like walking straight.

Maybe he could try praying?

Prayer is a conversation between you and God. You can tell Him, or ask Him, anything. Anytime, Hunt. Only remember, He is God and you are man.

John Brighton's response to Hunter's text about prayer the other night pressed in his mind and prompted Hunter to lift up his tangled thoughts, feeble as that felt, before he entered the battleground.

God, make her love me again. Not this other guy.

Was that . . . sufficient? Hunter pushed his fingers through his hair. He really needed a more detailed explanation. Maybe he'd better call John and get some clarification. Weren't there scripted prayers he could memorize or something?

Speaking of clarification and questions, why did God have this other guy show up and turn Janie's head in the first place? If He was going to have Hunter get sick and lose his place in the navy and come home, couldn't He make it a little easier to win Janie back?

It would all make sense then. And be worth it.

He is God, and you are man. Anyway, you and Hazel have reconnected. That's worth it.

So . . . God was God, and Hunter wasn't. Did that make his request a disrespectful inquiry?

Ugh. Hunter's mind was a knotted ball.

Footfalls on the boardwalk jolted Hunter out of the labyrinth of his thoughts. Chin jerking up, Hunter found a man in dark-green twill cargo pants and a gray button-down striding toward him. A glance at the patch on the man's left shoulder confirmed what the roiling in Hunter's stomach had already declared.

This was the man.

Hunter took him in with the sort of subtle detailed study he'd gained from backcountry living. Full federal uniform, including the green ball cap. Dark hair neatly trimmed, and clean shaven. As if feeling the comparison, Hunter ran his hand over the rough texture of his beard—something he'd indulged in since he'd been discharged from the navy.

Maybe Janie didn't like it. In their years together, he'd always kept the hair off his face—mostly because back then he was little more than a kid. Did the beard make him look wild and unkept?

"Good morning." Game and Parks guy dipped a courtesy nod and then reached for the café door. "Heading in?"

Hunter rolled his posture straighter. Not that he needed to. Thanks to the navy, he kept his shoulders square out of habit. "Can't miss Janie's cinnamon rolls."

Holding the entry open, the man allowed a small grin. "That's what I hear."

Hunter scowled. "Where did you hear that?"

Game and Parks shrugged. "Another ranger had an assignment this way a couple years ago. We tend to share the good off-the-map spots in this line of work. Perks of the job."

As he passed into the warm café, the aroma of cinnamon and freshly baked bread making his mouth water, Hunter did not like the way that last sentence landed. What other *perks* was this guy looking for? If Game and Parks thought he had an advantage wearing his uniform, he had another thing coming. Hunter knew from personal experience that Janie wasn't a particular fan of a uniform. She didn't want the life that came attached to it.

There. That should settle his tumultuous emotions. Janie flirting didn't mean much when it came to this guy. Maybe even Hazel had misread the whole situation. Or exaggerated it. His sister was a bit dramatic about some things. And she was terrible when it came to reading people.

Hunter strode toward the counter and plopped onto one of the stools. Game and Parks followed suit, leaning his forearms against the counter all casual and like he belonged there.

"Look who came back." Janie circled from the small dining space at the front of the café, her grin aimed at Game and Parks. Not at Hunter.

"Of course. Yesterday's lemon cake was amazing. Wouldn't take long for a man to become addicted."

Granite lodged in Hunter's chest. He'd come in yesterday? And the day before, for pie? This guy was definitely after something more than pastry.

Let the battle begin.

Rolling his fists, he fixed an unwavering gaze on Janie until she couldn't ignore him anymore.

"Morning, Hunter." Her smile faded into nearly nothing. Those blue gems held cool distance and maybe a touch of warning. "Cinnamon roll and coffee?"

"You know." She knew exactly what he liked. And she knew that he wasn't there for the food. Not entirely, at least. She knew every corner of his heart. She also knew, Hunter felt certain, that she was throwing darts at it right then. Sharp ones loaded with poison—the kind of toxin that would make a man writhe in agony.

Cruel. It was just . . . vindictive cruelty.

She had to know, and she was doing this intentionally. Janie had been able to read Hunter since they'd been fifteen and thirteen. It had been one of the reasons he'd never kept a secret from her. The exact reason, in fact, that he'd been stunned by her shock and anger at his desire to leave Elk Canyon.

Janie looked toward the floor and then shifted her attention toward the dining room. "Hazel snagged the table by the window. The one you usually like."

Was she . . . dismissing him? Telling him to get lost, let her flirt with Game and Parks alone?

Heck no.

"Think she was expecting a call from Bennett." Hunter crossed his arms and kept his stare pinned on her face. "I'll just let my sister have some time alone for that."

The man to Hunter's right cleared his throat.

Janie shot Hunter a quick scowl and then let sunshine back into her expression as she looked back at the other guy. "Two coffees. Two cinnamon rolls. Anything else?"

"Made my day already."

Hunter turned a slow glare onto Game and Parks. He was met with easy cordiality.

"Grady Briggs." The offer of his name was joined by his extended hand.

Hunter took it with a firm grip. Maybe a little firmer than usual. "Hunter Wallace."

"I guessed so."

"Did you? Why is that?"

"Hazel—you said she was your sister. I met her day before yesterday."

"Why would you remember Hazel or need to know me?"

"I'm running a study on the western spotted skunk up on the BLM land that borders your property. We tend to know who owns property where we're working."

"Is that so." Hunter kept his tone flat.

"Right. And we like to know the landowners—let them know we'll be working in the area. And I've been told no one knows the area like the Wallace siblings. We might need to borrow your expertise."

"We? Who else do you have coming here to sniff out the skunks?"

Game and Parks—Grady—itched his ear. "On this study, it's just me."

"So you'll be out wandering near our land on your own." Hunter smirked. "Good to know."

"It's not going to be a problem, is it?"

Hunter shrugged. Depended on how this guy behaved. Specifically with Janie. "My sister has been known to remove trail cams if they're aimed toward one of her traplines."

"I'd rather she didn't."

"Hazel hasn't done that in years." Janie smacked a mug in front of Hunter. Then she turned to Grady and passed the other mug in her hand straight into his. "You have nothing to worry about with Zel. And Hunter here will behave, because he needs all of his permits to go through." She shifted her look back to Hunter, letting it instantly morph from friendly to not so much. "And he wouldn't want any part of the government to delay that, would he?"

What was this? Janie was threatening him to behave? With a permit issue? What did she even know about that anyway?

"I have nothing to do with those things," Grady said.

Huh. Either the guy was a little slow and didn't recognize the ammunition Janie had just offered—even if it was a blank—or he recognized it and simply didn't want to use it.

Hunter ran a hand over his mouth as he passed a quick study over the other man. Grady's expression seemed honest.

Great. He was probably a good guy. One Hunter would instantly like in other circumstances.

Hazel tugged on the brim of her hat as she sent a surreptitious glance toward the bar. Janie's expression was like a summer afternoon in the hills—one minute sunshine and the next a thunderstorm. Wasn't hard to figure out which man got the sun and who received her thunder.

Hazel gripped her mug as a fierce surge of irritation billowed toward her best friend. How could Janie not see that Hunter wasn't over her?

How could she stand there and shower smiles on Grady-the-Game-and-Parks guy while Hunter sat right there?

The irony of her reaction wasn't lost on Hazel. Just a few short months—no, weeks—before, hadn't Bennett nearly begged her to reconcile with her brother? Instead she'd stubbornly held Hunter in contempt. Could she truly judge Janie for doing the same thing?

It wasn't her business.

Hazel fought to keep that fact center in her mind. Whatever was or wasn't going to happen between Hunter and Janie wasn't Hazel's business.

Goodness, that was hard though. Especially with this visceral reaction she had as she overheard Janie lay out a not-subtle threat to Hunter about permits. That was low—especially for Janie, who was, with every other person on the planet, kind and sweet and generous.

Only with Hunter had Hazel witnessed this bitter hardness from her lifelong friend.

Inside the front zipper pocket of her raincoat, a vibration distracted Hazel from her preoccupation. Unzipping the inner compartment, she pulled out her phone and felt a swirling mix of relief and anticipation at the name on the screen.

Conversations between her and Bennett had been stilted and bumpy over the past few weeks. But they were still talking. That was a relief.

Drawing a lungful of cinnamon-tinted air, Hazel tapped her phone and put it up to her ear. "Hey."

"Hi."

Hi, beautiful. Good morning, my mountain lioness. Hi there, love. Those were the ways Bennett usually greeted her over the phone. Or in person.

Not in the past several weeks though. The small, ever-present ache in her chest gave a quick punch. Hazel sucked in another quick breath, then put on a smile, as if that would make it all better. "How's Chicago today?"

A noticeable gap spread before Bennett responded. "Zel, we need to talk."

"I thought that's what we were doing."

"Yeah. I mean a real conversation this time."

Her pulse stammered. "I'm . . . I'm not sure what that means."

"I can literally hear you grit your teeth."

She swallowed. She was trying here. That counted, didn't it?

Bennett sighed. "The thing is, my dad has asked me to take in Nathan and Gemma."

"What?" That was nowhere on the radar of her fears and expectations for this conversation. Hazel picked through her scattered thoughts—some of which were relieved among the heavy smattering of absolutely shocked. "How could he expect that of you?"

In the space of silence that fell yet again, she could imagine him gripping his neck and then running a hand over his face. "It's . . . it's just the way he is." There was resignation alongside deep but subtle disappointment in Bennett's voice.

"You said yes, didn't you?" Hazel fought with the instinct to tell him this was a terrible idea. Things between Bennett and herself were strained already. How were they going to navigate this awkward and stormy section of their relationship with the added burden of two teenagers added to it?

"Yeah, Zel. I did." This time there was no subtlety in his disappointment. "Not right away. I thought hard about it and prayed about it. Talked with my mom. And I think this is what I need to do. They don't really have anyone else, and nobody understands how they're going to take this better than me."

He'd talked to his mom—but not with her. The arrow hit with a sharp sting.

"Hazel." Hunter's sharp use of her name jarred her from her blind stare at the window.

She turned to see her brother's deep scowl as he strode toward her.

"There's more." Bennett voice overtook the dead space on the phone just as Hazel held up a finger toward Hunter. "I'm going to move—"

"We're leaving." Hunter's command came dark and low. "Now."

Hazel's mind spun, and her heart throbbed, each beat a squeeze that shot painful electricity through her veins.

"—what's going on? Where are you?" Bennett's voice came back over the phone.

She swallowed. Fought the equally strong urges to yell and cry. Bennett was moving.

Leaving her. Because of his half siblings or because he'd given up on her? On them?

"Hazel?"

Clearing her throat, she lowered her head and pressed the phone harder against her face. "I'm at Janie's Café with Hunter. But he wants to go. Something is wrong. I need to go, or I'll end up walking back to Elk Lake."

"Oh." Defeat made Bennett's voice flat. "This was a bad time. I'm sorry. We can talk later."

"Bennett—"

"I've got some things to work out anyway." He made a noticeable effort to sound upbeat. "Just call me back when you're at the cabin and we can talk."

"But—" A toxic blend of crashing disappointment and irritation—at both her brother and at Bennett—swirled in her chest.

He was just going to . . . quit on them? And he couldn't understand why she didn't trust marriage . . .

"Tell Hunter hi." Then the connection went dead.

Hazel froze, keeping her face averted as she squeezed her eyes shut. That same horrible feeling washed over her. The one she'd nearly drowned in almost a year ago when Bennett had stepped back onto the deck of her cabin, suddenly remembering exactly who he was—and who she wasn't.

Not his wife.

Not anywhere close. Just some crazy, awful woman who had lied to him.

He'd despised her. And her heart had shattered.

Right then, despite the taste of irritation she had, her heart was crumbling all over again. Bennett was moving. Starting a whole new life all over again.

Without her.

A firm hand on her shoulder caused her to jump. She shot a look up to find Hunter's fiery expression on her.

"Let's get out of here."

Numbly, Hazel stood and followed her brother to the door. Without really thinking, she glanced back at the bar. Janie's gaze followed them. Distant and unreadable.

A storm had settled over Luna.

Six

Hunter had little patience to pick up their weekly goods from Mama B. The need to flee, to escape up to the lake, put his running shoes on, and start up a trail at double-time pace. With his inhaler, of course.

Or perhaps he'd leave it behind.

Maybe he'd run so hard that he'd collapse. At least then, in a fully blacked-out state, he wouldn't have the image of Janie's warm smile settled on another man taunting his heart.

He rubbed his chest, at the spot that would burn and wheeze as he pushed his stride. John Brighton had indicated that God's plans were good, even when they seemed bad. Was it irreverent to think that maybe finding reprieve in blacking out was good?

"Hunt, you look like you need some boxing gloves and a bag." Mama B didn't smile at her observation. "The one is still hanging upstairs. You know where to find it."

Hazel's glance slid toward Hunter, and he found retreat in her green-rimmed eyes. For the first time since they'd stalked out of Janie's, Hunter realized that the color of her eyes had changed since they'd arrived in town. They'd been full amber all morning.

"I don't have my inhaler with me." Hunter made himself keep bitterness out of his tone. It wasn't Mama Bulldog's fault that her daughter had sent him on a short trip to a dark mood. "Think we'd best head up the ridge, in case this snow decides to become unfriendly."

That wasn't likely. But then again, this was high country in Montana. One never knew.

Mama B held a suspicious study on him. "I'm guessing you met our new park ranger."

"Grady." Hunter shoved his hands into his pockets and shrugged. Casual as you please. "Yep. We met."

One salt-and-pepper eyebrow arched. "Nice guy?"

"Sure. But I'm sure you've already met him. Probably invited him over for one of your pepper pot roasts. Janie will bring some pie, and you'll have a lovely evening." Good job, there. Definitely kept the sarcasm on lockdown. Mama B would never suspect what had dumped kerosine on his attitude or who'd lit the match to set it off.

Hunter looked toward the rough floorboards, fighting to douse away his fiery mood.

"I wouldn't do that to you. Unless you wanted to come." With a stern expression, Mama B used both hands to scoot the box containing their weeks' worth of groceries across the glass counter. "That could prove interesting."

Hunter felt his nose flare as he drew in a hard breath. *Lock it down!* He forced his face up until his eyes met hers. "Sure. Why not? Name the date. Zel and I will be there."

With an unwavering look—one that blended compassion and frustration—Mama B held his stare and then shook her head. "This won't do you any good, Hunt."

This . . . this what? This pretending? This frustration? This determination not to look pathetic? Hunter wasn't sure what the older woman meant. But he knew what wasn't doing him any good.

Janie.

This persistent attachment to Janie. Especially when she seemed resolved to wreck him. He wanted her out of his head. He desperately needed to get the image of her flirting with Game and Parks entirely deleted from his brain.

Hunter rolled a fist and squeezed it tight. Had it been less than an hour ago that he'd determined to fight for her?

The firestorm in his mind and heart was full of contradictions, and Hunter couldn't make his thoughts make sense, let alone be consistent. Reaching for the box, he glanced down to Hazel.

She'd been awfully quiet during this brief stop at the Pantry.

Putting his energy into her might be a much better distraction than hoping he'd somehow lose consciousness.

"Let's go," he mumbled. If he could shove all the wound-up emotions about his own life to the back of his mind, he could focus on whatever was bothering his sister. That would likely be way more productive.

Hazel nodded and moved to open the door. The sleigh harness jangled an irritating sound and then Hunter was out on the boardwalk. Breathing in the snowy air, the cold in his lungs aided in dousing the flames in his chest, and his self-consumed frustration settled by degrees. He slid the box of goods onto the truck bed, and both he and Hazel climbed into the cab at the same time.

They were bouncing their way on the ridge—a solid ten minutes later—before Hunter felt like he had a grip on himself enough to address Hazel. Once again he noted that she'd not said a word. Just sat over there staring out the passenger window.

"Something happen?" he asked.

Hazel blinked. Her lips remained a flat line. And then she tipped her head until her temple rested against the glass. "We both stink at relationships, don't we?"

Rolling a tighter grip on the steering wheel, Hunter let that comment take a deep dive. All the way down to the place where honesty could rub a man's emotions raw. Especially when that kind of truth left him floundering in a pit of hopelessness.

Were the Wallace siblings doomed to failed romances and lonely futures?

Maybe they'd end up like Matthew and Marilla Cuthbert—the elderly siblings in Janie's favorite *Anne of . . .* something series.

Squirming in his seat, Hunter chuckled. More derisive than anything, but it was better than allowing the string of words that would probably not please God to roll off his tongue. "Yeah. I guess that's the truth." He glanced at her again.

Shoulders sagged in. Defeat in her expression. She looked like he felt.

"You and Bennett have a fight?"

She shook her head to negate that. Then she sucked in a shuddering breath. "He's moving."

Hunter's raging heart skidded sideways. "Moving?" Suddenly he was able to put his full focus on his sister, leaving aside his own frustrations and disappointments.

Nodding, she turned her face more toward that window. Likely so Hunter couldn't see her tears.

"Where?" Would Bennett just up and leave? "Why?"

Shrugging, Hazel took longer than a pair of heartbeats to answer. "I assume back to Chicago. To take care of his half siblings. His dad and stepmom are going somewhere or something."

Hunter felt his sister's despair settle in his own heart, and the ache was both for her and for himself. Bennett had become a good friend. And he was good for Hazel.

He couldn't leave. They needed him. With Hunter's fledgling faith in Jesus, and the memory of Bennett talking about redemption, Hunter felt strongly that he really *needed* Bennett there. Today was a prime example. Hunter had no real idea how a godly man should handle all this raging emotion regarding Janie and the Game and Parks guy.

If John Brighton couldn't be on site to help Hunter understand this new world of Christianity, then Bennett would have to help him.

God?

He wanted to finish that start to a prayer with *You can't let this happen*. But then he thought of his last shot-to-heaven quick prayer.

Make her love me again.

Suddenly Hunter heard how demanding that was. Could he really order the God of heaven and earth around? Like God owed him the life he wished for?

John Brighton's God was not a genie-in-a-bottle god.

Grant your every wish couldn't be how this worked. Not when Hunter knew himself to be a miserable creature who had desperately needed a savior. Not when he knew his own massive mistakes and failures.

God, I really need help understanding this all . . .

Was that demanding? It felt more like an honest plea than a demand . . .

Hunter rubbed his head, and then he put his attention back on his sister at the same moment she swiped her fingertips across her cheek.

Hazel had softened quite a bit in the past several months. Something that Hunter attributed to Bennett, and that was a good thing. But seeing her cry was new.

The ache in his chest ballooned. He reached across the space between them and gripped her shoulder. "We'll be okay, Hazel."

She covered his hand with hers. When she didn't respond, he moved to grip her fingers.

"No matter what, you've got me. Remember?"

"Yeah." Her answer came out breathy, and then she squeezed his hand.

That was a miracle in and of itself.

Thank You for it.

Allowing that gratitude to fall soft against the chilly steel in his heart helped. Hunter focused on that small measure of relief as he pulled up to Hazel's cabin, set the parking brake, and hopped out to take the box inside.

Once there, Hazel moved on autopilot to put away the groceries. "You want to come over for dinner tonight?"

Hunter repacked what she'd laid on the small round table for him to take to his camp. "Yeah. Better than a burnt hotdog for one." He paused, considering that. "Well, better if you let me do the cooking."

"I have trout. I'm good with trout."

That was true. If there was one dish Hazel had mastered, it was trout. Which was weird, because trout was tricky. Likely, Hazel had it down because she loved it, as had Pops, and Nan had taught her all the secrets. A bit of oil, some native herbs, and a dash of bottled lemon juice—which Nan would incorporate into as many dishes as she could, to avoid scurvy, because Pops hated just about every fruit and vegetable they could access.

Hunter nodded his agreement. "Trout it is. I'll do the rice."

She rolled her eyes, but a touch of amusement helped to soften the mossy green that rimmed the amber irises. Hazel had not mastered rice, and Hunter didn't like it crunchy, clumpy, or burned.

"Sundown?"

"That will work."

"Zel?" Hunter lifted the one-quarter-filled box. He waited to make his exit until she glanced at him again. "You going to be okay?"

She shrugged. "People change their mind."

Something she'd said not very long ago as a reason she'd rejected Bennett's sort-of proposal.

Hunter couldn't believe that Bennett had changed his mind—or his heart—about Hazel. Not when he'd seen the two of them together. Not when he'd heard the longing and conviction in Bennett's voice when the man had confided in Hunter that he wanted to marry Hazel. A sudden change of heart didn't fit here.

But he wasn't confident in that enough to say it out loud. What if it was just his desperate hope that Hazel wasn't right—that the Wallace siblings weren't doomed to lives of loneliness? Instead Hunter nodded and made his way back to the running truck.

Back at his trailer, he put away the few groceries and then wandered to the edge of the pond's shore. To his left a gentle wind rattled the millions of aspen leaves, creating a soft, familiar rustling that lent comfort. The deep-green wall of those leathery leaves had transformed to wide swaths of vibrant yellow.

Some things did change. And sometimes that was a good thing. Change was needed—part of the rhythm of life.

But Bennett? Had he really changed his mind?

Hunter could think of one sure way to find out the truth. Reaching into his back pocket, he palmed his cell phone and sent a call out to his friend.

"Hunter." Bennett answered right away. "I wasn't expecting you to call. Everything okay with the lodge?"

"Nothing wrong there." Hunter cleared his throat, an attempt to remove the bite in his tone. "My sister is upset though."

A muffled sigh came from the other end of the call. "Yeah. I should have discussed this with her first."

"So it's true? You're moving?"

"Yeah, but I didn't think she'd be upset about that part."

"How could you assume that? Chicago is a long way away, and she hates the city."

"Chicago?"

"Right." Were they talking about the same thing here? "You're moving back to Chicago. That's what Hazel said."

"It's not what I said." A pause rested in the back-and-forth. Then, "I told her I was moving to Luna. To be closer to the both of you because it's going to be complicated enough with me being guardian for Nathan and Gemma. I don't want the distance making things harder."

"Here? You're . . . you're moving here?"

"Yes, that's my plan. I must have been cut off when I was telling Hazel. It sounded like she was distracted."

Mild guilt plunged in Hunter's gut. That had been his fault. He'd been narrowly focused on leaving the café so he didn't have to witness Janie with Game and Parks a moment longer. He'd barked at Hazel, interrupting her phone conversation with Bennett, demanding that they leave. Now.

"Yeah . . . I'm sorry about that." Relief rushed to the spot that had just felt rotten. Bennett wasn't leaving. He hadn't changed his mind.

"Sounds like I'd better call Hazel and get this straighten out."

"That's a good idea. Like I said, she was pretty upset."

"Was she . . . did she say anything about me taking in my siblings for the next several months?"

"Just that you were. That's why you were moving—although she thought, obviously, that you meant you were moving to Chicago. She thought you were . . . giving up on her."

Bennett's end of the conversation sagged.

The silence stirred a touch of panic in Hunter. "Bennett, don't give up on her."

"I'm not. It's just . . ."

"I know. Weird. I get it."

Another beat of unsure silence went by. "I'm not giving up."

"Good." The measure of relief Hunter felt in that was shocking. It also proved to be motivating.

Bennett was going to keep fighting for love. Maybe Hunter needed to pick up his wounded and frustrated heart, take a deep breath, and keep going.

Seven

Janie reached into the sink full of bobbing apples, soaking in vinegar-tinged water, grabbed a deep-red Jonathan that filled her whole palm, and shook the water off. With her paring knife, she peeled it with the sort of gusto one might see in a contest.

"Are you going for a time record?" Mama asked, humor in her voice.

"No." Janie kept her head down, her eyes trained on that apple. The single, continuous strip curled around her knuckles. "Why?"

Mama stopped turning the apple-peeler-corer—the only one between the two of them—and turned to face Janie. "Maybe I should put a stopwatch on you. You might make the *Guiness Book*." This time humor wasn't the only thing threaded in her tone. A hint of prying emerged rather strongly.

Janie ignored it.

"Want to tell me what's fueling your bonfire?"

"No bonfires. Just peeling apples." Janie nodded toward the five-gallon buckets filling every area of the small house. She and Mama had brought them back from the U-pick farm they loved near Bozeman. Lovely variations of red, gold, and green filled the buckets—Jonathans, Honeycrisps, Ida Reds, and Ginger Golds. When they were done stocking the pantry with canned pie filling, they'd continue with steam juicing and sauce making. "We have a lot of work left to do."

"I've been peeling apples with you since you were probably too young to be wielding that sharp knife." Mama set her own tool down on her old Formica countertop. Then she covered Janie's busy hands. "I know a bonfire in my daughter's heart when I see one. What's going on?"

Shoulders slumping, Janie sighed. It was futile to deny Mama when she pried—which wasn't all that often. But when she did, she was all bulldog about it. Hence her nickname—Mama Bulldog. Well, that and the fact that if provoked, Mama would take on a bear and not quit until she or the beast was dead.

She could be that fierce. But that was an overflow of love. Sometimes in random moments such as this, Janie wondered how it was possible for a man to have walked away from Mama's resilient, beautiful heart.

Men were mysterious creatures. Dumb ones, at that.

"Janie girl. Talk to your mother."

She nodded. "You know that new park ranger who is renting Jeremy's ally house for the winter?"

"I do. Met him last week when he first came into town."

"Yeah. Me too."

In the dangling silence, Mama raised her brow. "And . . ."

"And I might have flirted with him."

Mama continued to look at her, a silent *continue* beckoning in her silence. When Janie did nothing more than blush, Mama leaned back against the counter and crossed her arms. "It's not a crime to flirt with an eligible man."

"I know." She tried hard to extinguish the heat in her cheeks. Why was she acting like a schoolgirl who had been caught cheating on a test? She wanted to claim that her reaction was because she hadn't a whole lot of experience "flirting with an eligible man." Men who were on the market to flirt with didn't frequent Luna all that often. And Janie didn't frequent anywhere else they might be.

But that excuse rang hollow in her conscience. It was *not* the real reason she felt out of sorts.

"Did he seem interested?" Mama pressed into the lingering silence.

"Yes."

"Is he, in fact, *eligible*?"

"I didn't see any signs of a ring."

"Then?"

Janie let out a low groan. "Hunter was there."

Mama pressed her lips together. Stange, she didn't seem one bit shocked. "Saturday morning, right? That would explain his stormy mood when he came to pick up groceries." For several heartbeats, she studied Janie. Reading her carefully, as though there might be instructions on how to best proceed. "It bothered you that Hunter was there?"

Janie hugged herself, her gaze drifting toward the linoleum floor. "It shouldn't."

"But it did?"

She nodded. Because she had done it, particularly, *because* Hunter was there.

"Why?"

"Because I snubbed him, and I flirted with Grady." She forced herself to meet Mama's waiting eyes. "On purpose."

"Ah. Because you knew it would bother Hunter?"

It was hard to own the truth sometimes. Especially when the truth was that Janie still had the capacity to act like an immature kid. She blew out a gusty breath. "Yeah."

"He's not over you?"

She shrugged. A verbal *I don't know* would be an outright lie, so Janie didn't say it. By the way he'd woven his fingers with hers, pressed his forehead against hers, and brushed the edge of her lip with the pad of his thumb when she'd gone up to see his trash trailer for herself, *no*, Hunter hadn't dumped her from his heart.

Then again, he could have been manipulating her, just as she'd accused him. So perhaps *I don't know* wasn't an outright lie.

That fire in her belly—the one Mama had commented on only minutes before—blazed hotter. Why did Hunter Wallace always have to mix up her life? She didn't like it. Didn't want it. She wished he'd just stayed away forever, like he'd planned.

Didn't she?

"Are you over him?"

"Yes." The answer shot like a spark from her lips.

Again Mama's eyebrows lifted. She didn't believe Janie. But rather than saying so, she reached across the gap between them and covered Janie's arm. "You're a big girl, Janie. I can't tell you what to do."

"That has never stopped you, Mama."

"From what I could tell, Grady is a nice man. And you know what I think of Hunter."

"That he's a wandering soul, just like—"

A single, sharp finger snap cracked into the space between them. "That never once crossed my mind or my lips, Janie Elizabeth Truitt." Mama went into full rebuke mode. "Those are your thoughts and yours alone. Things you need to deal with. And let's start by acknowledging some facts. When your dad left, he packed up and was gone. He didn't ask if I would go with him. He didn't *want* us to go with him. That's vastly different from the deal between you and Hunter, and you need to be honest about it."

Mama paused to let that truth seep in. Then planted her hands on her hips. "And if your resentment toward your father is driving this fear and resentment toward Hunter, then you need to deal with that and not drag Grady into the middle of that sort of mess. If you're truly over Hunter and honestly interested in this new man in town, then you don't need to feel guilty about it. Hunter is a grown man and will act like one. But if you're intentionally injuring Hunter and using Grady to do it..." Mama left the rest unsaid. Because she knew Janie could fill in the blank.

Then she was acting like a lousy person.

See. Mama had never held back from telling Janie what to do. At least, from telling her what she *thought* about whatever it was Janie was doing. Which was why Janie hadn't volunteered to talk about any of this with Mama.

Loosening her starched shoulders, Mama nodded, as if the conversation had been adequately covered. She reached one more time to rub Janie's shoulder, as if to soften the blow of those hard facts, and then moved back to the apples. "You're a fine woman with a big heart. I know you'll figure out what is right."

Great. That compliment felt more like... guilt.

Janie followed her mother's lead back to the apples and set her knife to peeling again. This time without the record-breaking energy. But her heart still writhed in her chest.

She *did* like Grady Briggs. He was handsome. He'd been polite and respectful—though a bit on the shy side. Maybe Janie liked shy. She couldn't say for sure—there'd been very few opportunities when it came to single men who held an interest in her.

Maybe she'd flirted because she just liked the guy. Maybe she'd been upset with Hunter because he had sat there, right next to Grady, and scowled at her, as if she didn't have any business liking another man.

How patriarchal of him. Hunter had no business telling Janie who she could like or not like. He had no authority to scowl at her flirting. He shouldn't have even sat there in the first place. Hazel had taken the table by the front window, after all. Hunter should have sat with her, way the heck away from the bar and away from where Grady had parked.

As she went through the mental gymnastics that involved Hunter and her emotional response, Janie's hands worked faster.

When Janie reached into the sink for a new victim to peel, Mama pinned a knowing look on her.

"What?" Janie huffed.

"Prayer. That's what you need. It's better than stewing. And it'd be a whole lot better than losing your thumb to an out-of-control paring knife."

"There's nothing to pray about."

"Nothing?" Mama laughed.

"Nothing, when it comes to Hunter."

"That may have been your problem these past years."

"What?"

"That you didn't pray about it."

"That's not..." True?

Janie stopped, her knife edge pressed against the sunny skin of a Ginger Gold. She'd prayed about her and Hunter back then, hadn't she?

Surely she had.

But... she wasn't sure. All she really remembered was that she'd been livid that he'd go do something as monumental as signing up for the navy without speaking with her about it. And that she'd been devastated that he didn't change his mind when she'd told him she wasn't going with him. And then she'd assessed him to be of the same ilk as her wandering, absentee father, which had been the death blow.

"Pray, Janie. And listen for an answer." Mama's instructions sank in deep.

As they went back to work, Janie stopped her mind from steamrolling over Hunter. But though Mama's instructions were wise and best, Janie found that actually praying about Hunter—about her and Hunter and what their relationship should look like now that he was back—was a wall too high to climb.

Instead, she asked God to remove the yucky feelings she had about her former fiancé. And then she pretended like that was enough.

By Monday Janie had found she could smother most of those yucky feelings. Enough to convince herself that God had complied with her wishes and set her free. She slid the four pies she'd assembled—two apple, one using the last of her juneberry supply and a spiced pear—into her large oven, set the timer, and moved on to making the dough for tomorrow's selection. Her food processor helped her make quick work out of creating eight more discs of dough, and she had them wrapped and placed in her refrigerator before the timer rang.

The warm aroma layered by apples, pears, cinnamon, cloves, and almond extract enveloped her kitchen with the sense of fall. Janie inhaled, delighting in the feeling of a job well done as the bell out front chimed. With a self-satisfied grin, she made her way to the door.

And her smile bloomed full at the good-looking man in a gray button-down ambling toward her pine counter.

"Good morning, Mr. Briggs."

His slow grin came across shy but pleased. "Just Grady. If I can call you Janie?"

"That seems like a good deal to me."

Stopping at the counter, he rested his hands on top, but he didn't settle onto a stool. And he didn't say anything further.

Janie pressed her lips together as the lull between them became awkward. "Can I get you some coffee?" she finally asked.

"Sure. To go." He itched a spot on his jawline. Then he fished a ten-dollar bill from his wallet and slid it onto the counter. "I'm heading to Yellowstone today."

"For the day?" Janie tried to ignore the splotch of red on his neck and turned away to pour his coffee when she couldn't hold back her grin anymore.

"For the next five days. I'm working the backcountry near the Mammoth Hot Springs area."

Janie set his coffee on the counter and secured the lid. "Five days? Where will you stay?"

"In my tent. I'll be on the trails pretty much the whole time."

"Oh." Talk about a wanderer. She brushed that thought aside, and when it resurfaced, she edited it. Not a wanderer. An adventurer. Not the same thing.

Another empty lull throbbed by. Unsure what else to say, and why she felt compelled to hold a conversation with this man who simply had come in for some coffee to go, Janie rubbed her moist palms down her jeans and summoned her *customer service* smile. "Well, stay safe in the backcountry."

He nodded. "Thanks." Then he picked up his to-go cup. And stayed right there.

"Something else I can get you?"

Clearing his throat, Grady scratched that spot on his jaw again. "Well. Maybe." He straightened his shoulders and dropped his hand to his side. "I mean, I had hoped that . . . What I mean to say is . . ." He cleared his throat again. "I'm sorry. I'm really bad at this."

"Okay . . ." Janie furrowed her brow, wondering how she could help this poor man out of his misery.

"What I came in for was to ask if you'd go on a date with me when I get back." Grady spat that out in a rush.

Her furrowed brow smoothed. Janie smiled full again. "A date?"

"Uh . . . yeah."

"I'd like that."

"You would?" He seemed genuinely shocked.

"I would."

"Even if I have no idea where to take you on a date around here?"

"I like hiking."

"You do?" His dark eyes sparkled with relief. "Me too." And then he shut his eyes and shook his head. "Obviously."

"There's a good trail south of town. It follows Elk Creek toward the Madison River."

"I've heard of it."

"Then let's do it," Janie said.

"Saturday?"

"I'll have to keep the café open until one, or the locals will have my head." Janie winked. "But after that I can close up early."

"Perfect." Grady lifted his mug and started for the door. "Thank you for the coffee."

"Grady?"

He stopped, hand on the handle. "Yeah?"

"Your coffee was only a dollar." Janie waved the ten that he'd left on the counter.

The smile he shot her way made her tummy flip. "I didn't actually come in here for coffee, and ten dollars is a steal for what I got." He lifted the to-go cup in salute. "See you in a few days."

Janie savored the warm, tickling sensation that raced through her as she made her way back to the kitchen. She made it all the way to the oven before Hunter intruded on her giddiness.

And that silly, wonderful buzz fizzled at the image of his dark, angry gaze. Ugh. Hunter ruined everything.

Hurt more than angry.

Janie ignored that whisper in her heart.

"I don't care," she declared to her perfectly baked pies. And she worked really hard to believe it.

Eight

"This is a *town*?" Gemma stood just outside of Bennett's Bronco, her hand on the open door, staring at the full length of Main.

The opposite car door slammed. "More like a ghost town," Nathan grumbled.

"People live here." Bennett came around the front of the vehicle and stopped beside Gemma, squeezing her shoulder. At least the girl had tried to keep up a decent outlook as they'd flown from Chicago to Billings, caught a ride from Billings to Bozeman from José, who had made the two-hour drive to pick them up, and then piled into Bennett's SUV to travel another two hours to Luna.

Bennett had second thoughts about making the full trip in one day, now that they'd planted their weary feet in the dirt of Luna's Main Street. The kids might have taken this otherworldly transition better on a bit of rest in between.

But he had an appointment with the Luna real-estate agent—who happened to be the sheriff's wife. And he had a driving desire to see a certain honey-haired mountain girl as soon as possible.

Looking down the boardwalk, past Luna's Pantry toward Janie's Café, Bennett searched the one-block-length street for that particular woman. Hazel had said she'd make it down from Elk Lake to meet them. His gaze was met with an empty dirt road and a vacant boardwalk and landed on the rising layers of mountains framed by gloriously fall-dressed trees. If he'd been the photographer he'd claimed he was when first he'd come to Luna, he'd have pointed his lens at that scene and clicked away. Stunning.

But not what he was hoping for.

Just as disappointment settled, a pair came out of the sheriff's office slash county jail—a woman and a man. Bennett grinned. There was no mistaking that leather Australian cowboy hat or the honied braid that draped over her shoulder. Bennett wasn't sure why she'd been in the county jail with Jeremy, but at that moment, when his heart squeezed with giddy pleasure and electric anticipation, he didn't care.

He set his stride to meeting her, his dark tennis shoes making a muted clap against the boardwalk, which contrasted with the much more pronounced smack of her boots against the wooden pathway. Jeremy held back as she neared the Pantry, and when she lifted her head, Bennett thrilled to see those golden eyes smiling at him beneath the brim of that hat.

And then she was in his arms. He pulled her in tight and buried his face into her neck, causing that hat to tumble to the boardwalk. Bennett inhaled the outdoorsy delight that was unique to Hazel

EIGHT

Wallace. All sunshine and pine, with a subtle hint of woodsmoke. Home.

"You came back," she whispered, her arms twisted around his neck.

"I'm still shocked that you thought I wouldn't."

"I'm glad it was a misunderstanding." Hazel leaned back, allowing him to swim in that lovely warm gaze. "I missed you."

Bennett leaned in to graze his lips across hers. "I missed you too." He took another sip—this time longer—from the sweetness of her mouth. "Almost a month is too long."

He hadn't planned on being gone that long. Two weeks max. But once he'd decided to take on his siblings, there were legalities to work through, packing to be done, and contacts to be made for yet another major move. The second in less than a year for Bennett.

"Now you're here to stay?" Hazel whispered, tentative hope in her voice.

A surge of joy met the tenderness in her question. "That's the plan." Bennett brushed another kiss on her cheek and then released her to take her hand. "Come meet the kids."

Her wary glance told him she'd not quite come to terms with this part. In truth, neither had he. It was a monumental thing, becoming a guardian. Being solely responsible for two young lives. Only a year ago, Bennett had lived for himself alone. Shifting his life and choices for the woman he loved was one thing. This was a little different.

He barely knew his siblings. But here they were.

Bennett resolved to make it work. And not just work, but to do it well. If there had been anything that had been consistent in his character, determination was it, and every time panic loomed in his heart, he leaned hard into it.

And as far as leaning hard into something, Bennett resolved, as he strode hand in hand with Hazel toward the pair of teens hanging back at the car, that he would press harder into God. He knew nothing but that he was going to need Him more than ever in the next several weeks.

José's promise of prayers—continued prayers—and anything Bennett needed, anytime, buoyed his sinking confidence. For now, he hoped José was praying for this introduction to Hazel. Heaven knew—and Bennett knew from prior experience—she could sure leave a person with a terrible impression. False, but awful nonetheless.

Then again, he'd not been exactly charming either that fall day nearly a year ago.

Three feet from the Bronco and still on the boardwalk, Bennett stopped, and Hazel came to a halt beside him. The best bet, he felt, was to begin with his sister.

"Hazel, meet Gemma." Bennett gestured toward the ginger-haired girl, who stood gawking at the Old West scene she would call home for the foreseeable future. "Gemma, this is Hazel."

Gemma turned to face Hazel, a timid grin curving her mouth. "You live up in those?" she pointed toward the western hills.

"I do." Hazel pointed toward Elk Canyon. "Up that way."

"Wow. Is it high?"

"My cabin is a little over eight thousand feet above sea level."

"Oh." Clearly that meant little to Gemma.

"We're currently at about six thousand feet." Hazel tried to help her understand.

Bennett squeezed Hazel's hand and then stepped toward Gemma. "Chicago is a little more than five hundred feet above sea level, if that helps at all. If your ears are popping or your head hurts, the elevation change might be why."

Or it could be that they were all exhausted. Bennett rubbed his temples, thinking he could use a large glass of mountain water and an aspirin himself.

"Oh," Gemma repeated. Then she rubbed her right ear. "This one hurts a little."

"We'll get you something for it." Bennett patted her shoulder. "Drink lots of water, okay?" Then he looked over the car. "Nathan, meet Hazel Wallace."

EIGHT

"Your lady friend." Nathan didn't even look up from his phone, his impassive tone both typical and grating. "I'm sure she's hot."

Bennett held a brief but hard look on him—which Nathan didn't care about because he didn't look up to see—and then shook his head as he turned to meet Hazel's reaction. As he would have guessed, Hazel wore a scowl, her lips pinched.

She was not one bit impressed. Part of Bennett wanted to watch that match play out, because he was 100 percent sure Nathan had zero idea what kind of beast his *hot lady friend* could be when provoked.

It'd be a little amusing to watch. Especially since Nathan's mumbled complaints had long since gotten on Bennett's nerves.

But maybe that would not be the best introduction to this new life they'd all been thrust into. Bennett searched for a distraction and didn't have to look far. Jeremy Yates stood in front of the Pantry, waiting his turn while the family met Hazel. At Bennett's small head movement, Jeremy approached, hand outstretched.

"Sheriff." Bennett shook the man's offered greeting with relief. "I assume your wife is somewhere nearby?"

"Leslie is waiting for you at the house she thinks would work best." Jeremy lifted his brown cap bearing a gold star and the words *Elk County Sheriff*, let the cool breeze ruffle his nearly black hair, and then returned it. "It's just a couple of blocks off Main. I can walk with you there, if you're up for it?"

"Good plan." Bennett looked over his shoulder, finding Hazel standing on the boardwalk, chewing her bottom lip, Gemma still a statue beside the Bronco, a fake smile plastered in place, and Nathan posted up against the back end of the vehicle, face buried in his screen. A great start for all of them. "We could all use a good walk after all that traveling."

"Right," Gemma said, like an overlit Christmas tree. Too bright. Too cheery.

Poor girl was scared to death, and Bennett couldn't blame her. What preteen wouldn't be, with her parents off to someplace in

Europe indefinitely and her new guardian a single, nearly thirty-year-old half brother she barely knew.

What had Chip been thinking?

Bennett placed his attention back on Hazel, silently pleading with her for help. Granted, he knew she was wildly uncomfortable with this scenario too. But she was a grown-up in this situation. And she knew what it was like to feel abandoned. If only she knew how to connect with other humans.

God, please help us...

Jeremy rescued them from the strained silence. "Shall we?" He gestured toward the county jail, which wasn't the direction Bennett had imagined they'd go, but that hardly mattered.

"Let's do it." Bennett waited for Hazel to draw up beside him and then took her hand. When Gemma filled the spot on his other side, he draped a casual arm on her shoulder. And then they waited for Nathan, who remained glued to the side of the Bronco, lost in his world of *Minecraft*.

"Nathan, we're going to see the house," Gemma said with sugar in her voice.

"Go ahead," Nathan mumbled.

"Nate." Bennett nearly barked his name. "You're coming too. Let's go."

"My name is not *Nate*." This time Nathan didn't mumble. He still didn't look up though.

"Good to know, Nathan." Bennett had forever been correcting people when they shortened his name, so he got that. But this snarky, lazy, disrespectful attitude was getting old superfast. Was this what his mother had put up with when he was that age?

A resounding *yes* clanged through his mind. Bennett had been the chief of disrespectful teenage boys, so this might be exactly what he deserved.

Bennett waited for another moment, puzzling over how to handle this. If he'd been Nathan in this situation, the more anyone demanded he do something, the deeper he'd dig in his heels. He glanced at Gemma, whose brow furrowed with a pensive stare at her brother. Then at Hazel, whose cool gaze might have been read as indifference if Bennett didn't know her better. But he did. She cared. She just wasn't going to allow Nathan the victory of knowing he could alter her course of action.

And there was the solution. As if a silent understanding had passed between them, Bennett nodded at Hazel and then started toward the county jail again. What was Nathan going to do if he didn't come with them? He knew no one. Knew how to get nowhere. Couldn't take off with the Bronco because Bennett had the keys. And Bennett suspected that Mama Bulldog had spied on the entire scene from the moment Bennett had parked. She'd keep an eye out.

Nathan could stay there by himself if he wanted. It really didn't make a difference.

When the group reached the county jail building, Jeremy gestured to the narrow dirt road that would lead north from Main, and they turned. Gemma glanced back, and Bennett could sense the tension in her already tight shoulders knot harder.

He leaned down to speak low. "He'll be fine. Maybe he just needs a minute by himself."

Gemma looked up at him, her copper eyes filled with worry.

Bennett squeezed her into a gentle hug. "There's not a whole lot here for him to get into trouble with, you know?"

"He could start a forest fire."

"Did he bring a match?"

"Umm . . . I don't think so. That probably wouldn't get through airport security."

"Then I doubt it." Bennett winked. "My guess? He'll wander after us the moment he realizes he's alone in a place that is very, very big, and very, very wild."

"Will he get lost?"

Bennett shook his head.

"Mama Bulldog has her eye on him, I can promise." Hazel's comment drew both Gemma's and Bennett's attention.

Though shocked that she would voluntarily speak to a stranger, Bennett felt gratitude rise. Hazel was trying, and he could kiss her for it.

Later, he would.

Jeremy Yates continued to lead the trio without comment until they came to a small, two-story, Victorian-style house. Though brick, it appeared to be in rough shape. The second floor—likely more of a loft area than an actual second floor—had been sided with peeling, jaundice-yellow gingerbread shake siding and was in grave need of new paint. Possibly, to be replaced altogether. But the roof appeared sturdy, and it was on a good-size lot that backed into a grove of aspens.

Bennett guessed that the main level was no more than nine hundred square feet. It'd be tight.

"This is three bedrooms?" he asked.

"Yes. Well, I'll let Leslie go into that with you." Jeremy waved them to the front door. "She's inside."

Releasing Gemma's shoulders and Hazel's hand, Bennett let the girls pass through the heavy wooden front door that Jeremy held open, and then followed.

"I'll catch up with you guys later," Jeremy said.

"Thanks for being our guide."

"Not a problem." Jeremy cast a leery glance over the house. "Hope this works."

Bennett doubted that Jeremy would worry except for the fact that he knew Bennett was a property investor who tended to have an expensive eye. But he didn't know that Bennett had grown up a whole lot more humbly than he'd lived as an adult. He could adjust. Probably.

The last thought fizzled as he stepped into the dingy home. Army-green carpet—torn in more spots than could Bennettcount on one hand—smothered the floor. Hopefully, beneath it there would be wood planks in decent enough shape to restore. The woodwork panels that came to chair-rail height had been stricken with Pepto-pink paint. The stairs, tucked into the far corner of this dark and bizarre front room, had also endured the merciless whims of a paintbrush—though that jaundice yellow from the front had been the weapon of choice there.

"Don't panic." Leslie Yates appeared from the large, wood-framed opening—sporting that awful yellow color—that must have connected to another room in the back. The kitchen? "It's a spectacle in here, but the bones are solid. You do flips, right?"

Bennett nodded, trying not to scowl. "Not usually when I live in them though."

And maybe even more to the point, *most* of his property-flip experience had been in vacation spaces—namely condos. Single-family, private-house flips, he'd discovered in the past six months, were different. Not harder different, but different nonetheless. And then there was the added fact that this was Luna. He had zero contacts in the area, and the nearest hardware store was an hour away.

It all made for a discouraging first impression.

Shoulders dropping, Lelsie nodded. "I get it. But the thing is . . ."

"There's not a lot to pick from in Luna."

Again, she nodded. "The only other property I have available that would maybe suit your needs is a trailer house on the other side of Elk Creek. But winters in a trailer house . . ."

"Yeah, no thanks." He'd visited Hazel in February and had a clear memory of the amount of snow that had piled up and over the deck at her cabin. Though he knew cold well enough, having lived in Chicago his whole life, he had no intention of doing mountain-level snow and cold in a trailer house.

With that thought, he wished Hunter the best of luck in his camper for the season. Oy. Maybe Hunt should reconsider sharing the cabin with Hazel. Surely by this point the siblings were past the feral impulse to kill each other.

Bennett turned a slow circle, his brain absorbing the obnoxious assault of colors with a filtering eye toward possibilities. Leslie was right—he did flips. He could handle this. Probably. This one would just require a little more planning. And flexibility.

And patience.

His examination landed on Gemma's bewildered—or perhaps horrified—expression.

"Not loving it, huh?" he asked her.

"It's . . ." She cast a worried glance toward Leslie. "Colorful?"

Leslie smiled, making her lovely face more attractive. For a skip of a beat, Bennett wondered how Jeremy had met her and how she liked living in Luna—because Bennett knew that Leslie had grown up near Billings. From all that he could see, the woman was settled and happy, and that gave oxygen to his own gasping hope for the same.

Love was worth sacrifice.

"It is that," Leslie replied to Gemma's comment. "The woman who lived here is . . . exceptional."

Hazel chuckled, drawing Bennett's attention. "You knew her?" he asked and then immediately wondered why that would surprise him. She wasn't *entirely* reclusive, and she had lived her entire life within reach of Luna.

"Marvel Elliot." Hazel raised a brow while she surveyed the madness of vibrant color. "She would give me a dime every Thursday when I stayed in town for school."

"Why?"

"She'd come into the Pantry for her groceries, her permed hair poofed out to its full five-inch length, and often wearing tiger-print leggings of some neon color, and say, 'Happy Thursday!' then press a dime to my palm. Then she'd say, 'Tell Essie hi from her Marvelous friend and that I expect her to come off the mountain sometime to see me.' She'd wave her ring-laden fingers over her head, like she was in a parade, and sashay out the door." Hazel laughed again. "I always thought she had come from the circus or something. When I asked Nan, she said Marvel came from the moon and might well be the reason this town was called Luna."

Bennett and Leslie both chuckled, and Gemma looked marginally less horrified by the house as she turned a slow circle in the middle of the room.

"I suppose some paint would fix a lot of this kray kray." Gemma's soft comment was likely her trying to talk herself into being okay with this.

Bennett appreciated her effort. He walked toward a rip in the carpet near the jaundiced-cased opening from which Leslie had emerged and bent to tug on the dirt-laden weave. Ah. Good bones, as Leslie had said. "There's pine flooring under this. We can hope its decent enough to refinish." He stood, sending an encouraging nod toward Gemma. "And you can pick your room first, since Nathan didn't come."

"I'm here." A low grumble came from the front doorway, followed by the boy with a hoodie tugged over his head and hands tucked into the pockets of his ripped skinny jeans. Bennett wondered how Nathan's city-grunge style would go over at Elk County High School. His guess? Not super great.

Concerns for another day. "Welcome, Nathan. Nice of you to join us."

Nathan shot a fiery glare at Bennett and then stepped into the room. His eyes widened, and he pulled his hoodie off his head as he took in the wild scene. "Sweet."

By his monotone, Bennett wasn't sure if he was being sarcastic or serious. He guessed sarcastic. Nathan was particularly fluent in mumbling sarcasm and off-the-cuff snark.

But then Nathan added, "Let's leave it."

"What?" That didn't sound sarcastic.

Gemma rolled her eyes. "You can't be for real, Nathan. It looks like my old Barbie Beach House partied a little too hard in here and the walls took the consequences."

Bennett didn't even want to consider why eleven-year-old Gemma went straight to a nasty hangover analogy, even if she'd nailed it. "We will definitely be getting rid of the . . . Barbie Beach House walls."

"Dude." Nathan tugged his hoodie back over his head. "Can't even . . ." He left the rest unsaid as he fished his phone out of his back pocket and sank his face back into the screen.

Bennett's chest tightened. Had the kid been serious? He looked back at the pink chair rail. Could Bennett live with that kind of visual assault every single day for the next . . . who knew how long? He looked at Hazel, hoping that for some unknown reason, she'd be able to help. He found Hazel's attention fixed on Nathan, and shockingly, she wore compassion.

"I think I might have a solution." Leslie spoke after a taut void had filled the house. "I know Bennett said Gemma could take her first pick of rooms, but . . ." She waved for them to follow her. Her cowboy boots made a soft clunking sound as she led them to the stairs, and then the click became sharper as she walked up the painted wood risers.

Bennett cringed. Man. Stripping that awful yellow paint to uncover the natural wood was going to be brutal. His knuckles already crawled with the dry itch that came from hot water, paint stripper, and a hard grip on a scraper for days on end, and that was just from the thought of it.

They reached the second floor—and Bennett's guess had been accurate. It was more of a loft than a true second story. Bennett hunched his shoulders and ducked his head to accommodate his over-six-foot frame to this less-than-six-foot ceiling. Leslie motioned for them to file through the door on the right.

Tie-dye.

The room was like a 1980s tie-dyed shirt. Colors spiraled on all four walls, and a disc ball hung in the center. Nathan lowered his phone and stepped into the middle while he gawked up at the ceiling and then the walls.

A slow, Jim Carey–Grinch-like grin crawled over his face. "Now this is what I'm talking about."

Gemma, not willing to step foot into that madhouse of visual cruelty, popped her fists on her hips. "Nathan, what in the world is wrong with you?"

He shot that grin—wider still—over his shoulder and winked at his sister. "Can you imagine Dad letting me do this?"

"Not on this side of death."

"Heh, heh." Nathan returned his broad smile to the shiny ball in the middle of the room. "Exactly."

Ah. Suddenly Bennett understood perfectly. *Whatever Dad wants, I want the opposite.* He knew that sentiment all too well.

"I want it," Nathan proclaimed.

"It's yours." Gemma shook her head. "I don't want to be caught dead in that sicko mess."

"All the more reason," Nathan said.

Leslie met Bennett's appreciative glance with a smile. "The other upstairs room is across the hall." She pointed.

Gemma spun around to investigate. Bennett followed, and Hazel waited between the two rooms at the top of the stairs.

The second bedroom was the same size, same basic layout, with a dormered window facing the opposite direction. But the walls were merely the Pepto pink that had had its way with the first floor.

Gemma blew out a dramatic breath. "We can paint it, right, Bennett?"

"First thing." Bennett nodded.

"There's some wallpaper at the Pantry you might look at," Leslie said. "Some really soft, pretty patterns. Mama B has good taste."

Gemma looked past Bennett and at Hazel. "Is that true?"

"I think so." Hazel propped one hand on the doorframe. "Her daughter, Janie, was always into trendy magazines and stuff. And her café is pretty cute. You could talk to her. I think she'd be thrilled to help."

This time Gemma's cautious look met Bennett's.

He shoved his hands into his pockets. "Whatever you want, Gem. We'll make it home for you. And I'd bet Hazel's right—Janie would lend a hand, and you would like her."

Gemma nodded slowly as she wandered toward the window that faced east. "At least the fall trees are pretty."

Hazel walked into the room and stopped beside Gemma at the six-paned window. "You have a good view." She tapped the upper right-hand pane. "See that dip in the land right there?"

Gemma nodded.

"That's Elk Creek. The sun will come up between the folds of hills that hem it in. It will be quite a morning show."

Gemma glanced behind her, then pointed at the empty space of exposed wood floor. "Maybe I'll put my bed there so I can see it."

"That's what I would do," Hazel said.

"I could use cream and soft greens. Maybe get a soft rug. It would be like pulling in the best of the forest." Gemma's tone hinted excitement as she looked at Hazel and received an approving nod.

Hazel surprised him. In the most delightful way possible. Then again, he remembered how she'd been with him when all he knew in the world was her—when he'd thought they were married. She'd been tender in his most vulnerable moments, like being out on the dock in the deep dark of a mountain night, shivering with fear.

"Here, Ben." Hazel had placed a palm on his jawline, turning his face so that he would look at her rather than the inky night. "Focus here . . ."

That moment had embedded in his mind, chiseled in his heart. It was the tenderness, the unmasked compassion, that she'd shown him in that awful moment that had stayed with him the most when he'd gone back to Chicago.

Hazel Wallace was significantly more than she let others see. He'd been enamored with the woman she'd allowed him to glimpse. And there she was now . . .

Bennett wondered if Hazel even saw this part of herself—the part that was warm and kind. The part that reflected the God in whose image she'd been made . . .

Awe and gratitude filled Bennett's heart as he watched his two girls interact. *My two girls . . .* Interesting that he already claimed them both that way.

Inhaling a long breath of the stale air in that old, rundown Victorian, Bennett felt his spirit lift. Though he had been, and was still, upset with his father for this careless move, he found peace in knowing his Father in heaven hadn't been surprised.

This was still new—trusting in God in the ups and downs of life—but Bennett had found more serenity in the past nine months of choosing to do so than he had in all the years he'd angrily told God that He'd failed and wasn't trustworthy.

Bennett leaned back so that he could peek across the stair landing and into the other room. There he found Nathan sprawled out on his back on the hardwood floor, staring at that disco ball. He let his attention trail back to the room where they stood, taking in Hazel and Gemma, both gazing out the window.

There was so much uncertainty. So many things that weren't settled and that could go terribly wrong, breaking his heart. He could come to love these kids, his heart growing fiercely attached only to have them leave and forget about him. Or reject him outright. He could lose the woman who had already rejected his marriage proposal.

And maybe that would happen. Every one of those devastating possibilities.

But this time was different, no matter the outcome. This time Bennett would run *to* God no matter what.

Not away. He'd tried that already. It had only led him straight into the dreadful darkness.

He'd hated the darkness. And he would never run away again.

Nine

The sound of water tumbling over the ancient rock bed and gurgling through the canyon, and the smell of crisp fall leaves, joined with the solid warmth of Bennett's fingers woven with hers to lend a sense of rightness to Hazel's tired mind. He was there again. Holding her hand. His blue eyes had held her with appreciation and, more importantly, with love, when they'd been investigating the Elliot house hours before.

He hadn't quit on her.

"You did well with the kids." Bennett lifted her hand and kissed her knuckles. "Thank you for coming down to meet them."

Relief teased loose the tangled mass of worry in her gut. He'd come back. Hadn't been so mad at her and hurt by her rejection that he'd decided to move back to Chicago and on with his life—without her. More than that, he was moving to Luna! So close that she could see him every day if she wanted to.

And now he was grateful she'd come down to meet his half siblings. Hazel could nearly giddy-sigh. "You're welcome."

They walked side by side, and she noted how much more surefooted Bennett had become when it came to trails in the past several months. This one, a wider path that paralleled Elk Creek as it ran toward the Madison on the south side of town, she hadn't been on since she'd been in school. Back then it had been her escape from town. If she hadn't been able to wander free up at Elk Lake, she'd found her way to the creek-side trail to set her wild heart free.

"By the looks of it, they are enjoying your wilderness," Bennett commented.

With scuffles and the occasional sound of scrub brush being disturbed, the two kids paced quite aways ahead of them.

"You seem surprised."

"A little bit. At least with Nathan. He was basically a zombie back in Chicago. I barely saw him because he was locked up in his room with his gaming all the time." Bennett stopped at a bush whose leaves bore a tinge of fall red and on them hung clusters of nearly black berries. He held a cluster in one palm and looked at Hazel.

"Chokecherries," she answered his unspoken question. "They're good for jams and syrups. Not great eating fresh though."

He nodded, brushed off his palm, and reclaimed her hand. He returned to their previous conversation. "Come to think of it, I'm a little surprised Gemma has taken to this place too. She's kind of . . ."

"Prissy?"

Bennett laughed outright. "Compared to you? Yes."

"Every woman is prissy compared to me."

Stopping in the shade of a brilliant-yellow aspen, Bennett tugged her hand and pulled it to his chest. "No woman compares to you." His dark-blue eyes searched her face, unveiled love in his stare.

A delightful shiver tickled down Hazel's spine. Along with a poke of guilt which jabbed her heart. She wanted him to look at her like this forever. And yet she'd rejected his proposal. Even Hazel could see the contradiction there.

Seeing it didn't mean she could change it.

"I'm glad you came back," she whispered.

"I don't know why you were afraid I wouldn't."

Hazel blinked and then looked down at her booted feet. The weight of the past month—all her worry concerning this man—provoked a slurry of emotions she could not keep back. Tears threatened, rimming her eyelids with warm liquid. At their last parting, they had left things uncertain and strained between them, and then Bennett had been gone for longer than planned.

She ran her palm over his chest and gripped his coat. "I hurt you."

"Yes." A gentle hand slid along her jaw and lifted her face so that she would meet his steady gaze. "Did you believe that my love is so feeble that it would collapse?"

Hazel winced. Truth? Yes—but not because she thought that only of Bennett. She believed it basically of everyone. People turned their backs on others they claimed to love for far less than a rejected proposal. Love was but a passionate reaction to physical attraction and chemistry and need. That didn't seem stable enough to endure through hard times.

Was that all love really was? Was that all *her* love for Bennett was?

She wanted it to be more. Something strong and unmoving, like the ancient peaks of her home. An abiding thing that she could count on. But that type of dependability didn't encompass people.

When people were involved, failure was certain.

"I aim to prove you wrong." Bennett brushed a kiss across her mouth. "We will hurt each other sometimes. Disappoint each other times. But good times or bad, Hazel, I'm not going to stop loving you."

Hazel wanted to believe him for all that lofty idealism. But it seemed too glorious to grab on to. "I'm sorry I hurt you."

The pad of his thumb traced over her cheekbone. "I shouldn't have proposed in that moment. That way. You were dealing with something really big with your brother, and it was impulsive of me to ask you right then."

There was an implication in his apology that unsettled her. Like he believed that someday she would change her mind about marriage. It provoked an uprising of irritation.

And a hint of softening curiosity.

Mostly, though, irritation.

Hazel covered his hand with hers, not wishing to embark on yet another disagreement so near to the ceasefire of the other. Then she stepped back. "The kids are pretty far ahead of us."

"How far does the trail go?"

"All the way to the Madison, if you want to walk that far. But that's more than twenty miles. And there's a bridge crossing that I don't think you'd like them to do alone. Actually, I don't think you'd like it at all."

Bennett looked down the trail. "Why not?"

"It's a narrow suspension bridge." The cable-and-plank bridge spanned more than thirty feet of space, fifteen feet above the widest part of the creek. It was minimally maintained and not for those with a fear of heights or swaying crossings.

Bennett liked neither of those, and Hazel didn't think they could trust the kids this soon. Particularly Nathan—though she'd quickly gained a soft spot for the fifteen-year-old boy. Everything about his *I don't care about you or what you think* vibe spoke a familiar story to her. One of a hurt, abandoned kid who had determined not to be exposed to that sort of pain anymore.

Nathan clearly fought to live on his own terms, and Bennett might be walking into a storm. Hazel doubted she could be much help to her boyfriend with that, but the least she could do was walk with him.

"Gemma." Bennett's call into the evening wilderness sent birds flitting from aspens and pines. "Nathan. Come on back. We'll go find some supper."

"Mama B said she'd buy Janie's deep-dish pizza for everyone," Hazel said. "She said to meet up at the café when we got hungry."

"That was generous of her."

It was, but not surprising. Mama B had a soft spot for stray humans—the same that Hazel had for stray dogs.

"Between her and my mom, hopefully I'll do okay." The tightness in Bennett's voice gave away the real fear he felt about taking on this responsibility.

Once again Hazel wondered why he'd agreed. On one hand she understood—he felt responsible, though he had no real reason to, and he wanted better for his younger siblings than his dad had offered to him. But on the other hand, Bennett barely knew these kids—and they him. What made him think this could work?

By his comment just now, he wasn't sure it could work at all.

His timidity about this reminded her of how he'd been after he'd hit his head last fall. Lost and utterly dependent on her. Not that he was lost or dependent on her now, but there was that hesitation in his expression. It drew compassion from a hidden well within and made her dare what she normally wouldn't.

"You could bring them up to the cabin while you wait for the house papers to go through." She swallowed, wondering even as she spoke how she'd adjust to having so many people invading her space when she'd lived alone all these years.

The kids appeared from the distance, making their way back.

"Thanks, but I'm not going to do that," Bennett said. "We'll be fine at the hotel."

That remained to be seen. Hazel had seen Bennett's jaw clenched when he'd checked into the Creekside Inn. The rooms left a whole lot to be desired for people used to a Super 8—or so she'd overhead a traveler say at Janie's. She couldn't imagine what the owner of luxury resorts, such as Bennett Crofton, thought of the dark space, dingy walls, old shag carpet, squeaky double beds, and cracked avocado-green sink.

Hand in hand, Bennett and Hazel walked toward the trailhead.

Actually, she could imagine Bennett's impression of the inn. It was likely running the same vein as what he'd said about her place when he'd first arrived last year as a "client."

"I mean to tell you that it's disgusting to think about sleeping in the same space some mountain man strung out his dead animals."

The replay of that conversation as they'd ridden up to the cabin made Hazel giggle.

"What are you laughing about?" Bennett asked.

"I was just remembering how you were when you found out the shack had been where Pops had hung his pelts."

Bennett wrinkled his nose and shook his head. "For the record, that's still disturbing. You shouldn't make grown men sleep in something that small and awkward anyway. Adding the pelts layers a whole new level of horror to the experience."

They came to the trailhead and stopped at the dirt parking lot where Bennett had parked his SUV. Hazel looked up at him. "How did I end up with such a squeamish man?"

"I'm normal, not squeamish." He tapped her nose. "And I believe you told me that you chased a raccoon out of my sleeping quarters and fell in love with me."

"No. I said *you* fell in love with *me*."

"That's right. I did." He kissed her cheek and then winked. "And I'll be fine at the hotel, don't you worry. After all, I've survived worse."

Hazel playfully pushed his chest even as she laughed. Bennett reached around her waist and tugged her close.

Gemma came jogging up the path and into view. She hesitated when she saw them standing so close, obviously worried she'd interrupted something private.

"Nothing to see here." Bennett released his hold, brushing Hazel's nose as she stepped back. "Is Nathan coming?"

"No." Nathan's snark came just loud enough to be heard. "Nathan fell into the river and is drowning."

Gemma joined Hazel and Bennett at the parking lot just as Nathan came into view.

"That's not funny, bud," Bennett said.

"No one would care."

Hazel's heart pinched. Bennett reached to pat his shoulder, but Nathan ducked away.

"No touching." Nathan rolled his shoulders, as if trying to shed the offense. "I'm not the touching kind of person, and we don't have a touching kind of relationship. So hands off."

Bennett held up both palms. "Got it." Then he fished his key fob from his pocket and with the press of a button, his Bronco beeped a hello. "Pizza, anyone?"

"Oh yeah!" Gemma's enthusiasm made up for Nathan's mild shrug. "Is it deep dish?"

"Uh..."

"It's almost as good as Lou Malnati's," Hazel said into Bennett's hesitation.

"How do you know about Lou Malnati's?" Gemma asked.

Hazel shrugged. "My brother had it mailed when he was in Chicago several years back. Janie, my best friend, decided it was bread from heaven, and she and her mom—we call her Mama Bulldog—set out to make their own version. It's pretty close. Janie serves it on Fridays at her café during the fall and winter."

"Look at that." Bennett slid into the driver's seat, and everyone else entered the car as well. "We didn't leave everything behind."

"House. Friends. Big-screen TV. Lake Michigan. Private pool. Starbucks." Nathan listed his protest, tabbing each deadpanned item off with his finger.

Bennett looked at Hazel. She shook her head and ignored the boy's contrary attitude. From what she knew, he was entitled to a bit of resentment. Heaven knew how she'd be if someone tried to take her out of Elk Canyon.

Actually, everyone knew how she'd be—pulling stunts on helpless men that would land her in jail.

She had no room for judgment.

Ten

The sun rimmed the western peaks as Hunter took the last curve on the road into Luna. It had been a while since he'd enjoyed a Friday evening in the old café. The last time he had, in fact, Janie hadn't yet taken over the business—it had still been under the direction of her great-aunt Lucy. Back then, Friday night fare was pot roast and potatoes, just like every other evening.

According to Hazel, Friday nights at Janie's Café were deep-dish pizza nights.

TEN

A bulge of satisfaction billowed in his chest as Hunter pulled alongside the boardwalk across from the county jail and parked. *He'd* been the one to introduce Janie to Chicago deep dish, and as he'd hoped, Janie had loved it. So much so that she'd apparently spent over a month working on a copycat to serve at her own establishment. And all of Luna was forever grateful.

You're welcome for that. The smug thought was directed more toward the six-hundred-plus souls who, whether by choice or lack of choice, called Luna home. When his mind fixed onto Janie though, the smugness fizzled, and pride warmed his heart.

She was something, that Janie Truitt.

As Hunter stepped onto the boardwalk, that admiration seeping from his mind and filling his heart, he drew to a hard stop.

That would not do.

He'd spent the week trying not to think about Janie. Trying to dispel the deeply disturbing image of her sweet smile pinned on a man who was *not* him. The effort had been agony. And largely fruitless. The only way, in fact, he could imagine that he could succeed in not caring about her flirting with Grady was that he not care about her.

At all.

Janie would be like a faceless stranger on a sidewalk in some city. A nameless passerby who drew from him exactly zero emotion, good or bad.

That would be his strategy—he would wear an armor of indifference.

It was time to don the shield then, because the woman was just down the walkway. Through that door marked *Café*, just past the bell that chimed a little too cheerfully, and likely in the kitchen that smelled like heaven.

Hunter sighed, running a palm down his bearded face, as if he could literally make his expression blank with the swipe of his hand.

She is nothing to me...

The kick of his pulse argued that point, but Hunter ignored it. He pushed his stride forward, markedly less eager than moments before, and made his way to the gathering he was to be a part of.

He pushed through the door marked *Café*, ignored the happy tinkling above his head, and decided that *heaven* was certainly an exaggeration for the aroma of baked bread, perfectly paired tomatoes, garlic, and onions, and melted cheese that caused his mouth to water, and categorically denied that his heart stuttered when a pair of forget-me-not blue eyes met his involuntary gaze from the door of her kitchen.

She is nothing to me...

The electricity in his veins proclaimed that to be the lie it was. Even so, Hunter repeated it in his mind.

"Hunter." Bennett's smile on his name allowed Hunter a reason to shift his attention and let his smile free without mistaking it for something it might or might not have been.

"Bennett! You're back."

"I am. I brought reinforcements." Bennett's hand rested on a young red-haired girl's shoulder. "Meet my little sister, Gemma."

The girl's smile matched Bennett's, all charm and persuasion, even down to the dimple that likely melted Hazel's stubborn heart. With one glimpse Hunter had little doubt that if she chose to, Gemma could work that adorable grin to gain whatever she wanted. He hoped she wouldn't be that type.

"And that over there"—Bennett pointed to a boy in a black hoodie and stonewashed ripped skinny jeans that likely cost well over $200—"is my brother, Nathan."

"Half brother," Nathan mumbled, not looking up from the phone he held lengthwise. "And that hardly counts, since we've only met, like, five times."

Hunter shifted his glance from the boy who clearly wasn't happy with this situation to the man who had been stuck with it. Bennett's attention held on Nathan, a look of frustration marking his features.

"Nathan is just grumpy," Gemma proclaimed with extra sunshine in her voice. "He doesn't do well with change, and he doesn't like meeting new people." She settled a pleading look on Bennett. "Don't worry. He'll come around."

"Sounds like someone else we know."

Though Hunter had spoken with a teasing intent, he had an immediate and strong aversion to the situation as it was playing out. Namely, that Gemma, the younger sister, was protecting Nathan, the older brother. Having lived through a different but similar ordeal, Hunter believed strongly that the boy was shirking some God-given responsibility. He should have been protecting his sister, not the other way around.

The instantaneous impulse was to dislike the boy.

"Pizza is served." Janie came around the counter with four loaded plates magically balanced in her two hands. Her smile hit Bennett, then Hazel. Gemma and, though the boy couldn't possibly have seen it, Nathan. When she looked at Hunter, she paused.

No glorious smile. But there was something soft in her eyes . . .

Hunter turned toward Gemma as she slipped into a chair at the table beside the window. "What do you think of Montana so far?"

She sipped on a glass of ice water, then summoned that winning charm. "I like the mountains."

"They are a sight, aren't they?"

"I like . . ." Gemma bit her bottom lip as she searched for something else to remain upbeat about. "Well, the view from my bedroom is pretty."

"That's good." Hunter glanced at Hazel, searching for help.

"She'll get to wake up to an eastern creek view," Hazel said.

Look at her, being friendly. Helpful.

"We went to the creek this afternoon," Gemma said. "It's pretty."

"Did you hike?"

"Yes. I think I'll need better shoes next time." Gemma stuck out a foot and wiggled her thin-soled slip-on canvass shoes. They bore the stains of dark silt among the sparkles embedded in the coral and white stripes.

As Hunter nodded and nearly replied with something about Mama B's having a selection of sturdy footwear in the back of her store, a presence behind him summoned an involuntary warmth to ooze through his limbs. Even before he looked around, he knew the only woman who could draw that sort of physical response was standing there. Close enough to touch. Near enough to crumble his flimsy resolve.

Why did he always respond this way? How did a small blue-eyed woman possess the power to turn his military-trained body and mind to a puddle of warm goo?

Before he met her eyes, he allowed the replay of her smile aimed decidedly *not* at him to flash through his mind. The mush hardened to ice. And that was what he wanted as he met her gaze.

"Pizza?" Her expression grew guarded, as if she sensed his stiffened response.

"Sure." Hunter kept cool stream in his tone. Indifference. That was what he was going for. He wasn't going to give her that power anymore—not to turn him to a melted puddle nor to drive him to maddening frustration. He took the plate she held out, allowing their fingers to meet and forcing his stare to remain apathetically locked with hers even while the impact of contact ricocheted up his arm.

"Thanks." Then he turned back to Gemma. "Can I join you?"

Gemma nodded, Hunter sat, and Janie stood nearby for more moments than necessary. Her lips pressed, her gaze dropped to the spot near her feet, and she swallowed. Then she pivoted and walked back toward the counter, her steps slow and without spunk.

Something inside Hunter's chest twisted—like he'd just wounded his best friend. But he fought against the impulse to relent. After all, it'd been a long time since he and Janie had been anything close to resembling friends at all, let alone the best kind. And she had known exactly what she was doing the other day when he'd sat at her counter with Grady beside him, aiming her scowls at Hunter with the same precision she'd placed her smiles on Grady.

If Janie wanted reconciliation, she could seek it. If she wanted Grady, then she would have to accept cool aloofness from Hunter.

TEN

She couldn't have both Hunter's warmth and Grady's attention. Hunter just didn't own the might and goodness to live that way.

Janie rolled her shaking hands into fists and tucked them tight against her stomach. Hiding in the cool pantry located in her kitchen, she pressed her back against the series of built-in shelves and exhaled a controlled breath.

It shouldn't make her queasy, the way Hunter had given her a front as cool as the northern October breeze. But the hard switch in his demeanor made her world spin. As she lay her head back and shut her eyes, she felt the sensation of his forehead pressed to hers. The thrilling tickle of his thumb grazing the edge of her bottom lip triggered a flush of heat to wash over her body.

Why would she allow herself to relive that moment? That had been weeks—no, months ago. It wasn't helping. It only drove a sharp ache deep in her heart.

The thing was, though, that she could handle Hunter's anger with her. That she could manage by firing anger right back. But the way he'd been tender all those weeks ago? She wasn't sure what to do with that.

Worse? This new cool detachment. He'd looked at her just now as if she'd been a stranger in whom he had no interest. No one of consequence. No one who stirred anything in his heart.

No anger.

No love.

Nothing whatsoever.

In his distant gaze, she'd merely been the girl serving pizza.

Janie opened her eyes and stared up at the ceiling as a sense of emptiness yawned in her heart. What was this feeling of loss? She and Hunter had broken up years ago. She'd cried all the tears. More, he'd been *gone* for most of the time between then and now. Why should she have this new sensation of emptiness?

Because Hunter had decided he didn't care? Hadn't he already proven that by leaving?

No, he'd cared back then. Evidenced by how angry he'd been.

Which meant, by her own measure of anger, she cared too. Cared enough still that the thought of him being aloof toward her made her grieve all over again.

They couldn't exist like this, not if Hunter was going to live in Luna. Janie couldn't stand the distant chill and the emptiness it provoked. She had to find a different way—*they* needed to find some other means of existing in this small town together. A better way of dealing with each other.

Crossing her arms, she rubbed her shoulders. If she wanted something different, she would have to be the one to make the first change. Heaven knew Hunter had found his solution. That wasn't going to work for Janie. But doing things like intentionally flirting with another man while Hunter sat there watching hadn't helped. And finally willing to tell the truth of it, Janie admitted it hadn't been kind at all.

It had been entirely mean.

That wasn't who she wanted to be. Not in general, and not to Hunter. So she would try kindness, and maybe then she and Hunter could find their way back to friendship. A nonvolatile, more-than-mere-strangers, *kind* friendship.

There. That was what she wanted. Friendship with Hunter. That way they could live in Luna and not make each other miserable.

With resolve sliding in place, Janie blew out a breath of relief and let herself out of the pantry. Once in the kitchen, she plated four more slices of pizza, which looked more like pie than what one got from a typical delivery service, and arranged the plates two to a hand to deliver them to the dining room.

Janie served two other patrons who had come in for Friday night deep dish, and then Bennett and Hazel, who hadn't received their plates on her last round.

"Thank you for doing this," Bennett said. By the relief in his voice, he meant it from the depths of his heart. "I hadn't thought through what we'd eat tonight."

"It's my pleasure." Janie wiped her hands on her apron. "Plan on coming in for breakfast tomorrow."

"Only if I get to borrow your kitchen to make omelets." Bennett winked at Hazel.

Janie nodded. "That is certainly not one of my specialties, so you can have at it." She glanced at Nathan, who slouched in his chair, his plate scraped clean. "Can I get you another slice?"

He shrugged. "It's almost as good as Chicago's . . ."

"I'll take that as a compliment—and a yes." Janie picked up his plate and then moved toward the other end of the table, where Gemma and Hunter sat. Gemma's was clean. Hunter hadn't started on his pizza yet. Likely, he'd waited for Bennett and Hazel.

Hunter was considerate like that.

With that gentle thought, Janie managed a smile for him. "Do you want a warm slice, Hunt?"

His eyes snapped up, his light-brown gaze meeting hers. Startled. By the use of his name or her noncombative tone?

"No," he said after a heartbeat. "I'm good. Thanks."

Janie nodded. "How about you, Gemma? Could you eat another slice?"

Gemma patted her stomach. "I think I'd better not. That was amazing, Miss Janie. And also, Nathan is wrong—that pizza is every bit as good as Chicago's. He wouldn't eat it otherwise."

Janie laughed. "Thanks."

Gemma's smile could warm a December day. The girl, Janie had surmised, was as easy to like as her brother was easy to become annoyed with. Both, she guessed, were working really hard at stuffing back emotions they didn't want to surface—each using different means.

Just like a pair of siblings she knew. Her attention drifted back to Hunter just as Gemma turned toward him.

"Lake Shore Splendor has a great vibe. Good choice." Gemma dipped her head with all the confidence of an experienced marketer. "But I think you should have a groundbreaking party."

Hunter's brow moved with a thoughtful lift, and then he nodded. "That does have some appeal, Miss Gemma. What would you suggest?"

"Invite everyone you know, obviously. And—what do you have to do up there? Can you swim in the lake?"

Hunter chuckled. "We've had several hard frosts, and yesterday I saw thin ice at the shoreline. So I wouldn't recommend that."

"Right." Gemma became entirely pragmatic as she tapped her chin with a pair of perfectly pink-tipped fingers. "Swimming is out. But the water is still open . . . Do you have boats?"

"One old canoe over at Hazel's cabin."

"Well, that's a start. How about fireworks? Can you do that?"

Hunter snapped. "That's it!"

"Perfect. Then you'll have to have an evening party. Fireworks and food. What can you make?"

Janie snorted, drawing both of their eyes. At Gemma's slight mortification, she laughed outright. "Hunter can burn meat and slap together peanut butter and jelly. That's about it."

Hunter tried to scowl, but the moment his eyes connected with Janie's, she saw him break. Ah, there he was. The man whose eyes could tell her his secrets. And a smile that could stop the world.

He laughed. "Janie isn't wrong."

"You could do the food then." Pointing at Janie, Gemma offered the solution as though it were as easy as one plus one.

Sometimes one plus one made two broken hearts.

Janie blinked. Hunter swallowed and turned his face toward the table. His shoulders bulged under his flannel shirt, tension rippling hard in his silence. Then he lifted his chin, repositioned his smile into the neutral *I don't care* zone, and looked at Gemma. "Janie is busy here."

Kindness . . . friends.

"I could do it," Janie said.

TEN

The scraping of forks against plates coming from the other side of the table stopped. Three sets of adult eyes turned up to her. Two hopeful. One stunned.

"You—" Hunter's mask of indifference slipped. He wet his lips and rubbed the trimmed beard along his jaw. "You would do that?"

Ah... this. This could pave the way for something fresh between them. Not romance—that wasn't possible for them.

But friendship.

Janie touched the muscled arm beneath that soft shirt. "Sure. I'd be glad to."

The world did stop. For just a moment. Janie decided that it was to reset—to let the old die so that the new could have a fighting chance.

"Fantastic!" Gemma spoke into the space with ignorance as to what had just passed. "It's set then—a groundbreaking party for the Lake Shore Splendor lodge, catered by Miss Janie. I'll help you with the invitations. I am excellent at PR."

The round of chuckles from all sides of the table held a tinge of nerves. Or maybe that was just Janie. Either way, this was happening—and it was a good opportunity.

Groundbreaking... for more than a lodge. A new beginning. One in which Hunter and Janie could be friends.

Janie felt good about that.

Eleven

Hunter hung back after Bennett and his little instant family clogged down the boardwalk toward the Creekside Inn at the edge of town. He rubbed the back of his neck while a cold breeze came off the peaks to the west, a breath of snow carried on the air. More than likely they'd wake up to a dusting of fresh snow in the morning.

Bennett's band reached the inn, and Hunter watched his friend wait until the kids passed into their room, then reach for Hazel. When the pair came together for a kiss, Hunter turned away. The stirring in his chest became a mix of twinging ache and yearning.

Shoving his hands into his pockets, Hunter turned to peek through the window at his back. A lone figure moved inside, wiping tables, pushing in chairs.

Ah Janie...

She confounded him.

Just when he'd resolved to let her go the only way he knew how—to lock up any sort of emotion concerning her—she volunteered to cater an event for him. Why would she do that?

Hunter knew exactly what he wanted to be her motivation. Did he dare believe it possible?

Before he could talk his longing heart out of that hope, Janie looked up from her work, caught him watching her through the window, and smiled.

There was no talking him out of it now. Hunter held her gaze while determination came forth like Lazurus from the tomb.

Janie lifted a wave, and Hunter mirrored the gesture. Then she turned and made her way to the back, shutting off the dining room lights as she went.

The wind grew stronger, but Hunter remained planted. If anyone wondered, he'd claim he was waiting for Hazel, which technically was the truth. His sister had ridden a horse down to town earlier that morning, but it was already dark. She'd need a ride back to the cabin if she didn't want to spend the night in town.

But the real reason Hunter remained rooted outside of Janie's Café had very little to do with his sister. New life expanded in his heart and mind as he allowed everything about Janie to sink back into the vacant hole she'd once filled.

Those beautiful blue eyes. That warm-as-melted-sugar smile. The way she made his head swim and his heart soar. He wasn't done fighting to win Janie back.

He would never be done.

Next morning dawned as he'd expected—with a fresh sheet of brilliant white covering the land. It'd gotten downright cold in his camper, and he felt the snow in the mild buzzing of his body. A strange quirk of his since childhood—he'd always known when it snowed at night. Always. While in town, he'd look at what Mama B had in stock for buddy heaters.

With his old winter coat in place and cup of steaming coffee in hand, Hunter stepped out of his trailer to meet the freshness of the day. Along with the knowledge of the silently falling snow, he'd lain in his cot with the hope of Janie's smile giving him a mild high.

This morning he'd go down around about after the Saturday morning rush—which should be just before noon. Most fall Saturdays, Janie made chili—at least that was the story in town. Hunter was looking forward to that—if Janie made chili the way her mom made chili, he'd ask for seconds and save one of the portions to take back up to the camp. But before he did that, Hunter planned to be in Janie's kitchen. Helping her, if she'd let him. Talking plans for the groundbreaking. And making progress in his renewed resolve to win her back.

Kitchen scenarios could play perfectly into that. He'd wash the dishes—proving he wasn't completely useless when it came to meal prep. And he'd look for a perfect opportunity . . . Maybe she kept a dish she needed on high shelf. Or maybe she'd need help lifting a full pot of soup from the stove . . . He'd find some way to show her that life could be better if they were together.

And if that hypothetical scenario allowed him to touch her . . . He let his imagination linger there. His body warmed as he imagined reaching around her to retrieve that too-high dish. That near, he'd inhale the scent of apples and vanilla from her hair—a crisp but earthy rich aroma that would pull him closer.

His heart stuttered as he let this pretend scene play out further. It might or might not have ended with his lips brushing the warmth of her neck.

If helping her allowed him to touch her, all the better.

Hunter sipped his coffee, not really needing the added caffeine charge that morning. Snow crunched softly under his boots as he wandered toward the edge of the pond. Slowly he pulled his mind away from that intoxicating make-believe kitchen scene and focused on the reality he had. Stillness filled his senses. The quietness. The cleanness.

It felt hopeful that morning, and Hunter turned his thoughts toward the verse that John Brighton had texted him two days before. He pulled out his phone from his coat pocket, tapped until he found that text, and read the verse again. *Trust the LORD with all your heart; do not depend on your own understanding.*

Two days ago Hunter had been in no mood to *trust* anything. He'd been in a mood to throw things and glare at anyone and everyone, including John when he had FaceTimed for their weekly Bible Study.

John had advised prayer and patience. As much as Hunter wanted to grow in his new faith and to become a steadier man like John, he also wanted to let the world know that Janie's flirting with Grady made him crazy, and he wasn't going to pretend otherwise.

Man, he'd had a little-boy fit about it all.

Standing there alone, Hunter laughed inwardly at himself. He'd call John and apologize and tell him that he'd been right. Hunter should have just trusted that Janie would come around again. God had it all in hand.

"Hey, God, I'm still new at this." Hunter set his mug down on the overturned cut log next to his campfire ring. The contact of the hot ceramic against the half inch of snow made an instant ring of wet wood. "Thanks for working it out—I'm sorry I didn't trust that You would."

Good thing Hazel lived a solid quarter mile away on the other side of the ridge. She'd think he'd lost it, standing outside in the fresh snow talking toward the sky like Someone was up there listening. Then again, if she witnessed him talking to God like this, maybe he'd know better how to tell her about his newfound faith in Jesus. That would be a good thing, because Hazel needed Jesus as much as Hunter needed Jesus, and Hunter was pretty sure everyone around them would agree.

"Show me how to tell her, will You?"

Hunter chuckled as he stuffed his phone back into his pocket and retrieved his coffee cup. He'd go in and grab the Bible John had mailed him and reread all of Proverbs 3, spend some time thanking God for the new day and fresh hope, and pray for Hazel. Then he'd split some wood before he made his way down to Luna.

Everything was going to be like this blanket of snow. Clean and beautiful. He just needed to trust God.

Janie gathered the four plates left on the counter and piled them into her dirty-dish bin. The morning had been the usual—busy, and that was a good thing. She'd heard more than one disapproving groan, however, when she'd told her usuals that she'd be closed for the afternoon.

"But it snowed," old man Jasper argued. "Snow means chili, don't it?"

"Usually." Janie employed her sweet smile. "Today, though, I have a prior engagement."

"With who?"

"Who said anything about a who?"

"Engagements involve two people, little missy." Jasper's eyes lit with a smug knowing. "Going up to Elk Lake to see a returned navy man, ain't ya?"

"No, sir, as a matter of fact, I'm not." Janie refilled his coffee mug and set his bill on the table. "Enjoy your coffee now. I'll have chili for you next week."

"Huh." Jasper pressed his elbows against the table and leaned forward. "If it ain't that mountain boy, then he's gonna be real upset to find out who it is you're closing up early for an *engagement* with, seeing as he left the navy and came home for you."

With her back turned to the old busybody, Janie drew in a quiet, controlled breath. Sour heat rolled in her gut, but she glanced over her shoulder with a stern glare. "Hunter is busy with his own life. And he certainly did *not* come back to Luna for me."

"That's not how things look to me."

Says the old man who can't see straight enough to match his shirt buttons correctly. Janie smirked and then turned away, nearly laughing at the ongoing cockeyed apparel that Jasper was famous for. If he ever showed up with a correct button-down, everyone would suspect he'd had a woman involved, because the man hadn't been able to match up those things in ten years.

Rather than lipping off to her elder, as she had the impulse, Janie shrugged and scurried to the kitchen. The amusement that had tickled her about her old patron's clothing mishap died as that sour sensation crawled from her gut up to her throat.

Hunter . . . *he's gonna be real upset . . .*

Janie didn't doubt it, even if she believed he'd only be upset because of some feral, doglike possessive streak that plagued all men. *Mine!*

She had no interest in being a man's dog bone.

Did she really think that lowly of Hunter? That he saw her only as a prize to claim, that he was a selfish, possessive man driven by ego and a need for gratification?

Those were some pretty severe accusations. By the knotting of her stomach and the hard lump in her throat, Janie knew they were neither accurate nor fair. Especially when only yesterday she'd settled that she did want to establish a *friendship* with him.

Bitterness can make you blind.

Mama's admonition seeped into Janie's thoughts, and with them a strong conviction.

Lord, I'm still angry with Hunter, but I don't think that I am being entirely fair to him.

A measure of relief eased her upset stomach as she confessed that truth. Janie sighed into it. She closed her eyes and whispered the rest of her prayer. "Help me to be fair—to see him without bitterness fogging my vision."

The ringing of the front bell let Janie know that Jasper had finished his coffee and exited her café. With a hard breath meant to expel what remained of her twisted emotions, Janie dipped her dishcloth in the bucket of warm, sanitizing water, wrung it out, and returned to the dining room to clean up. She wiped the counter down, collecting crumbs as she did, and then moved to start on the tables in the far corner.

Another tinkling of the bell sounded.

"I'm sorry. I'm closing early to—" Janie straightened to look at her customer and then stopped. She swallowed at the sight of Hunter standing there, beard neatly trimmed, hands tucked into his black North Face coat. She cleared her throat as she dusted away the feeling of being caught. "I'm closing early today."

His brow furrowed, concern seeping into his steady gaze. "Everything okay?"

"Of course." Her voice had gone up two octaves. Dang it. Janie painted on her sweet smile. "Everything is perfectly fine. I'm just taking the afternoon off."

"Oh." Hunter nodded, honest relief allowing his lips to relax. "I'm glad to hear it. Do you have plans?"

"Um . . ." Heat crawled up her chest and oozed into her neck. "I do, actually."

Hunter's easy smile directly contradicted her earlier accusation of him being possessive. "Good. I'm glad you're taking the day off. You deserve a break every now and then."

She waited for him to ask what she was going to do. He didn't. More proof—he didn't see her as something that belonged to him. Someone to manipulate and control.

Hunter had his faults, but he wasn't that sort of man. He'd never been that sort of guy.

"Can I help you clean up so you can get out of here?" He stepped toward her, holding his hand out for her cleaning rag.

"Thanks," she squeaked, and then wiped down the next table, double time. "I got it though." Goodness, she was acting super weird. There was no way Hunter wouldn't notice that she was being weird. She rolled her shoulders back and faced him. "Was there something I can help you with? I think I have a cinnamon roll left. I could go—"

"No. I don't want to keep you from your afternoon off. I had just come to talk to you about the groundbreaking, but that can wait."

"Oh." Her heart squeezed.

Hunter took three strides closer and touched her elbow. "Thanks, by the way, for agreeing to help me. It means a lot."

Had her offer to help come off as something she hadn't intended?

No. She was overthinking this, just like she did when it came to anything involving Hunter. "Of course."

The pop of a car door shutting nearby sounded, and from the corner of her vision, she saw a man passing the big front window and then stop at the front door.

Grady.

Panic shot through her chest as that bell above her door rang again.

Hunter turned to see who passed through, and his jaw visibly tightened. His hand fell from her elbow, and he shoved it into his pocket.

"Hi, Janie." Grady looked at her and then eyed Hunter. "Am I too early?"

Oh dear. There was no way Hunter could misunderstand that—and neither was there a chance Janie could tamp down the heat that was sure to paint her cheeks crimson.

"Not at all. Let me just finish—"

Hunter reached toward her and snatched the rag from her hands. "I got it."

Janie stared at him. His eyes didn't smile, but he didn't scowl at her either.

"I got this. Key is in the pantry, right?"

Janie felt numb as she nodded. "Where Aunt Lucy kept it."

His lips pressed into a line, Hunter nodded. "I remember."

Her ears rang as if she'd been in the path of a blast wave. Inside, her core quivered. She glanced a Grady and found him watching her with a quiet look of uncertainty.

"Off you two go," Hunter said, false cheerfulness in his voice.

False, only because she knew him.

Grady dipped a solemn nod toward Hunter. "Thanks."

Janie wiped her hands on her apron, then untied it. Hunter reached to take it.

"I can finish here," Janie stammered.

"I told you—I got it."

She met his eyes for only half a breath and then looked away, because what she saw there made her chest ache. A blend of betrayal and hurt. She didn't like the feeling that she deserved either.

Honestly, she'd rather he'd have stormed out mad. Then she could just label him a selfish jerk and not feel bad at all.

Twelve

Bennett looked up from the wobbly table he'd been sitting at for far too long and squinted to see out the heavily streaked window facing Main. A figure came around from the back of Janie's Café, shoulders slumped in his black coat, hands punched into his pocket, and face cast toward the dirt road.

Hunter Wallace had never carried himself like a man beat down. The lack of his hard-earned military posture sent up warning flags, and the fact that he'd just come from the back side of the café exploded curiosity.

Bennett needed a break from looking over legal documents anyway. And the kids definitely needed to leave the dark space of this tiny room and the screen trance they'd been under.

"Let's get out of here." Bennett pushed his chair backward, only to feel the snap of one of the wooden legs give way beneath him. Great. Something he'd have to replace. Standing, he looked around at the room in which he'd barely slept, what with taking the awful cot, listening to Nathan snore, and worrying that Gemma was going to burn out all her sunshine before she started her new school. Every piece of furniture in this dump needed replaced.

The whole place needed a revamp. If it wouldn't look like he was trying to compete with Hunter's lodge, Bennett might have taken on that flip.

No, he had enough going on, financially and personally. He didn't need one more project right now.

Gemma sprang off her bed, pushing her painted toes into those now-dirt-stained Toms. "Are we hiking again?"

Bennett shook his head. "Think we'd better go see what Mama B has for sturdier footwear for you." He picked up the papers he'd been reading and signing. "And maybe we'll check to see if Leslie is available to go over these."

"On a Saturday?"

Shrugging, Bennett grabbed his recently acquired Yellowstone hoodie and ducked into it. "She told me we'd get this process done ASAP so we can get into the house."

Looking around the room with a wrinkled nose, Gemma nodded. "Good. The sooner the better."

His sentiments exactly. Bennett smacked the bottom on Nathan's black Air Force 1s. "Let's go, bud."

Nathan pinned a glare on Bennett. "What?"

Heaving a sigh, Bennett reached for patience. This had gotten old fast. How were they going to survive each other? "Let's. Go."

Nathan tugged on his ear, removing an AirPod. "What?"

At least he hadn't been ignoring Bennett. "We're going out. Come on."

"Out where?" Nathan didn't move.

"Outside." Bennett walked to the door. "We need fresh air. And to do something other than sit."

"There's nothing in this hellhole to do."

"Watch your mouth."

"What? Hellhole is bad language to you?" Nathan sat up, rolled his eyes, and stomped his feet on the floor. "Where are you from, the fifties?"

"The nineties, genius. And you don't need to call this place a hellhole when you haven't even given it a chance."

"Wow." He brushed out the narrow doorway without a jacket over his Smashing Pumpkins T-shirt. "You'd have a cow if you knew what I thought of this hotel room."

Bennett could guess. It was likely not far from the not-so-pretty label that had scrolled through his mind when they'd checked in yesterday.

"Might want a sweatshirt," Bennett said. Did Nathan know his favorite grunge-rock band with the most depressing messages ever was older than Bennett? Likely not. Nor did Nathan know that Bennett had also spent way too much time drowning in the blackness of songs like "Bullet with Butterfly Wings" himself. Enough to have tattooed in his brain that final, life-sucking lyric . . .

But praise God, Bennett no longer believed that he couldn't be saved. Now, he desperately knew that he'd *needed* to be saved.

"Was Dad this uptight when he was a preacher?" Nathan's snarky question caught Bennett off guard.

Bennett hadn't even known Nathan knew their dad had been a pastor. "I don't really remember."

"How could you not remember?"

"He left when I was young. Before that I rarely got into trouble, so it wasn't an issue either way."

"Ah. So that's why you and Gemma get along so well. You're the compliant type."

"I was for a while."

"Was?" Nathan snorted. "Whatever." Shaking his head, he stuck his AirPod back into his ear.

Be careful, little ears, what you hear...

Bennett's heart squeezed as he imagined what kind of lyrics were blaring into Nathan's brain. He realized, now more than ever, how much impact a song could have. How much influence words could have.

Death and life are in the power of the tongue. That was in the Proverbs, wasn't it? Bennett made a mental note to look it up later. And to meditate on the truth of it, because he knew going forward he was going to need to hang on tight to it with this little instant family he'd gained.

"Which of these is Mama Bulldog's?" Gemma pointed toward the line of facade fronts along the boardwalk across the road, effectively pulling Bennett from his heavy thoughts.

He motioned toward the center building. "The Pantry."

"She has the biggest shop in town!" Gemma employed her cheerleader voice.

Would Elk County Public School have cheerleading for junior high students? Doubt weighed Bennett's mind. Issues he could deal with later.

He followed the bubbly girl to the store, Nathan trudging five feet behind him. Once inside, Mama B greeted them with her smiling blue eyes.

"Hello there, Croftons."

Gemma clapped her hands. "We're famous!"

"Bennett is certainly a celebrity in Luna." Mama B winked. "Therefore, his siblings must also be known."

"I'm Gemma. You must be Mama Bulldog. Hunter told me about you. Oh!" She slapped a hand over her mouth. "Am I allowed to call you that, or is it only for special people who know you?"

"I declare you special." Mama B dubbed Gemma's shoulders with her hand. "However, I will need your name to make it official."

"Gemma." She bowed to receiver her "knighting," before pointing to Nathan. She grew serious. "That's my brother, Nathan. He won't like being declared *special*."

"Got it." Mama B raised a wave. "Hello, Nathan."

Nathan must have heard his name, because he jerked his chin in a *'s'up* gesture. That was as good as it was going to get.

"We're in need of sturdy shoes for Princess Gemma here." Bennett landed his hands on Gemma's shoulders.

"Right. I've got a few." Mama B waved them toward the back and then led the way.

Along the back wall there were exactly five styles of footwear. Thick strap sandals, low-rise hikers, high-top hikers, cowboy boots, and mud boots.

"Umm..." Gemma chewed on a pink painted nail. "Are there any options that are... cuter?"

Mama B laughed. "Cute gets a dirt bath real quick around here. But we can check a catalogue and see what we can order."

Gemma sent a pleading look to Bennett. It was all puppy eyes and sweetness.

Bennett was pure putty. But did it matter? Dad had left a large expense account—his usual course of action to cover his lack of being a good, present father with copious amounts of money. "Let's get something you can use now, and then we'll look at the catalogue."

With a happy nod, Gemma squealed. "Compromise! I love it."

Oh good heavens, he'd have his hands full with her every bit as much as with Nathan, just for opposite reasons. By the smirk Mama B shot him, she very much agreed. But she didn't pursue that, opting instead to work on size and fit with Gemma.

"I thought I saw Hunter come in," Bennett said.

"You did." Mama shot him a look that said *warning*. Then she looked toward the stairs behind the counter. "He's upstairs, working something out on the punching bag."

Bennett nodded. "Can you..."

"Sure. We'll hang out and try on shoes and maybe even look at some skis."

Bennett scowled at that. Skiing wasn't on his agenda anytime soon, and he doubted that Nathan, who loathed anything that required he detach his hand from his phone, would strap on some slippery sticks and see how he and gravity got along.

A fun discussion for another time. Rather than mull on it, Bennett took the narrow wooden stairs two at a time until he reached the loft. From a room to his left, he heard the muffled sounds of low grunts and rhythmic hits. By the speed of those punches, Hunter was working things out hard. Bennett let himself into the twelve-by-twelve room, finding Hunter stripped down to his white T-shirt and jeans, hands protected by thick gloves, and sweat soaking the fabric on his back.

Bennett's presence unknown, Hunter launched into another series—jab-jab-cross-lead uppercut. With his shoulder, he stabilized the bag, then threw that series again—faster. His feet moved, and as the bag swung, he danced a small circle until he faced Bennett. After the uppercut, Hunter used both gloved hands to stop the swinging bag, then he braced his head on it, his chest heaving hard. A quiet wheezing filled the room.

"You okay?" Alarm seized Bennett as he jogged forward.

The wheezing grew louder, but Hunter nodded his head against the bag.

"No you're not." Bennett looked around the room. "Where's your inhaler?"

"Coat." Hunter gasped.

Bennett spotted the black coat on the floor beside the door, Hunter's gray flannel a puddle of fabric beside it. Tossed off in a hurry, by the looks of it.

Something had sure set Hunter off.

Holding on to that clear fact to ask about later, Bennett dug in the pockets of the coat until he found Hunter's Albuterol, then spun back to his friend, who still sagged against that hanging bag, clinging to it as if that was the only thing keeping him from face-planting onto the floor. Shaking the inhaler as he went, Bennett jogged to Hunter.

His wheezing hadn't lessened. In fact, it sounded more severe. A full-on attack. This was what the doctor in Nevada had been concerned about—and why the navy had medically discharged Hunter. His life had been altered forever by that illness.

Bennett sucked in a sharp breath as grief surged in his chest for his friend. Life could be so unfair.

Hunter took the inhaler, but as soon as he tried to stand upright to inhale, he staggered backward. Bennett caught him and then repositioned so that he could shove him upright with his shoulder. "Come on, buddy, breathe." Real fear set in. The nearest hospital was almost an hour away.

Luna needed Bennett's mom—this entirely solidified that fact.

Hunter exhaled, clearly trying to control the instinct to panic. Once his lungs were empty, he put the inhaler to his lips, puffed once, inhaled deeply, and held his breath. Bennett remained at his back, feeling the man's weak body tremble and the hard pounding of his high heart rate. Quite possibly too high. Hunter held his breath for what seemed like way too long, then exhaled and took another puff.

At least that exhale didn't rattle the room quite so fiercely. And the frightening blue tinge around Hunter's pale lips was fading.

"Want to sit?" Bennett asked.

Hunter nodded, and Bennett eased him to the floor. Once Hunter leaned forward, bracing his arms against his knees, Bennett was fairly sure Hunter wasn't going to crumple into a pile of unconsciousness. Bennett settled beside him, listening with degrees of relief as his friend's breathing grew easier.

Over a full minute passed. It felt like life hung in the balance.

"Thanks," Hunter wheezed softly.

"Were you trying to work yourself to death?"

He shook his head. "Trying to work some mad to death."

"Did it help?"

Hunter sat up, ran a hand over his sweat-drenched hair, then shook his head. "Not sure." He leaned back, slumping against the exposed shiplap on the wall and rubbed his chest. "Gave me a headache—or made the one I started with worse. Sort of wish you'd just let me pass out."

"That's not gonna happen." Bennett stood and walked over to where Hunter had shed his coat and shirt and picked up a water bottle that sat among the clothing. Then he returned and sat so that his back pressed against the wall. "Want to talk about it?"

Hunter accepted the water and took a long slug. He wiped his mouth against the shoulder of his already wet shirt and then sighed. "Janie is out with Grady right now." His face turned toward Bennett, revealing sad, tortured eyes. "Like a date."

"Ouch." Bennett winced. "I thought I saw you coming from the back of her café?"

"Yeah. I told her I'd finish cleaning the dining room and lock up so she could get going."

"That was . . . generous."

"It was either that or lose my head." Hunter gulped another drink. "I've done that too much, I think."

"So you kept all the mad inside, closed the café for her, and then let it out on the punching bag?" Would Bennett have that much self-control? "That's better than some men might do."

Hunter sat forward again, draping his arms around his propped-up knees. His shoulders rounded as he hung his head forward. "I don't get it, Bennett."

"Do you and Janie have . . ." Hunter and Janie had obviously a convoluted history, and neither one appeared to be over whatever had passed between them. Hunter had quickly softened his anger toward Janie. Janie though? The woman seemed not to know what to do with Hunter. One moment Bennett would catch Janie gazing at Hunter like a woman enamored. The next she was glaring at him with all the fierceness of a mama bear.

How could love be so hard?

The question that had tied Bennett up in knots over the past several months—because he knew the difficulty only too well. How could he love Hazel with every inch of his heart and yet it wasn't enough for her to trust him? How could she claim to love him and yet she refused to give him a lifelong promise?

But this conversation wasn't about Bennett and Hazel. Bennett trained his wandering mind back to Hunter. "I mean, did you have a reason to think . . ."

"She offered to cater my groundbreaking. Just came right out and said she'd do it. And smiled at me." That last sentence came from Hunter as if he'd been punched.

And Bennett got that. A woman could reach clean into a man's chest and take full ownership when she smiled at him. "Yeah, I was there. It was . . . nice." Had Janie meant to play a cruel game with Hunter's heart? Though he'd witnessed her fire and snap aimed at Hunter, Bennett doubted Janie was that harsh. Sometimes what women intended as simple kindness, men took as something more. "But that—"

"I know." Hunter growled. "Trust me, I know she didn't mean to make me believe it meant a fresh start. Janie's been mad at me for a long time, but she's not cruel. I'm stupid to think this, I guess, but I took it like a sign." He looked back at Bennett, the torture in his gaze now compounded with childlike confusion. "Bennett, you said before you thought I was brought back here for redemption. And I believe it—with Hazel, there's already been that, and that's flat out amazing considering she refused to even answer my phone calls for months. And I've come to see that I need God—I need to be saved. John showed me how Jesus came to take my guilt and save me." He tapped his chest. "I believe that—and I sort of think you do too."

Bennett stared at him, stunned at how well Hunter put his new faith. "Yes. I do. My faith is a revived thing, and I'm still kind of stumbling around in the dark, trying to live the way I believe God wants me to. But the base is there—that I have faith in Jesus as my Savior. I'm glad to hear that He's your Savior too." More than that simple statement conveyed. Joy burst in his chest at knowing Hunter's eternal life was secure with Christ.

But there was the conundrum that seemed to plague all Christians: How did one make sense of the messiness of life? How did they live now, with the heartaches and the disappointments—not to mention the weakness of the flesh?

Hunter nodded, then looked back at the floor in front of him. A length of quiet extended, and Bennett pondered those big questions, as well as what exactly had triggered Hunter's extreme response to Janie—and why his new faith seemed to amplify it.

"Hunt, I'm not following here. Tell me how believing in Jesus is confusing you about Janie." Even as he said it, Bennett knew there were all sorts of ways to make that kind of connection. His own faith, and the desire to live a different life—a godly life that didn't make sense to others—had stirred up some powerful issues between Hazel and himself. Things that were still not resolved.

Following Jesus affected every aspect of life. And the truth was, some things were made more complicated by that faith.

"I took Janie's kindness the other night as a sign." Once again, he met Bennett's gaze. "Not just from her, but from *God*. Because I got a text earlier this week from John Brighton. He was sharing Proverbs 3:5–6, where God says to trust Him and He'll work it all out. That's in the Bible, Bennett. And I thought that . . ." Shaking his head, Hunter rubbed his neck.

"Oh. I see." Bennett leaned hard against the wall behind him. He got it—all the way deep in his heart. Bennett understood this confusion. "You hoped that since you believe God now, and He said to trust Him, that God had worked it all out, and your relationship with Janie would fall back into place."

"Yeah." Hunter slammed the half-empty water bottle down beside him and pushed up to stand. "Stupid. How simple could a man be?"

"I get it, Hunt." Bennett followed Hunter to his feet. "I'm not sure that's stupid. Maybe just . . ."

"Stupid."

"No. Shortsighted. But I think every believer has run into this kind of disappointment before, on some level or another. It's not stupid—it stirs up legitimate, hard questions."

Bennett couldn't help but think of his dad. What had triggered Chip's abandonment of his faith? Honestly, Bennett had never been all that concerned with that question. The one that possessed more of his mind—and his emotion—was how his dad could abandon *him*. It took him nearing thirty years old before he could take a wider view, understanding that Bennett Crofton wasn't the central character of the world's stage. Not even, really, of his dad's story.

Humility. That was what had to happen. Nothing like God showing a man exactly how quickly He can take everything—including his memory—to bring him to his knees. There was an Old Testament story about something similar happening to a king . . .

Bennett tucked that thought away for later, when he could look it up.

"One of the biggest reasons I walked away from my childhood faith was because I had believed that God wouldn't let my dad leave us. But then my dad left. Started a whole new life that didn't have anything to do with my mom and me. I think, looking back, that as mad as I've been at my dad all these years, I was livid with God."

Hunter took that in, not saying a word. For several long moments, there was only the pulse of vulnerability between two men who didn't often peel off the layers of their hearts for anyone, and the fragility of young faith confronting the harsh reality of a messy, broken world. In the drawn silence there seemed to be an unvoiced question.

Will you still believe . . .

Hunter turned and stepped to a small window overlooking the alley behind the Pantry. "How do you figure this?"

Will you still believe . . . if the life you hope for here isn't how things go?

A pulse of fear surged at that whisper to his heart, and Bennett crossed his arms over his chest, digging a hard grip into both of his biceps. *If it all goes badly, will you trust I'm still good?* A lump bulged in his throat. It felt like a loaded question. This time, though, he had this one thing to hold to: *God is good. Even when life felt not so good.*

He shall wipe away every tear... That was in Revelation—the end of the story. Bennett and José had talked about that when Bennett had called his friend seeking prayer and godly advice. Bennett had been so angry with his dad for doing this to the kids, and he'd bit a harsh question about how were Gemma and Nathan ever going to know God when their dad was so lousy?

God is greater than the sin that overwhelms. Our own and that which is committed against us. The physician of our hearts and lover of our souls is more than able to redeem them all. Your life now... doesn't it proclaim it, Bennett?

Every broken heart mended. Every mess made clean. Hearts made new.

Redemption revealed in perfect beauty. Just . . . not yet. Bennett and José and Hunter, they had to live here and now, in the *not yet*. But there was such a hope in that promise of full redemption, even if it did feel so very far off.

Bennett relaxed his clenched fingers. "I don't know all the answers, Hunt. All I know is that I might be the central character in my own narrative, but I'm not in the bigger story. My life—and yours and Janie's and Hazel's—it all matters to God. He cares about all the details. But in the mix of our choices, and a world that is wrecked, and God's greater story at work, sometimes our hearts are going to be broken. Some things aren't going to make sense. That is life with sin in a fallen world."

"What then?"

What Satan, the world, and even some people meant for bad, God intended to use for good—another story from the Old Testament. This one, Bennett knew. It was found near the end of Genesis.

The whispered question resonated again. *Will you?*

"Then we still must choose." Bennett gulped, then he tipped his head back, casting his eyes upward. "You and I, we have to choose." *As for me...* "I'll still believe." The statement was a promise—one that God had gently requested for quite a while.

And Bennett hadn't given it.

Oddly, his mind saw the moment he'd told Hazel he wanted to marry her. The expression of fear in her eyes, the withdrawal of her heart he'd felt as keenly as the piney breeze that had stirred his hair, they both still made his heart writhe.

She couldn't—or wouldn't—give him the promise.

Oh God...

Bennett sagged back against the wall, the full force of Hazel's doubt about his faithful love landing next to the lead weight of his own lack of faith in God.

The rejection—Hazel of Bennett, Bennett of God—it was the same.

I'm sorry. Please heal this doubt...

Thirteen

Hazel looked at Hunter's text, wondering why he'd not stopped by earlier in the day to see if she wanted to go to Janie's Café with him. He'd done so faithfully for over a month. It had stung, as the hours wore on into the afternoon, to realize he'd left her behind.

Again.

Not the same thing.

As these little pricks of irritation had surfaced lately, Hazel had begun naming them for what they were: insecurities. Often, irrational insecurities.

THIRTEEN

It was a big step for her to not just stew in the annoyance, letting it fester until it was full-blown anger. Quietly, she hoped Bennett would notice. Hazel didn't like that he often saw her as a child. Mostly, she didn't like the realization that many of her fitful reactions were that of a child.

It was time to outgrow that little girl afraid of being trapped and abandoned.

The phone on the table next to her Sherlock Holmes book vibrated again, reminding her that she'd not yet answered Hunter's message. She scanned the text from Hunter again.

I came down to town this morning—I'm sorry I didn't stop to see if you wanted to go. It's a long story—and I don't want to talk about it. But Bennett has permission to start work on the Elliot house. I thought I'd help. You want to come?

For a moment Hazel wondered why Bennett hadn't told her that he was going to start on the house. But she'd seen him with the kids last night—he was exhausted and overwhelmed, and Nathan was going to push him to the end of his patience and beyond. Hazel would bet on that. A little bit of grace from her was certainly required.

Look at her, not overreacting!

She smiled a congratulatory grin to herself as she picked up the phone to answer her brother. *Yeah, I'd like to help. Spare me the long ride to town on horseback?*

He replied promptly. *On my way.*

As she gathered her shoes and flannel-lined denim jacket, Hazel thought about how much easier it was to get to town and back now that the road was passable and Hunter had a truck. Pops had been stupid-stubborn about not using the old access road or owning a vehicle. Stuck in the old ways, clinging to them like they'd be his salvation.

Sort of like his granddaughter . . .

Ironically, Pops had used the road to get his alcohol fix. Hazel didn't know who his supplier had been, but by the evidence of bottles she'd found, she knew he had one.

Stubborn and hypocritical. Ouch.

Hazel punctured the air with a huffy breath. "Fine. I admit it. I'm too stubborn for my own good."

Scout yipped an applause bark. Moose eyed her from the corner, a gentle look of *That's fine. Practice...*

"Okay, Moose. I know. I'll get there." Eventually. Probably. Maybe she'd be able to admit faults out loud to others—like Hunter. Or Bennett.

It was hard! Living alone had locked her in some tight habits—one of which was a total disregard for others.

Yikes.

Another was a complete lack of trust.

There, her chest twinged as her mind couldn't help summoning the image of Bennett's gorgeous, gentle blue eyes. So full of love. And begging her to love him back.

"I do love him back," she told Moose, as if he were the one she needed to answer to. In a way, the dog was. Bennett had become Moose's person, and since the day Hazel had rejected Bennett's proposal, things hadn't just been strained between Bennett and Hazel, they had been off between Hazel and Moose too.

Or maybe Hazel was slightly nuts. Could this be normal—this anthropomorphic relationship she had with her dogs?

Whatever. She and her dogs had a connection—whether other people thought that was weird or not didn't matter.

Hazel returned to the discussion at hand. "And I do trust Bennett."

Lying on the floor, his chin tucked between his paws, Moose merely looked up at her, raised his eyebrows, and then huffed as he looked away.

He was calling her bluff. Dogs didn't lie. They didn't fight dirty. They didn't accuse without cause.

Which left Hazel with the uncomfortable truth: she didn't trust Bennett. Not with her whole heart. She believed he loved her... for now. Believed that he wanted a life with her... at the moment.

Forever?

Hazel wasn't sure she believed in that sort of promise. Not like she didn't think people stayed together for their whole lives—she'd watched her grandparents stick it out. But a love that lasted, that made a lifelong commitment a joy and not a prison?

That was the problem. Promises came with tethers. There couldn't be freedom in a lifelong commitment. Could there? It just couldn't be guaranteed, at least. People changed—usually for worse.

Goodness, that sounded harsh, especially when she laid it up against Bennett's sincere proclamation of love. And it made her feel awful when she replayed his understandably angry response to her accusation that he was after her land.

How could she have said that to him? Talk about worse . . .

Hazel growled at the tail chasing of her thoughts. She shut her eyes, bouncing her phone on her forehead, as if jarring her brain could fix what was inside her heart.

"How am I this much of a mess, Moose?" She opened her eyes and looked at her old friend.

Raising his large white head, he panted and then made the great effort to get his legs beneath his massive body to lumber to her side. A short whine followed by a grunt came just before Moose planted himself on his hind end.

"You still love me, right, boy?"

That massive head pressed onto her lap.

"More than you love Bennett?"

Moose sighed.

"Okay, but equal to Bennett?"

He pulled his head from her lap and pushed his front paws forward, sliding against the pine floor into a lying position.

A nonanswer.

"Maybe we could try it, don't you think?" Hazel bent forward to pet the thick fur of Moose's panting side.

Moose picked his head up. *I'm listening . . .*

"Bennett could move in here while he's working on the Elliot house."

That chin clunked back on the floor. *No dice.*

"Yeah, I guess there's the kids to consider." A pang of something close to jealousy hit her as she thought of Bennett's little instant family—one she wasn't a part of. Hazel ignored it, not wanting to consider why she'd feel insecure about that. "It'd be pretty cramped, and I'm not used to people all the time." Not to mention, Bennett had already turned down that offer last night.

A puff of air left Moose's lungs, and he rolled to his side. Utterly unimpressed.

"What?"

The dog side-eyed her, then looked toward the bunkroom where Bennett had stayed over the summer when he'd visited.

"Fine. You're right. Bennett wouldn't go for it."

I'm really trying to be a better man, Zel. A godly man. Can't you get behind that? Something Bennett had said to her last summer, when he'd told her he wouldn't be sharing her bed on his visits anymore.

Bennett was already a better man than she'd first met last year. Why did that mean they couldn't enjoy the physical pleasure of their love? And anyway, it was silly that Bennett would be opposed to moving in. Wouldn't it make sense to see if they could stand living together before they decided marriage was a good idea?

Something in Hazel's heart dropped in opposition to her logic. It felt like . . . disappointment. In herself.

The sound of tires against dirt and rocks set her free from the labyrinth of her dizzying thoughts. Relief took the place of that unaccounted disappointment, and Hazel leaned down to pet Moose once more before she popped to her feet. "Come on, old man. You're going outside because I'm going to town to see a man about a house."

Moose lifted his head with eagerness.

"His house. We're staying here."

With a string of grunts and a few whines tucked in for good measure, Moose clumped to the front door. Hazel opened it the same time Hunter stepped out of his truck. Ice and Cream scampered outside, no regard to people or older dogs, barking an overly enthusiastic greeting. Scout trotted to the deck and then sat at

Hazel's feet, watching her for instructions. Moose walked with his slow, purposeful stride, stepping down the front steps and toward Hunter. Once at his side, he planted his large backside into the ground.

"Hello, old friend." Hunter laid one large hand on Moose's head, his fingers getting swallowed in the thick fur. "Are you keeping my sister in line?"

Moose glanced toward Hazel, then turned smiling eyes up to Hunter. *I do my best.*

Wasn't that the truth?

With a small finger motion to Scout—her silent instruction to come—Hazel left the deck and met Hunter on the ground. "Is that what he's supposed to be doing?"

"It's why I left him with you."

She squinted at Hunter. "You left him because you couldn't take him."

"Think what you want, little sis."

"Huh." Hazel jammed her arms into her denim sleeves and turned to her pack of dogs. "Stay. Be good. Leave the raccoons be." She pointed to Ice, who had gotten into a scrape with a mama coon only last week. He still had the missing fur patch on his shoulder to prove it.

Hunter walked around to the passenger side of the truck and opened the door. Hazel followed, musing at how her brother somehow had become a gentleman, and she wasn't sure what to make of that.

Had Janie noticed?

Hazel doubted so. Especially since Janie seemed to have found a new object of her friendly, flirty smile. Glancing at her brother as he slid behind the wheel, she hoped Hunter wouldn't flip out if anything transpired between Janie and the Game and Parks guy. He'd sure had gone sour and silent last weekend when he'd witnessed Janie flirting with the other man.

Didn't Janie realize Hunter had never gotten over her? Didn't she know Hunter well enough to know that at this point, he likely never would?

A sharp pin of conviction poked Hazel's heart. Who was she to be judging Janie? Wasn't she claiming to love Bennett and yet doubting that they'd last long term?

Not doubt. Fear. That wasn't the same thing, was it?

"Bennett has big plans for the house." Hunter spoke as he guided his truck toward the access road.

Relief grew wings and flapped away the circular nonsense in Hazel's mind. She grabbed on to the alternate topic with all her heart. "He'd have to. Have you seen the inside?"

Hunter's serious expression loosened into mild amusement. "I haven't. But I remember Marvel Elliot, so I'm betting it's colorful."

"Like a set of highlighters exploded all over the walls."

"Nathan probably loves that."

"Actually, he did." Hazel met Hunter's sarcastic glance with a nod. "Only because it would drive his dad nuts."

"His dad isn't here."

"The thought of it was satisfying enough."

"He's gonna be a handful, isn't he?"

Hazel shrugged. "I think that he just needs to find his own feet and know that he can stand on them."

Hunter's brow raised. "Look at you. Reading people."

"Just Nathan. Gemma . . . She so sweet and peppy that I might end up in a sugar coma ten minutes into being with her."

"I like her. She smiles."

"Like a young Janie?"

Shoulders immediately stiffening, Hunter's easy expression chilled. "Yeah. I guess."

"Janie still smiles."

"Not at me."

At the Game and Parks guy. Hazel could almost hear her brother's hard lament in the stiff pause that hung between them.

"Hey, Hunt?" She peeked at him, cautiously intruding on his personal misery. Hunter glanced at her. "Things work out sometimes. You know?"

"Sometimes." Hunter released one hand from the steering wheel and nudged her shoulder. "Seems like things are back on track with you and Bennett."

Hazel stared out the windshield as the small town of Luna came into view. High-pitched roofs dotted the Elk Creek valley, interrupting the sea of vibrant yellow aspens that were quickly turning brown and would soon become large clumps of naked branches standing boldly from a blanket of snow. On the opposite side of the creek, the valley stretched in a series of shallow treeless pastures. A handful of ranch-style houses dotted the rich, rolling grassland, and a grid of log fence, built in the A-frame style, separated one ranchette from another. All of them snugged up against the rise of purple-gray peaks that hemmed in the southern and eastern sides of the valley.

It was like a world set apart. Isolated and beautiful.

Those boundaries don't bother you? Hazel puzzled at that question—one that ribboned through her mind but didn't seem like one she'd think up on her own. Why would the security of the hills surrounding her home and life bother her? They kept the valley set apart and pristine.

Hunter turned his truck left before he got to Main and followed the narrow dirt road two blocks east until he came to the old Elliot house. Parking parallel to the Victorian on the front yard, he shut off the truck. "Ready to scrape paint?"

"Is that what we're up to?" Hazel scrambled out of the truck, happy to get out of her head, and followed Hunter to the front door.

"Yep. Starting with Gemma's room—because Bennett promised. Bye-bye bubble-gum pink. Hello Gentle Wisdom. Gemma's words."

Hazel wrinkled her nose up at Hunter. "Gentle Wisdom?"

A genuine grin—a welcome sight after the conversation in the truck—cracked the dark shadow of his bearded face. "That's what the paint card called it. Gentle Wisdom. And the wallpaper she picked out for the slanted roof part of her room is called Soft Vines. So I guess she'll be all twined up in soft wisdom." He winked and shrugged. "Could be worse."

"Clever. When did you start paying attention to things like this?"

"I have a poetic side."

"Hidden by flannel, a beard, and deadly aim."

"I spent a few years without the flannel and beard. And anyway, I wasn't always a jerk, and you know it."

Hazel couldn't deny that fact—especially now that she knew that some of the biggest things that she'd held against him, he'd actually done to protect her.

Turned out Hunter had always been intuitive and caring. Which made her a lucky sister after all. Now, if only Janie could remember the version of Hunter that she'd cared about . . .

Since when was Hazel so wrapped up with happily ever afters? Hadn't been so long ago that all she'd wanted was to secure her land and have the rest of the world leave her alone.

The door in front of them swung open, and Gemma bounced onto the covered front porch. "Hi, guys! Ready for renovation?"

"We're not tearing any walls apart today." Bennett stepped out of the house behind the bubbly girl.

Gemma stuck out a pouty lip that didn't appear too serious.

Bennett shook his head. "She spent the past two hours, while I was signing papers, watching that renovation show in Texas. Now she's got it in her head that we need to gut the first floor."

"It would be fantastic. All open concept. New windows, fewer walls . . ."

"Tell the truth, Gem. Had you ever even heard of *open concept* before today?"

"Well . . ." Gemma peeked at Bennett with a sheepish but still determined grin. "No. But it would still be great."

Bennett held a stern look down on his younger sister for all of two heartbeats, and then he melted. "You might have a point. But it's not happening right now."

"I'll take that." Her winning look made Gemma's copper eyes dance.

Hazel pressed her lips together, trying to suppress a laugh as she looked up at Bennett. "Putty."

"Hush." He snagged her arm and drew her toward the entry. "You're here to help."

"I am being helpful." Hazel stepped into the house, and her mouth drifted open as she scanned the front room. All the awful green carpet had been lifted and cleared, leaving dirty gray-brown floorboards exposed. "I see you started without us."

"Yeah. I tugged on the loose corner over there"—Bennett pointed toward the wall that separated the front room from the back of the house—"and kept pulling. Apparently whoever laid the carpet didn't like glue. Or padding. It was tacked down with a few nails, and I'm guessing held in place by heavy furniture."

"Lucky for you." Hunter passed from behind Bennett and Hazel. "Gemma, get me a brush. Let's get this show started."

"Oh! My kind of man."

All three adults froze. Hazel looked from Bennett to Hunter—both of whom suffered pink-stained cheeks, Hunter's standing out boldly against his beard.

Gemma turned to look at the trio standing in weird silence. "What?"

Bennett cleared his throat.

Hazel burst out laughing. "You're eleven, Gem. You don't have a *kind of man*."

Rather than looking embarrassed or put out, Gemma tossed him a sassy smirk. "You don't know many eleven-year-old girls, do you?" She waltzed up to Hunter, dusted a paintbrush across his chest, and then danced her way to the stairs.

Hunter stood wide eyed, the paintbrush Gemma had pushed into his chest still held there with his own hand. "What on earth?"

"Heaven help me," Bennett muttered. "I thought she was going to be the easier one."

"Oh, Benji." Hazel shook her head. "I told you. Putty. That's what you are. Anyway, I'm pretty sure she was teasing. It's fun to watch grown men blush."

"Eleven-year-old girls should not know that." Bennett scowled at her. "Did you at that age?"

"I was gutting small animals at eleven, Bennett."

Hunter chuckled. "She also had a crush on Slater Hopkins, a senior at our school, when she was eleven."

"What?"

Hazel ignored Bennett's false outrage and shook her head at Hunter. "Every girl at any age in Elk County had a crush on Slater Hopkins when he was in high school."

"I think I need to meet this Slater Hopkins."

"Good luck. He's out in California working as a stunt double." Hunter shifted his attention to Hazel and smirked. "Last I heard, he was living with his boyfriend."

Hazel shrugged. "He was pretty to look at."

"Am I pretty to look at?" Bennett's blue eyes danced.

"Must be. Hazel stares at you more than anyone I've ever seen." Hunter walked toward the stairs and patted Bennett's back. "Including pretty-boy Hopkins." Then he turned and bounded up the stairs.

Bennett's laughing gaze stayed pinned on Hazel. "Is he right?"

"I don't stare."

"Do you think I'm pretty to look at?"

Hazel huffed, grabbed the canvass bag of paintbrushes, and moved to head up the stairs.

Bennett caught her by the arm before she could charge by him. He leaned down and whispered, "I think you're pretty to look at."

There was no beating back the flash of heat that flooded her cheeks.

"And you're right. It is fun to watch someone blush."

"I didn't say someone. I said grown men."

"It's fun to watch a mountain woman blush."

Hazel tried with all of her might to frown. "I think flirting is a family trait."

"Maybe so." Bennett pressed a kiss to her cheek. "But just so you know, I reserve all of my talent in that department for you."

She couldn't hold back the giggle that bubbled from her chest.

"Ah." Bennett pulled her against him and wrapped both arms around her. "That's what I was after."

Circling an arm around his waist, Hazel snuggled against him as they gently swayed. "A laugh? That seems like a puny goal."

"I love your laugh, Zel. It's like finding a rare gem. And it's been a stressful week." Seriousness weighed his tone, a sharp contrast to a few moments before. "I could use something light and happy."

Hazel leaned back and looked at him. Those beautiful eyes that—for the record—were quite pretty to look at, had lost their smiling sheen. She cupped his jaw. "I want to help you, Bennett."

He nodded. But there was something reserved in his wordless response. Like he hoped for something more. Rather than pursuing whatever that was, he leaned down and touched his lips to hers. Then he let her go, took her hand, and moved toward the stairs. "Shall we paint?"

Fourteen

Janie leaned back on her hand and took in the fall afternoon. A breeze rustled through the tops of the spruce trees at higher elevations, stirring the air with a whisper of autumn before dropping to the aspens. Those golden leaves—what remained on the branches—shimmered in the sunshine as they quaked, making a sound like soft rain. Inhaling, she closed her eyes and imagined that she was completely at ease in this lovely moment.

But she wasn't.

Swallowing back a discontented sigh, Janie lowered her chin and returned her attention to the peanut butter and jelly sandwich and banana lunch that Grady had provided. It'd been thoughtful of him to pack something for their hike. And this vista at a bend in the creek had all sorts of sweet outdoorsy-date vibes.

But she wasn't feeling it.

Even when she really focused on those romantic vibes, which were right there in front of her, Janie couldn't make them root and force them to grow. Because every time she tried, an invasive weed named Hunter Wallace sprouted in her mind.

They'd come to the creek often when they were younger. First as a pair of kids—along with Hazel—out looking for something to do after school. Fishing was Hazel's preferred activity. It helped her not feel quite so displaced when she had to stay in town. Hunter had a thing for carving branches. He'd find tree litter scattered on the forest floor and whittle them into arrows or carve faces into the soft pine and aspen wood. Janie had just liked being with them.

As they grew older, Janie liked being with Hunter. Not that she'd outgrown hanging out with Hazel, but there had been a defined moment that had changed things between Hunter and Janie. One that refused to die in her mind.

He'd come down from Elk Lake alone—which wasn't too common. And he'd stayed with Mama and Janie for five whole days. Mama's expression had been stern, and she'd watched Hunter carefully during the first few days. Her only explanation was that Hunter had been hurt—which had been true and Janie knew it, because it was one of a handful of times that Mama had made the nearly hour-long drive to Big Sky to the doctor. She'd taken Hunter along.

Two days went by before Janie cornered Hunter. They'd gone to the creek trail together, just them. At the shoreline, Janie tossed rocks, trying to attain the coveted foot-tall splash. Hunter didn't even pick up a single stone.

"*What happened?*"

Hunter scratched his hair behind his right ear. "I fell and cut my back."

She'd seen him do that before—the itching behind his right ear. Settling her hands on her hips, she cocked one eyebrow. "Let me see."

Though Hunter scowled, a rush of pink filled his face. "It's fine."

"I want to see it." Janie took on Mama's squinty eyes and don't-talk-back-to-me tone. And it worked.

Hunter held a long look on her, and something in his eyes reached straight into her heart and claimed it for himself. Forever. Then he turned, tugging the back of his sweatshirt up. His grunt was the only indictor of pain, but that might have been because she didn't see his face. She saw only that fierce jagged rip in his flesh. The home-pulled stitches were uneven, but they held the damaged flesh together. Fiery red surrounded the wound.

Janie reached and touched his back several inches below the wound. Initially his muscles flinched hard beneath her fingertips. But then he exhaled, and the body under her touch softened.

She didn't say a thing after she removed her hand, and Hunter carefully dropped his shirt into place. But when he brought his gaze back around to meet hers, she met his eyes.

"What really happened?"

His gaze widened. "I fe—"

She shook her head. "I've played bull with you for years. I know your tells, Hunter, even if Mama doesn't."

Hunter visibly swallowed, and his brown eyes sheened before he shifted his stare toward the river. "Pops was drunk." His voice hardened, but his lips twitched. "He came back to the cabin drunk and in a fury."

Janie's heart froze inside her chest. The block of ice was both painful and numbing. "He cut you?"

Shaking his head, Hunter blinked. "No. A bottle got broken, and I ended up rolling onto a glass shard."

"Were you fighting?"

Pressing his quaking lips tight, it took a moment before Hunter nodded. He spun, pinning his tormented gaze back onto her. "You can't tell."

"You have to tell!"

He shook his head and gripped her shoulders. "No. Pops rarely does this. And he was so ashamed that he took off into the woods as soon as he came to."

"Hunter—"

"No!" *He leaned down, his hot breath painting a path across her forehead.* "The state will remove us if anyone finds out. That would kill Hazel, and you know it."

"Mama would take you both."

"There's no guarantee that they'll let her. Don't you remember what happened after my parents died?" *His pleading held fire as his grip on her arms tightened.* "They placed her in Billings, Janie. Billings! And we almost didn't get her back. She's still messed up because of it."

Janie shrank as she blinked back tears, and Hunter softened his hold.

"Please, Janie." *His hoarse whisper hinted tears.*

How could she deny him? "Is Hazel safe?"

"Yes. I made sure she was. And I will again, if I need to."

Biting her bottom lip, Janie tried to think how she could get her friends out of this awful situation. But there wasn't an answer. Nothing clean or easy or obvious.

Hunter pulled her close and then wrapped her in a hold that was both possessive and needy. "I trust you, Janie." *Then he pressed a kiss to her head.*

So many emotions turned in her heart and mind she couldn't even name them all. But what she did know for certain was that she would protect this boy and his sister with every shred of strength she owned.

"I'm here for you, Hunt." *She twined her arms around him, careful to avoid the cut on his upper back.*

Hunter sagged against her even while keeping her firmly against him in his embrace. "I need you," *he whispered.*

Something warm and delicious swirled in her chest. "I'm always going to be here for you."

Apparently, that was a vow Janie could not break.

"Do you not like grape jelly?"

Jerking from her trancelike stare across the river, Janie forced a smile as she turned to look at the man she'd come to the creek with. "I like grape jelly fine." Just, usually not the store-bought kind. Mama had been making her own since forever, and this factory-jarred stuff was vastly different. But Janie jammed the half of sandwich she had in her hand into her mouth and took a hearty bite.

Wonder Bread was also not her fave. But they didn't need to go into that either.

"Did you come here a lot as a kid?"

"Yeah. We spent nearly every decent day after school out here."

"We?"

"Hazel, Hunter, and me."

Grady shifted in his spot near the trunk of an aspen tree, propping an elbow on his knee. "Ah, so you grew up together."

"Yes."

"Did you have a falling out?" He took a bite of his own sandwich, clearly expecting that she would have a story for him to hear.

"Not really." At least, she and Hazel hadn't. She and Hunter . . . *falling out* didn't even begin to describe the mess between them.

Grady wiped his face with a cloth kerchief. "Oh. It's just, there seemed to be some tension between you and Hunter. At least the first time I met him. I thought maybe he volunteered to close your shop for you as a peace offering or something."

Janie swallowed. No, Hunter hadn't been holding out a peace offering. He'd misinterpreted the olive branch that she'd offered him.

"He had come down from Elk Lake to discuss food for his groundbreaking party. I'm catering it." Janie slipped what remained of her sandwich into the baggie and closed it. With the fire burning in her belly right then, trying to eat was futile. "He didn't know I was closing early."

"Or going out with me." A single dark brow raised on Grady's face.

Brushing the crumbs from her fingers, Janie shrugged. "Guess not."

"Does it matter?"

Man, this guy was fishing hard for a first date. She pushed up to her feet and stepped toward the gurgling water. "No."

Behind her, she heard Grady packing up what remained of their picnic. Then she heard his booted feet crunching on the rocky shoreline. He stopped beside her, his bicep nearly brushing her shoulder. "I'm sorry, Janie. I don't mean to be nosy."

She turned to look up at him, finding kind eyes looking down on her, set in a handsome face that any girl would be lucky to look at every day of her life. Janie made her lips tip upward and hoped the small grin didn't look strained.

Grady turned and brushed her hand with his large fingers. "I just want to know if I'm getting in the way of something."

"No." Maybe. Probably. Yes. But she needed someone to get in the way.

Her quick response was rewarded with a smile, and Grady dared to wrap her fingers with his.

Warm, gentle grip. Janie narrated the feel of it to her heart so that it would do the appropriate flip.

No gymnastics.

"So if I work up the courage to ask for a second date, it might not end in failure?"

That was pretty sweet, and her heart woke up enough to melt a little. "I doubt your requests for a date ever end in failure." She squeezed his hand.

His smile grew.

Her heart warmed.

This might work.

"I'm always going to be here for you . . ."

She didn't have to break that promise. Maybe it just would look different than those two kids way back then had in mind.

And maybe that would be okay.

Fifteen

At the top of the stairs, Bennett paused long enough to peek into Nathan's room. There he was, sprawled out on his back in the middle of his empty room, staring at that ridiculous disco ball.

Bennett shook his head. At least this time he wasn't staring at his phone. "We're painting Gemma's room. How about helping?"

No response.

"Nathan." Bennett stepped into the tie-dyed space.

Nathan jerked his head toward Bennett and tugged an AirPod out of his ear. "What?"

"We're going to work in Gemma's room."

"Good for you."

"Come on, man. You can't just lie there all day while we work."

"Bet."

Bennett blew out a long breath. "Is this how it's going to be?"

"Probably. Unless you leave me alone."

Was this a battle worth fighting? Bennett listened to the easy conversation happening in the room across the hall. Hunter had asked Gemma about her school in Chicago, and Gemma was prattling on about cheerleading and swim club—things that Bennett couldn't promise her when she started attending Elk County Public School.

That now-familiar weight pressed down in his chest. *God, I don't think I can do this.*

He focused on Nathan again. Let him be. More than likely he'd be more of a pain in the butt rather than a help anyway.

"Enjoy your disco ball, then." Bennett turned and left the room.

"You know I will."

The response was likely intended to grate on Bennett—and held the strong possibility for success. But Bennett exhaled slowly, clenched and unclenched his fists, and chose to let it go.

Crossing the hall, Bennett found Hazel stirring a can of barely green paint called something Wisdom—which reminded Bennett to pray for exactly that. As he did so silently, he joined Hunter and Gemma at their washing-the-wall job, taking up a rag from a bucket of warm water as he went.

"Can I get a new duvet?" Gemma aimed her eager, winning expression at Bennett.

Yet again he was reminded of how often he'd used charm to get his way. Man, he was going to have to figure out how to curb this habit in Gemma. No one with such a sweet face should wield that much manipulation.

"What's a *duvet?*" Hazel asked.

"It's like a bedspread case." Gemma folded her hands together, squishing her cleaning rag in between her palms. "Please, Benji?"

"Bennett."

Gemma glanced at Hazel—likely because the girl had heard the woman use Bennett's forbidden nickname.

"And no, I don't think so. The moving truck should get here in a day or two, and we'll use what you had in Chicago."

"But my old room was pink."

Bennett glanced at the bright pink on the walls. "Then maybe we're wasting our time."

"Not this color of pink." Gemma wrinkled her nose. "Soft pink. Pretty pink."

"What color is your bedding?"

A dusting of *soft pink* spread over her freckled face. "Gray."

"I'm fairly confident gray will work with Wise Owl green."

"Gentle Wisdom."

Bennett shrugged. "Exactly."

Gemma produced that cute pouty lip along with a pair of pleading puppy eyes. Dang, but the kid was good at being adorable. Did it matter if he let her pick something new? It was all coming from Dad's account anyway...

Bennett glanced at Hazel, who watched him with crossed arms and an amused smirk. *Putty.* He steeled against Gemma's charm—not that he minded Hazel knowing he was a softy. That was way better than her original evaluation of him as a spoiled, self-centered city boy who couldn't survive the mountains. Being a softy had earned him the privilege of knowing the softer side of Hazel Wallace, and that was a rare prize indeed.

But boundaries were needed. He met Gemma's pleading look again and shook his head.

Gemma's shoulders sagged, and she snapped her fingers. But with the next breath, she was back to sunshine. "Oh, okay. Gray will work ... for now." She looked up to Hunter and winked.

"Gemma, stop flirting with Hunter. He's literally more than twice your age, and my friend."

"Are you literally more than twice my age?"

"Literally."

"How old are you?"

FIFTEEN

"If I said I was close to thirty, would you think I was old?"

"Thirty is definitely old." She popped her hands onto her hips and tipped her head. "But I don't believe you. You don't have any gray hairs."

Hazel snorted.

"Oh good grief, Gem." Bennett stepped beside her and slipped a hand over her mouth. "I'm begging you—please stop."

Gemma laughed. "Okay. I'm done. For today. But Hazel is right—it is super fun to watch old men blush."

"Great." Hunter shook his head. "I've moved from *grown* to *old*. I'm not sure I should thank you for that, Bennett."

If it stopped his little sister from flirting with his friend, Bennet wasn't sorry.

"Hello?" a woman's voice called from the first floor. "Anyone home?"

Bennett exchanged a look with Hazel.

"That's Janie," Hazel said.

A sense of dread locked in his chest, and he shifted his gaze to Hunter. The man's demeanor shifted—where he'd been relaxed and easygoing, now his jaw had locked tight and his shoulders had stiffened.

Hazel must have read her brother's reaction as well. Her eyes, which had been amber since the moment she'd walked into the house, had faded and now held a ring of mossy green. That was interesting. Before Bennett had gone to Chicago, Hazel would have immediately taken Janie's side in any and all conflicts between Janie and Hunter.

Things could sure change quickly.

Setting the wet stir stick against the rim of the paint bucket, Hazel stood up and turned to leave. Bennett trailed her, and they both clambered down the stairs. Janie stood in the middle of the empty front room, eyes wide as she took in the highlighter vibrance of the walls.

A man stood behind her. Bennett didn't even know his name, but he felt an immediate dislike for the guy.

"Hi, guys!" Janie grinned wide. A little too wide. "We heard you were able to start work on the house and thought maybe we could lend a hand."

Hazel turned those now nearly-all-green eyes up to Bennett. The room hung in an uncertain pause. Did Janie know that Hunter was there? Certainly she didn't know that her going out on a date with another guy had sent Hunter into an asthma attack by way of a punching bag.

Would that matter to her?

Bennett had to believe it would. Janie wasn't heartless.

"I'm Grady." The stranger stepped forward and held out a hand.

Bennett swallowed, glancing at Hazel as he tried to piece together what to do. He met Grady's palm with his own. "Bennett."

"Janie's told me about you—that you're taking in your younger siblings for a while. That's generous of you."

Though he tried to smooth it away, Bennett frowned. Those two younger siblings were right up the stairs and in hearing distance. Bennett knew keenly what it was like to grow up with the father they had—one who cared more about success, money, and personal pleasure than about what his actions did to his children. Nathan and Gemma didn't need to feel like a charity case.

Grady didn't have a level playing field to begin with when it came to Bennett's estimation, but he was already slipping further down.

"Is . . ." Janie's too-bright smile faded. ". . . are the kids upstairs?"

"Yes."

"We're painting." Hazel held a look on her friend that Bennett was familiar with. It was the none-too-happy look.

Janie's brows pulled together. "Can we help?"

"Not sure how many will fit. Hunter and Gemma." Hazel crossed her arms and let an intentional pause drop. "Bennett, Nathan, and me. That's already a roomful."

"Oh . . . oh." Janie bit her lip.

"Miss Janie! Isn't this the craziest place? I mean, so bright in here, right?" Gemma skipped down the steps. Ignorant of the chill in the room, she danced to Janie's side, linked her arm around hers, and tugged. "Come see my room! That way you can appreciate the before and after. I'm thinking of having a reveal party. Wouldn't that be so fun?"

Janie glanced at Hazel, and Hazel sighed.

That was that. Gemma had Janie halfway up the stairs, and Hazel followed. Bennett waited for Grady to pass in front of them, and then he brought up the caboose.

There was no stopping this train wreck.

They were adults. All of them. Right?

Hunter's back was turned to the group by the time Bennett came through the door. His shoulders rippled as he scrubbed the walls with an intensity that might just send him into another breathing fit.

Gemma chattered away, pointing out the view out her dormered window, where she'd put her bed, saying that Bennett wouldn't agree to new bedding, but she wasn't giving up on that . . . She worked her way around the room and came to the paintbrushes.

"Problem." Hands on hips, Gemma spun to Bennett. "You only got five brushes." She counted each person in the room. "There are six of us. Seven, if Nathan ever decides to be useful."

"It's not a problem." Hunter kept his attention only on Gemma, scratching his hair behind his right ear, and managed what was clearly a forced grin. "I've got to go, Princess Gemma. But your walls are clean and ready to become wise."

"Really? But—"

Hunter didn't wait to entertain Gemma's protest. He moved his attention to Bennett, carefully avoiding Janie. "You can get my sister back to the cabin, right?"

"Of course."

A single nod and one more dark look sent Hunter out of the door, down the stairs, and out of the house.

Collision averted. Even so, Bennett felt the fracture of impact. He couldn't imagine that every other adult in the room had missed it.

The world just kept being a mess.

Sixteen

Hazel had never painted a whole room. Or even half of one. The soreness in her back and shoulders hit her with surprise. One would think that a lifetime of hauling and chopping firewood would have given her a pass.

It hadn't. She rubbed her left arm as she stepped up the two front steps to the cabin.

"Sore?" Bennett's hand covered the spot she'd been massaging.

"Yes. But you can't laugh."

He chuckled. "I recall a dunk in the frigid lake helps with sore muscles."

She shot him a warning look—only half-serious—while Gemma leaned against the railing on the deck at the cabin.

"Look at that!" Real wonder painted the girl's voice.

Hazel turned to see what Gemma was in awe of. The rich tangerine and velvet purple pinks of the western sky reflected off the glass of Elk Lake.

"It's amazing, isn't it?" Bennett wrapped both arms around Hazel's shoulders, tucking her back against him.

"This is why you moved from Chicago."

"Well . . ." He pressed a kiss to Hazel's temple. "I'd say it was a side benefit."

"Ew." Gemma wrinkled her nose. "We don't need to know everything."

"Says the girl who spent half the afternoon flirting with a man twice her age."

Nathan trudged up onto the deck. He pinned a hard look on Gemma. "You did what?"

Gemma shrugged. "It was harmless."

He shook his head. "Don't act like Mom."

Yikes.

"Don't act like . . ." Gemma looked him up and down. "Yourself. Maybe find a better version of you while we're here, hmm?"

At her back, Hazel felt Bennett's deep sigh. She found his hand and slipped her fingers between his. "My brother and I always bickered," she whispered.

"That's not surprising."

"But we're okay now."

"Prayers and miracles." He kissed the top of her head, his tone serious. And grateful.

Hazel wasn't sure what to do with that. On one hand, she felt somehow valued knowing that Bennett had prayed for her and Hunter to reconcile. On the other, what did God have to do with it anyway? She was a fix-your-own-problems sort of girl. She didn't like the thought that she'd needed divine intervention for anything. Even if it was obvious that she had.

Besides, if God did have something to do with Hunter and her reconciling, why had He let them fall apart in the first place? Or for that matter, any of the bad stuff that had happened in their young lives?

Leaning away from the man at her back, Hazel opted not to dwell on those complicated questions, denying even that they truly bothered her—though she didn't know why she felt it necessary to deny that. Bennett let his arms fall away, and she turned to enter the cabin. "It feels like a night for cider."

"And s'mores," Bennett added.

"Sweet!" Gemma employed that everything-is-great high-level energy. "It's like going to camp all over again."

It was a cover-up. Hazel was certain of it now—and if it was anything like what she'd witnessed in Janie after Hunter joined the navy, Gemma was going to crash hard when this over-the-top positivity stopped smothering her pain.

Glancing at Bennett, Hazel wondered if he knew his little sister well enough to detect the mask. Were men intuitive like that? Bennett seemed to be.

And look at her, being intuitive about people again! It was a bit like reading her dogs or her horses.

Maybe. Maybe she'd had the ability all along but people wore her out too much to discover it before now.

"You went to camp?" Hazel asked.

"Of course! Every year."

"This is nothing like camp, Gemma." Nathan rolled his eyes. "Starting with the fact that we don't get to go home."

"You're always such a downer."

"You're always so delusional." Nathan took his earbuds out and tucked them into his hoodie pocket, then looked at Hazel. "Our *camp* is five weeks long, in Maine, and features personal trainers who specialize in health and personal training for tennis, competitive swimming, and golf. We are served brunch on Sundays, and every

Friday night is a required dinner-attire evening." He waved his hand around the small front room of Hazel's cabin. "*This* is nothing like that."

"But we have a bonfire every evening. And on Saturday we have *s'mores*." Gemma stuck her tongue out, as if she'd made her point.

"Is that where you were before I came to Chicago?"

"Yes." Nathan spat the word like it was wormwood on his tongue.

They'd been five weeks in Maine, and Bennett's dad couldn't find enough time to go to marriage counseling/retreat or whatever it was they were doing during that time span? Hazel glanced at Bennett, finding his brows knit together sternly. She'd wager he was thinking similar thoughts.

And redoubling his determination *not* to be his dad. *Which might be why marriage—and abstinence before marriage—is important to him.*

Yeah, but . . .

But those weren't thoughts she needed to wrestle with right then. She headed to her tiny kitchen, retrieved an open jar of Janie's homemade apple cider from the fridge, and poured the contents of it into a saucepan. She covered it and placed it on the stove.

"Okay. Fire." Hazel turned to face the small family. "Outside or in?"

"Ohhh! Outside." Gemma clasped her hands together and swooned. "So we can see the stars. They're so bright! Don't you think they're dazzling, Nathan?"

"Dazzling." Nathan mocked her choice of word, shaking his head. There might have been a peek of a grin he worked to keep down though.

"Got it." Hazel headed to fill the fire pit, located on the near side of the dock, just off the lake shore.

"Watch the cider—don't let it burn," Bennett instructed and then followed Hazel outside.

Together they layered tinder and kindling in the center of her stone pit and then created a small teepee with slender pieces of seasoned pine.

"You're getting good at this," Hazel said.

"Learning from a pro." Bennett winked.

"You'll be one yourself before long, now that you're a full-fledged Montana man." Hazel reached for the book of matches she had in her back pocket. "How long do you think before Gemma's sun-bright energy snuffs out?"

Bennett blew out a long sigh. "I don't know. Is it selfish of me to hope it doesn't?"

"I doubt she's normally this . . . chipper."

"No. I mean, she's generally happy. Dad praises her for it. And tells Nathan he wishes he'd be more like his sister, which helps nothing." Bennett gestured toward the house. "But this is next level."

Hazel nodded. "But you don't want her to find a more normal level? It's gotta be exhausting for her."

"I appreciate that she's trying to make the best of things."

"Even if it's fake?"

Bennett sat back on his haunches and ran a hand through his hair. "I don't know. No, I guess. I'm just not sure what I'm going to do when she crashes. Hopefully, by the time that happens, she and I will have a real relationship to work from, and Nathan will have come to terms with all of this, and I won't worry that he's going to try to hitch a ride back to Chicago or something."

Hazel struck the match, lit the tinder, and waited for the flame to catch. Orange tongues grew and spread, licking up the kindling like greedy little things. When the first pop of a larger piece of kindling sounded, she felt confident the fire had taken. She moved to stand behind Bennett to rub his shoulders.

"Just tell me how to help."

"You're doing just fine." He covered the hand she'd laid on his shoulder.

She grunted. "Who would have imagined?"

Bennett looked back at her, then stood. "Me."

"You would?"

"Yes." His look held on her, long and meaningful in the semidarkness. Then he took her hand and wove his fingers between hers. "I imagine so much with you, Hazel."

As warmth filled her chest, Hazel swallowed. She didn't have to wonder too hard what he meant by *so much*.

Marriage. Family. Till death do they part.

Her? The mountain woman who was more likely to drive a man mad than make him want to stay? The girl determined never to be trapped ever again?

It seemed absurd. And yet, oddly, standing there with him, her heart felt raw with the wonder that not only did this man love her so much that he'd continue to pursue her even after she'd hurt him with her rejection, but incredibly, this taste of family with him was *good*.

Could it be good? Forever? The slim possibility felt as tantalizing as it did dangerous. Hazel wasn't sure if she should indulge in it or run.

Luckily the kids chose that moment to bound out of the house, mugs of cider in hand, and make their way toward the fire. Well enough, that—the break away from the surge of emotion would give her a chance to get her head on straight.

Nathan handed Hazel a warm mug.

"Thanks."

He grunted. Took a sip. Was it her imagination that his tense posture relaxed?

Elk Lake could do that—ease away the strife of life off the mountain and take a person to an unexpected place of solace. Hazel had witnessed it several times over the years as a hunting guide. Men would come up with the weight of the chaotic life born from too much noise, too much responsibility, and way too many possessions, and let it tumble from their shoulders as the simplicity of a campfire, an unbelievable night sky, and the quiet whispers of trees in a mountain breeze unknotted all the unnecessary complications.

How was it that she still had her own life complications?

Hazel glanced at Bennett, then let her vision travel over Gemma and Nathan. Complications?

Yes. But not the sort she wanted unburdened from.

As that mystery settled in her mind, she turned her gaze up to the crystalline evening sky. Blackness had captured the eastern portion, as a hem of yellow orange held on to the west. Just a few more minutes and the color would all wash away, leaving the darkness to rule alone.

No. That wasn't so. On an evening they'd shared out on the dock late last January, she'd reminded Bennett of that, pointing out that the velvet black was merely the deep background to set off the white fire of the stars, allowing them to shine their best light.

The contrast of opposites was stunning.

A hand wrapped around hers, strong and warm. Knowing Bennett's touch, she laced her fingers with his while she continued to take in the beauty above.

"It just doesn't get old, does it?" Bennett asked.

"No." She turned her grin to him. "Especially when you're not afraid."

"No more fear." He winked.

"Hey, not to interrupt the sweet nothings going on over there"—Gemma made a mocking *ew* face—"but I recall a promise of chocolatey gooey goodness."

Bennett laughed and then rested his mug between a pair of river rocks in the fire-pit ring. "Right. I've got the s'mores supplies in the car. How about you come give me a hand?"

Gemma found a spot for her cider, and then the pair of them strode away toward Bennett's car.

Silence extended as Hazel stood on one side of the ring and Nathan on the other. He sipped his cider, one hand tucked into his hoodie pocket, and stared at the bouncing orange and yellow flames.

"You always live here?" he asked.

Surprised he said anything, Hazel nodded. "Since I was a girl. My parents lived in Luna, which is where I originally lived until they died."

SIXTEEN

"I didn't know your parents died."

"Yes. When I was just a girl."

He took a longer swig from his mug. "Sometimes I think . . ." Nathan didn't finish that.

Hazel imagined how he meant for it to end. That it would be easier if his parents had died? Man, that was a twisted, painful thing for a kid to think.

Had Hunter had such moments, thinking such hard things about Pops?

What made some men so selfish and unkind? What drove them to do mean things to the people they were supposed to love and protect?

With sudden clarity, Hazel realized she'd qualified that question with *some*. Not all. Some. Because Hunter wasn't one of those men. After several years of believing the worst of him, Hazel knew the truth without a doubt. Hunter wasn't that man.

Bennett wasn't either.

Some men were kind. Some protected. Some were selfless. Some loved well.

As the power of that revelation surged through her veins, Hazel refocused on Nathan. *Grow up to be the good kind, kid.*

Maybe that was why Nathan and Gemma were there. To see something different, to experience something different. Not just the mountains and the quiet and the unbelievable night sky. But a whole different life. Perspective. So maybe they would be different people. They wouldn't have to walk their parents' paths.

Just like she didn't have to walk the same way her Pops had gone.

Nathan leaned to set his mug on the ground. "Since there's no one out here, can I take a leak in the woods?"

Hazel blinked. Then she chuckled. "Go for it. Just keep the firelight in sight."

Nathan turned, his shoulders hunched and both hands tucked firmly in his pockets, and took himself into the woods. From the opposite direction, Gemma's bubbly voice drifted in the darkness, followed by Bennett's deep, soft chuckle.

For a minute or two, Hazel had a respite from being surrounded by people. She breathed in solitude. Strange... she felt the weariness that came with constant human interaction. But she also felt somehow a rightness and even a joy for having been with *these* people. They hadn't entirely drained her to the point that she needed at least a week by herself to recover.

A shuffling of rocks and dirt sounded moments before another vocal exchange between Bennett and Gemma. The pair neared and then stepped into the small ring of yellow light created by the bonfire, each carrying something for s'mores.

"And now for the main event," Gemma said.

Bennett broke apart the four pack of long metal forks he'd purchased from Mama B, along with the rest of the goodies' supplies.

Gemma ripped open the marshmallows and snagged a fork from her oldest brother. "I am an expert at toasting."

"Like you were an expert at painting?" Bennett asked wryly. Gemma had proclaimed so down at the house. It was soon discovered, as she'd slopped paint randomly against the clean walls, allowing thick trails of dripping green to run down the length and onto the floorboard, that she most certainly was *not* an expert. Or even experienced at all.

A sheepish grin met Bennett's raised-brow look. Then she shrugged. "No worries, bro. I've been doing this every summer since I was six."

She'd been shipped off to a five-week summer camp since she was six? Hazel didn't know much about growing up in a *normal* family, but that seemed off.

Bennett took Gemma's comment without showing a sign of concern. Instead, he stabbed a mallow and passed the setup to Hazel, then repeated the process for his own.

They each had a gooey mess consumed and were licking sticky fingers when Bennett looked around, as if something was wrong. "Where's Nathan?"

"He went into the forest to...um...you know..." Hazel would just spit it out like the backwoods girl that she was, but she wasn't sure Bennett wanted her to be *that* mountain woman in front of Gemma. Would it embarrass him? Irritate him?

Who knew. This being an adult-in-charge thing was whole new territory.

"How long ago?"

How long had it been? Couldn't be too long.

"Zel." Bennett's tone took on a demanding quality. "How long has Nathan been gone?"

She shrugged as irritation collided with panic. She wasn't actually responsible for these kids. But where was Nathan? How long had he been out in the dark woods alone?

Feeling small and stupid, Hazel peeked at Bennett across the fire. "He left shortly after you and Gemma went to get the s'mores."

Bennett winced.

"Nathan goes off on his own all the time. No worries," Gemma inserted.

"Goes off on his own where?" Bennett asked.

Gemma shrugged. "Sometimes to the arcade. Sometimes to grab some fast food. One time he even took Dad's Miata down to the shoreline. Dad wasn't very happy about that—mostly because Nathan had done some street racing and the tires were a little burned up."

Bennett crammed a hand into his hair. "Gemma, has Nathan ever been on his own in a place like this?" His furrowed brow hooded over a wild look.

Panic strummed through Hazel. She should have known better. Nathan was a city kid, and a displaced one at that. The sun had gone down, and the moon hadn't broken over the horizon yet. It was dark. Like pitch-black dark. There wasn't a way for a kid like Nathan to get his bearings if he lost sight of the campfire. Ten steps in the wrong direction would render him lost in the forest. A half mile in the wrong direction could put him in serious danger.

"Zel." This time unfettered fear pitched Bennett's voice.

"I'll get Scout."

"Can she track him?"

"She's our best bet for that." Hazel looked at Gemma, who stood wide eyed. "Stay by the fire in case he comes back. I'll give you a flare. If he shows up and we're out of cell range, go to the dock and fire it over the water." She turned her attention back to Bennett. "The flashlights are in the cabinet above the sink. I'll call Hunter."

Bennett turned and jogged to the house while Hazel dug her phone out of her denim jacket pocket. Gemma started calling Nathan's name, and Hazel called Hunter.

"Nathan wandered off." Hazel didn't bother with *hello* but dove straight into it when Hunter answered.

"Which way?"

"He went toward the corral last I saw him. But it's dark, and it's been a while."

"I'll head your way."

Hazel hung up as Bennett came out of the cabin with three flashlights. Scout bounded after him, glad to have been let outside with the people. Ice and Cream also trotted behind Bennett.

He handed her a flashlight and gave one to Gemma, who intermittently rent the air with a loud call for her brother, then gestured toward the sled dogs. "Can I take one of these guys?"

"Sure. Take them both. I don't know if it'll work, but if you've got something of Nathan's with you, grab it. They're not bloodhounds, but maybe they'd pick up something."

"Worth a try. I think his gaming bag is in the car."

Hazel nodded. "Their leashes are in the tack room, if you want them."

"Will I need them?"

"Probably not." Hazel turned her attention to the husky-mix dogs and pointed toward Bennett. "Go with Benji. Help him find Nathan."

The pair cocked their heads, turned to look at Bennett, looked at each other, and then jogged to Bennett's side.

"Good dogs." He bent to scratch Cream's head. "Let's find Nathan."

SIXTEEN

Hazel looked at Gemma, finding her sunshine had disappeared behind a dark cloud of fear. Gemma bit her lip, let it free, and then called for Nathan again. This time her desperate voice trembled.

Hazel stepped close and squeezed her shoulder. "We'll find him."

"He probably took off on purpose."

"It doesn't matter right now. We'll find him. Hunter is coming. He'll show up from over there." Hazel pointed in the direction of the trail that went over the ridge separating the big lake from the pond. "I don't want you to be startled when he comes out of the trees. Okay?"

She nodded.

"We'll find him, Gemma." Hazel motioned for Scout and set off toward the corral. *Please, let us find him.*

It was a refrain she silently repeated well into the night. Never once did it occur to her that she was praying. Perhaps more significantly, it didn't occur to her that all her hope hung on a God she wasn't fond of to intercede when she didn't believe that He cared.

All Hazel could do in between calling out for Nathan, checking her phone for good news, and traipsing through the woods was repeat that plea.

Please. Let us find him.

Seventeen

Hunter squeezed his phone, using the flashlight app to shed light on the ridge trail as he made his way toward the cabin. His mind spun in several different directions, the relay of events that day causing havoc in his heart.

Pray and surrender, Hunt. And don't forget—I am here and praying for you. John Brighton's closing words to their conversation anchored his otherwise tossed-in-the-storm thoughts.

Imagining Janie out on a date with Grady had nearly sent him to the ER. Literally, thanks to this lifelong lung damage he had. Seeing her with him at Bennett's project house nearly had Hunter right back at the punching bag. Only this time there wouldn't be anyone there to make sure he recovered. And for a hot minute, Hunter thought that might be a decent solution.

Instead he'd taken himself back up to Elk Pond, worked up a sweat splitting some firewood, stopped short of having another attack, and retrieved his phone to call the one man he knew who would give him solid advice.

John hadn't let him down. Consoling, understanding, but also unmovable in his belief that God saw Hunter, knew his heart, and would work all things—even through the utter devastation of losing Janie forever, if that be the case—according to His good will.

"That's a hard thing, holding to a faith that says God is good, even when the pain tells us otherwise. But, Hunter?" John had paused, ensuring Hunter was listening with more than his ears. "God *is* good. And He'll do good in your life. I think you've already seen that in the hard things that have happened in this year alone. Allow Him to do His work, and maybe through you, He'll reveal His love and goodness to the people you love and want His salvation for."

Hazel. That was who John was referring to, and he was right. Hunter hadn't found the right way, the right words, to share with Hazel his surrendering to Jesus. But he wanted to. With Hazel, though, it would take more than words.

She would have to witness God's splendor.

Rounding the final bend in the trail that would empty from the pines onto the small plane that contained Elk Lake, Hunter paused. He listened, hoping to hear something that would indicate Nathan's recovery. When nothing but the rustling of aspen leaves reached his hearing, he cupped his hands together and lifted Nathan's name onto the cold breeze.

He held still. Listened. Still nothing.

Lifting his face toward the starry sky above, he whispered a prayer. "Jesus, You see him, don't You? You know exactly where Nathan is. Please show us. And please keep him safe."

He stepped forward and then paused again. "And, Jesus? Show us your splendor right here at Elk Lake. My sister—she's lost, like Nathan. Only she doesn't know it. Will You send Your search and rescue out for her?"

It was tempting to stand there and keep praying. He had a lot more he needed to tell his Savior. About how much his heart hurt because Janie was moving on—and how angry that made him, and that he felt his self-control slipping every time she was near or he thought about her with another man.

But the mission was Nathan, and Hunter reached for his military training to stay the course.

"Nathan!" Hunter called for the boy as he moved toward the end of the trail.

Was there something? There, to his left. Up the steep scramble of scrub oak. Turning toward that rise, Hunter called again. "Nathan!"

He leaned forward, tuned his hearing for anything not common to the area. Yes! There was something . . .

Help.

Is that what he'd heard? It wasn't the breeze, was it? A bough scuffing against another limb up by the upper part of the creek?

"Help!"

No. That was definitely a voice. A desperate, frightened boy's voice. Hunter leapt into the scrub and pushed his legs up the steep slope, bushing stiff branches from his path and ignoring the sounds of tearing fabric and the sting of cuts against his arms. "Nathan! Stay put. I'm coming."

Man, how did he get up there? That was the opposite direction of the corrals—which was why Bennett and Hazel hadn't looked this way.

More pressing, had Nathan seen the rocky ledge that overlooked the lake, or in the pitch of darkness, had he walked straight off it, tumbling onto the rock slide directly below?

God! Nathan's call had come from that direction. *Please . . .*

Hunter reached a small leveling point, and he turned slightly left toward that granite outcropping. From where he was now, he'd be beneath the overlook. "Nathan! Where are you?"

"Help!" This time the call was absolutely clear. And terrified.

"Where are you?"

"Rocks . . ." His voice cracked hard.

He'd fallen. Hunter felt certain of it. Why hadn't he, or any of the others, heard it? Surely Nathan would have shouted, wouldn't he?

For Hunter's part, it was distinctly possible that he'd been too lost in the chaos of his head. An absolute failure for a rescue mission. *Focus. You always focus.*

As Hunter reprimanded himself, his mind went rogue, jumping to the memory of his parents. They'd fallen to their death in a sudden storm, leaving Hunter and Hazel orphans. His grandfather had used that same black granite rock face his parents had fallen from to end his own life.

Now Nathan?

No. Not Nathan. *God, help me get there in time . . . No more tragedy at Elk Lake, please!* Hazel couldn't handle it—she'd lock herself away, worse than before, and never believe that there could possibly be a good God who loved people. Bennett didn't deserve it—wasn't he there with the kids, trying to show them a better way of life than their father had demonstrated?

And Hunter? His faith was so young. How would he handle such a disaster right now?

He didn't want to find out.

"Nathan? It's Hunter. I'm coming. Talk to me, bud."

"I'm here."

Hunter picked his way over the scree field of jagged granite, scanning the ancient avalanche litter with his phone light. "I'm not seeing you. Keep talking. Are you hurt?"

"Yeah. My leg." Pain soaked Nathan's voice. "I think it's busted."

A sigh—largely of relief because a fall from the ledge should have been much worse than a broken leg—left Hunter's lungs. "I'm getting closer. Just keep talking to me."

"I see your light. I'm above you."

Hunter shifted his phone and scanned higher up.

"Here! I'm here—you just shined the light on me!"

Hunter jerked his hand back. There. Nathan waved both hands over his head, signaling for attention. Hunter scrambled upward, wishing he had the footing of a mountain goat as he slipped and stumbled over the uneven and jagged rise. "I see you, buddy. Just sit tight."

The climb took much longer than Hunter liked, and it came with several scrapes on his hand and a twisted ankle from bad footing. But he reached Nathan. Scanning the boy with his light in one hand, he gripped Nathan's shoulder with the other. The boy shivered violently—from cold or from shock, Hunter wasn't sure. Likely both.

When his flashlight illuminated Nathan's right leg, Hunter's stomach dropped. It was bad. Very bad. Ripped jeans soaked in blood. The bone had cut clean through Nathan's leg.

Nathan quaked intensely. Hunter moved the light from the injury back up to the boy's face, finding it sheet white—including his lips.

"Stay with me, Nate." Hunter shook his shoulder. "I'm going to get you out of here, and you're going to be okay. But I need you to focus on staying with me."

"My leg..."

"Yeah, I know. But you're going to be okay. Focus on that, not on your leg, all right?"

With an audible gulp, Nathan nodded.

Hunter unzipped his light Columbia coat, unbuttoned his long-sleeved flannel, and ripped a section off the shirt. Bending back over Nathan, he paused before he touched him. "I'm going to wrap this tight above the break, okay?"

Nathan winced.

"It's gonna hurt like... heck."

With a deep grimace, Nathan nodded and then gripped Hunter's thermal undershirt.

Guess that meant he was ready. Hunter wrapped the strip of cloth tight, grabbed a nearby twig the thickness a little more than his thumb, and used it as a windlass. Nathan moaned deeply, barely suppressing the shout of pain.

Once the tourniquet was secure, Hunter took a screenshot of his phone so he could relay the time to the medical people. "Okay, buddy, breathe. That part is done. I'm going to call Bennett and Hazel, and then I'm going to see how best to get you to where a vehicle can reach us, okay?"

Nathan slumped back, breath heaving, and nodded.

"Don't move." Hunter tapped his phone to call Bennett, all the while moving the light to scan the area above them. Nathan hadn't fallen from the overlook—he'd missed it by only a couple of feet. "Thank You, God," Hunter breathed.

"What's that?" Nathan asked in a meek tone.

"I was thanking God—both that we found you and that you missed the outcropping that overlooks this rockslide. Had you gone off that . . ." Hunter wasn't sure how Nathan *hadn't* gone off that. The trail led right to it. "Thank You, Jesus," he breathed again.

"Tell me you've got him," Bennett said over the speaker.

"I've got him. He's hurt, and we've got to get him to the hospital over in Big Sky."

"How do I get to you?"

"Drive the access road toward the ridge, and park where it switches back to go down to town." Hunter had a plan to get Nathan to that point. In optimal situations, they'd walk there in less than ten minutes. Obviously this was significantly less than optimal. "I'll call you when I get him out of the scree field. Don't panic when it takes us a while. We'll get there."

"Can I help you after I park the car?"

"Yeah. Grab Hazel and have her lead you toward the old trapline trail."

"Got it. Can I talk to Nathan?"

"I'm here," Nathan said.

Hunter didn't need to shine the light on the boy to know he grimaced. The pain rang clear in his voice.

"Man, it's good to hear your voice. Hang in there, okay, Nathan?"

"Yeah."

"You're in good hands."

Nathan looked up at Hunter, a mix of pain and fear in his eyes. "I know."

Hunter squeezed his shoulder. "I'll get him out of this, Bennett. But keep praying. He's got a long road in front of him."

With the phone call over, Hunter handed Nathan his cell. "I've got a plan, buddy. We're going to go up the same way you came down. It's a scramble though, and I'm going to have to carry you."

Wide eyed, Nathan nodded. "Can you do that?"

"Yeah. But we're going to try it with you on my back. It's gonna hurt."

"I can handle it."

"Yeah?"

Gritting his teeth, Nathan nodded.

"I need you to hold the light so I can see where we're going. Can you do that?"

"Yeah."

"If you're going to pass out, you've got to tell me, okay?"

"I'm not going to pass out." For the first time since Hunter found him, determination overrode the panic and terror in Nathan's voice. "I can handle it."

Hunter nodded, keeping a firm look on Nathan. "Yes you can. Ready?"

Nathan reached for Hunter's shoulder. He grunted as Hunter moved into position, and when Nathan pushed off the rocks and onto Hunter's back, a painful grunt sounded from Nathan's chest.

But he held a firm grip around Hunter and kept the light shining forward. Hunter began the scramble back up to the trail, trying hard not to make the pain in Nathan's leg worse. He couldn't imagine how the jostling didn't hurt, but Nathan's grip remained firm, and the light stayed steady.

Once they reached the top of the boulder field, Hunter hefted them both up. It took his arms pulling, his knees and feet pushing, and every bit of his strength, but he got them safely over the drop and back onto the trail.

One miracle at a time.

Please, God, don't stop them now...

With strength he didn't know he had, Hunter jogged the trail, making his way to the spot where he'd need to veer off to find the vehicle. Not once did he need his inhaler. It didn't even occur to him that he might.

He'd failed already. Bennett leaned forward in the hard chair of the waiting room, dropping his head into both hands. His elbows pushed hard against his legs, but he was only vaguely aware of the pressure there.

How could he have failed within two days of this unsought arrangement?

A pair of strong hands, small and gentle, kneaded his tightly bound shoulders. "It's going to be okay." Hazel pressed against him as she leaned to offer comfort.

Head still in hands, Bennett shook his head. "I lost him." Tears blurred his vision as he turned to look at the woman beside him. "How could I have lost him?"

Hazel shook her head. "Nathan is fifteen. And he wandered off into the darkness without a clue where he was going. You didn't lose him. This is *not* your fault."

"I can't pin blame on a kid when I was given responsibility for him."

Sitting up straight, Hazel took his face in between her firm hands. "He is fifteen, not five. And he admitted that he was trying to find the road to leave."

A shuddering breath slowly left Bennett's chest. He heard what Hazel was saying, but he couldn't shake the heavy weight of guilt that proclaimed this was his responsibility. That Nathan was back in the OR of this tiny hospital, hopefully undergoing a successful surgery to realign his fibula and stitch up his opened leg, and that was entirely Bennett's fault.

Or worse, the ugly, niggling accusation that Hazel had been negligent in allowing Nathan to wander out into the woods alone in the first place.

No. This wasn't Hazel's fault.

But was it Nathan's? He was just a kid. A city kid who didn't know any better.

"Zel isn't wrong, Bennett." From the row of chairs across from Bennett, Hunter offered his low consolation. "Nathan is old enough to make choices—good or bad. No one—you or Hazel—could have known that he intended to find the access road and hoped to make it to the highway."

The enormity—and stupidity—of Nathan's failed plan pressed hard against Bennett. What had made the boy think he could *hitchhike* his way back to Chicago? Insane.

And really, really dumb.

But Bennett should have suspected he'd try something like that. The kid lived in a world of virtual reality, thanks to his unending screen time. He had no concept of the wilds of Montana, no understanding of the dangers of real life.

Clenching his fists, Bennett bounced his forehead against them. "I can't let this happen again."

"What are you going to do—tie a rope around his waist and trail him wherever he goes?" Hazel asked.

"Maybe." He sat back, slumping against the chair. "If that's what it takes."

Bennett could feel the disapproval from the Wallace siblings as they exchanged a look.

Hazel settled an expression that somehow combined compassion and resolution. "Pops used to say that when a guy acted like he had something to prove, it was usually because he needed to prove it to himself."

"I don't know what that means in this context. Nathan wanted to leave because he didn't want to move to Montana in the first place."

"I think Hazel might be right."

Bennett glared at Hunter. "Still not making sense. And the ramblings of your backwoods grandfather aren't helpful right now."

"Nathan has been a pain in the butt since you got here." Hunter crossed his arms. "I'm guessing he was a pain long before he left Chicago—and not just with you." He paused waiting for confirmation. He must have taken Bennett's lack of response as exactly that. "Which means he feels like he's got something to prove."

"Whatever. Right now I have to deal with a broken leg that requires surgery, so . . ."

Hazel crossed her arms and turned in her chair to face Bennett. "Teach him how to stand on his own two feet. Show him that he can."

"Great. I'm sure that will help. Then he'll be gone for sure, and I'll never find him."

"No he won't. He'll know he can take care of himself like a man should, and he won't feel trapped. He won't feel like he's got to figure it out on his own."

Bennett scowled at his girlfriend. Since when did she know all about fifteen-year-old boys and how to take care of them? She barely understood her own brother.

But . . .

No. That was foolish. Anyway, Bennett wasn't even sure what these Wallaces were talking about. Wilderness survival lessons? Military boot camp? Both were right up Hunter's alley—but not Bennett's. And even if they embarked on such a scheme, who knew but it would only equip Nathan with the gumption to do something even more stupid.

"Feeling helpless is an awful thing." Hunter glanced at Hazel, regret flashing in that look, and then returned to Bennett. "And it can make a person do crazy things. What if we showed Nathan how to be a man—how to take care of himself and how he can care and protect the people who matter to him. Suddenly he's not trapped. Not strapped to total dependency on your dad's money. Not dependent on someone else to make choices for him. He'd be free to stand on his own, become who he wants to become."

"We?"

Hazel slipped her hand into his. "We're here with you, Bennett."

Bennett let his eyes slide shut, the warm moisture lining his lids threatening to roll. "I don't know..."

"Just give it some thought," Hunter said. "You'll both have plenty of time to think about it the next few months while he recovers." He stood, stretched, and patted Bennett's shoulder. "I'm going to find some coffee."

Nodding, Bennett sat straighter. "You could head back to Luna. There's no reason we all need to stay here."

Hazel's grip on his hand hardened. He heard her silent declaration loud and clear—she wasn't going anywhere.

Hunter's look slid to Hazel, then he nodded. "I'll stop and check on Janie and Gemma."

"Thanks. I appreciate it." It was truly a generous offer, considering the wreck Hunter was when it came to Janie right then. "And, Hunt? Thanks for getting Nathan out of there. I hate to think... if you weren't there..." Bennett choked on the lump in his throat.

Hunter patted Bennett's shoulder once and then stepped back. "Let me know how the surgery turns out."

Bennett nodded, and Hunter turned to go, leaving Hazel and Bennett alone in the ER lounge to wait out the long night ahead. Bennett turned to look at her. "You could go with your brother. I'll be okay."

Those amber eyes, rimmed with a thick ring of mossy green, held fast to him. He felt her strength of resolve like an anchor in the midst of this dark storm. "You're not alone, Bennett."

He leaned to rest his head against hers. As she held him, he wondered if she really understood love, even as she poured it out freely on him. Or if she'd ever believe that she was not alone either. And he wouldn't let her be so ever again.

It was her and him for the rest of his life. He vowed it.

Eighteen

Janie brought two mugs of rich raspberry hot chocolate to the sofa, where Gemma snuggled. Wrapped in Janie's thickest, softest blanket—the one with colorful fall leaves scattered in the print—Gemma sniffed and wiped her wet cheek.

"Here we go, sweetie. Guaranteed to warm you clear through to your bones and soothe those frazzled fears." Janie passed her favorite mug to Gemma. Once the girl clasped it, Janie ran a hand over her auburn hair, smoothing the sneaky flyaway strands. "I just got a text from Hazel. She says the doctor came out and they were able to reset the bone cleanly. They're stitching him up now, and then he'll be moved to a room to sleep for the night."

Gemma sniffed again and nodded. "I wish Bennett's mom was here already. She could have helped."

"It would be nice to have a medical professional right here in town." Janie smiled, lowering to her overstuffed chair and tucking her feet beneath her. "But the truth is, Nathan needed a hospital. I'm certain that Bennett's mom would have agreed."

"Why can't Nathan just make the best of things?" Gemma dropped one hand into her lap with a huff. "Dad always does whatever he wants. Begging, throwing a fit—it doesn't matter. Dad plows on. Nathan knows that."

What to say to that? Janie only had a distant view of Mr. Crofton—but even that gave her a glimpse of a man she didn't like. Bennett never spoke a whole lot about his dad, but the little bit that Janie gathered—mostly from Hazel—told her that Bennett didn't want to be anything like the man. And this? Sending his two teenage kids halfway across the country to live with their estranged half brother?

Not too admirable.

"Sometimes we just feel like we need to get away."

Her father had.

Hunter had.

Janie swallowed against the resentment that sprouted in her chest.

"I don't know why Nathan would care so much about going back to Chicago anyway. All he ever does is play video games. Or get into trouble with his worthless friends." Gemma air quoted *friends*. "I'm the one who had things going at home. Cheerleading. Swimming. Real friends who didn't use me because of my dad's fast cars. If I can be positive, seems like he can too."

"Some people just don't have the personality to look for the bright side."

Gemma sighed. "I guess." She ran her fingers over the softness of the blanket, then looked up and met Janie's eyes. "Can I tell you something?"

"Sure."

"It's really tiring sometimes."

"Looking on the bright side?"

She nodded. "Sometimes I just want to cry and say it's not fair. Maybe even throw something."

Janie held on to that sincere, desperate look and let it sink into her heart. Oh, how she knew how that felt. Painting smiles over storm clouds, laughing instead of crying . . . This girl was her soul sister when it came to that. The only exception for Janie had been Hunter.

With him she'd let stone-cold mad settle into place and kept it there. Perhaps because he was the only person on earth with whom she'd ever truly been her whole broken, not-always-sunny self. Even Hazel didn't know the layer that cried at the loneliness. That still felt the ache of abandonment left by her dad's leaving. The stifling imposter syndrome and feeling certain that at any moment she'd fail and everyone would know that she'd never had it in her to be successful in the first place.

Gemma was an eleven-year-old, red-haired, copper-eyed reflection of Janie's secret self. What would eleven-year-old Janie wish for right then?

She knew exactly what. Janie unfolded her legs and stood. "I think you should do that."

"What?"

"Right now. I've got some rolls to check downstairs in the café's kitchen. You'll have the whole apartment to yourself. Go lock yourself in the bathroom with that pillow." Janie pointed to her small fuzzy throw pillow. "Throw it at the shower. The mirror. The door. Whatever you feel like. Let it all out. Everything you feel about your parents taking off for Europe, having to move to Montana, your brother getting hurt. All of it. Yell. Scream. Do what you need to do."

Wide copper eyes stared up at her. "You . . . I . . . really?"

"Yep." Janie tucked a loose tress of Gemma's hair behind her ear. "I'll be back in about ten minutes. The place is yours. Let it out."

Janie planted a kiss on the top of the girl's head. Then she headed for the door leading to the stairs, leaving a stunned Gemma Crofton sitting on her sofa. Hopefully with the freedom to pour out some real emotion so it didn't become toxic sludge inside her beautiful young heart.

Janie flipped on the kitchen light and opened her side-by-side refrigerator. Yep, there were those rolls, just as she'd left them earlier that evening. Ready to bake in the morning and then be served to the after-church crowd, along with her peppered pot roast. Satisfied that all was well—and more importantly, that she wasn't a liar, saying she was going to check on the rolls—Janie shut the cooler doors and leaned back against them. Tipping her head back and crossing her arms, she allowed a long exhale.

Lord, it'd been a day. It felt like a week had gone by in less than twenty-four hours. First, with Hunter showing up at the café and finding out she was going out with Grady. That had bothered her way more than she'd anticipated. Truth be told, it still bothered her.

Then the afternoon with Grady . . . had been a perfectly nice afternoon. A nice hike, a nice picnic, with a nice man. Why did that evaluation feel . . . flat?

Janie shut her eyes. "What am I doing?"

The empty kitchen gave no response.

"God, what am I supposed to do?"

Still, only the gentle hum of the refrigerator at her back . . .

And a muffled knock at her back door?

Janie pulled herself straight, head tilted to hear and eyes studying the solid back door.

Yes, there it was again. Someone was at her back door. With a heart jolt at the possibility that yet another catastrophe had hit, Janie scurried to answer the knock.

Brown eyes peered at her from the thickness of the night. Oh man. He could still take her heart captive when he looked at her like his soul was bare, his heart was raw, and he needed . . .

Her.

A tremble rolled through her middle. She swallowed, pulling open the door wider. "Hunter." Why did his name make her heart skip? Why did her imagining that he'd come to claim her again send fiery electricity through her veins?

She must be tired. Exhausted. After all, it had been a *very* long day.

"Hey. Is it okay if I come in?"

Since when did he ask such things? Especially when she'd clearly opened the door to him?

"Of course." Great. Her voice cracked. Like she was nervous about him picking her up for sophomore homecoming or something equally juvenile. Clearing her throat, she brushed up her friendly smile. Good reminder—she'd determined to seek friendship with Hunter so they could at last cease this volatile seesaw of emotions between them.

Hunter nodded, then stepped into the heart of her kitchen. His shoulders rippled with tension, and when he turned to her again, strain pulled at the corners of his eyes.

"Is Nathan okay?" Rising concern filtered in her voice.

"Yeah." He rubbed the top of his head. "It sounds like it's going to be a long recovery, but he's okay."

"Thank God you were there." Janie stepped nearer, the sizzle of her initial response fading into the reality of what had happened. What if Hunter hadn't heard the boy's cry? By Hazel's quick account, she and Bennett were looking for him in the opposite direction. They wouldn't have found him.

Then what? Broken, bleeding leg, high altitude, temperatures diving below freezing. Not a recipe for a city boy lasting through a mountain night.

Hunter's lack of response intrigued her. "Hey—you okay?"

He nodded. Then his lips trembled, and he pressed them tight.

"What is it, Hunt?"

"I shouldn't have heard him." Brows raised, he settled a serious look on her. "Honestly, Janie. The wind was going the other way.

The stand of pine and aspen between us . . . I really shouldn't have heard him. I hadn't even really been listening for him until that exact moment—I had been too lost in my head about some other things."

Other things . . . Did that mean her? Was it pure arrogance that she guessed it did?

She'd seen him at Bennett's house before he'd skedaddled out of there. His jaw had clenched hard, and he'd itched behind his right ear, then claimed he had some other things he needed to do.

Geez, Janie. The world isn't all about you—focus on the matter at hand.

"You stopped and listened, and suddenly you heard him?"

"I stopped and prayed, and it was like his cry for help came to me. I think I heard him, but every time I hit rewind and replay that moment, it seems . . . beyond me."

He'd *prayed*? In all the years that they'd been friends and then dated, Hunter never once had claimed that he'd prayed. Even though Mama had taken Hunter and Hazel to church as often as they would cooperate—which wasn't much—God hadn't meant much to the Wallaces. They were too self-sufficient. Or maybe too jaded by brokenness. Either way neither sibling had been interested in faith.

Hunter's penetrating study felt like a message in the silence. One Janie wasn't certain how to decipher. Rather than dissecting it, she returned to the part about thanking God Hunter had recovered Nathan.

"Thank God you heard him, however it happened."

"Yeah. It's just . . . stunning. This faith, this trusting God is new to me, and I'm stunned to discover that He really does *act*."

Whoa. That was a whole lot of big news to take in at once! When . . . how . . . why?

"Is church still at nine tomorrow?"

Speechless, Janie merely nodded. Hunter mirrored that wordless response. And then . . . more palpable silence.

Was he going to tell her what happened? Why, after all these years, he was crying out to God for help, and now he wanted to go to church? Maybe he was waiting for her to pry . . .

"How's Gemma?"

Just when Janie was ready to take the deep dive into those profound questions, Hunter switched gears. She worked to mentally change tracks with him. "She's trying to be sunshine and rainbows."

He shook his head. "She's gonna crash, isn't she?" His words sank in with an unspoken acknowledgment—*you would know. I know you would know.*

"Yeah." Janie leaned back against the counter, feeling both known and exposed at the reality that Hunter understood her so deeply.

Would another man ever understand her the way he did? The things she'd wrestled with her whole life? The things that had broken her heart? Could Grady?

If she let him. That was the question though—*if.*

But there was Hunter . . .

Janie tried to ignore the painful, sweet stirring in her heart. *Friendship.* That was what she was willing to try for with Hunter. Just friendship.

The silence felt like a rubber band stretched taut. Distance and tension grew between them.

Hunter stepped backward, pinning his back against the pantry door opposite her. "How was your date?"

Did he have to work to put the cool, nonaffected tone into his question?

"Fine?" Shoot. Janie was pretty sure that had come out as a squeak. She cleared her throat and lifted her chin. "We just hiked part of the Elk Creek trail."

"Upper or lower?"

"Lower. Then we had a picnic."

He nodded, his attention focused on the floor.

"You helped Bennett all day?"

"No, not all day. Just most of the afternoon."

This time Janie nodded. And stared at the floor. She crossed her arms. Shuffled her feet.

"Is there a time we can talk about food for the groundbreaking?"

"Sure. Anytime."

His brows lifted at that, a stern *no* in his chilly look.

No, he didn't want to stumble into her when she was going out with Grady. No, he didn't want to witness that one bit.

It was a small town though. If she continued dating Grady, Hunter would have to come to terms with running into them. Unless he decided to hide up at his lousy camper all winter.

He would. Janie felt instinctively Hunter would do exactly that, and it made her sad.

She sighed. "I can make time on Monday morning, if that would work for you."

"Thanks." Hunter stood straight and took three steps toward the exit. "Suppose Mama B would let me crash in my old room? Hazel will need a ride when she and Bennett make it back."

"I'm guessing she was planning on it."

He nodded. "Thanks for taking Gemma. I know it helped Bennett, and he appreciates it."

"Of course. I'm glad to do whatever they need."

Hunter reached for the door, began to pull it open, and then stopped. When he turned, he settled those brown eyes directly on her. "Are you going out with him again?"

If ever she knew how one of those hares felt in a Wallace trap, this was the moment. Sharp, burning pain clamped around her with a sudden force that threatened to steal her breath. And that steady gaze fastened on her, all blazing and tortured at once . . . The ache edged her close to nausea. All Janie could manage was a shrug.

Hunter nodded, then turned to leave.

"You can sit with Mama and me in church tomorrow," Janie said in a rush, nearly choking on the swell in her throat. She didn't want him to leave with this awful piercing sting throbbing in her gut. She didn't want to shut her eyes tonight only to see the angry sadness in his. She needed him to smile at her—even just a little. Or say *okay*. Anything was better than . . .

Hunter shook his head. "Thanks for the offer."

And then the door closed. Janie sagged against the counter behind her, one arm wrapped around her middle. A single rogue tear seeped against the side of her nose. Friendship shouldn't hurt like this.

Hunter lay in the soft bed that he'd spent much of his younger life in. The warmth of the log-cabin quilt covered him with weighted comfort, the smell of Pine-Sol and Old English furniture oil feathering against the memories of a few years of feeling steady. Mama B had that effect on him, and staying in her home wrapped him with the same security.

A blessing, since his heart had waged war all day.

Janie had moved on. After all these years of focused anger, she'd let it go, let *him* go, and had moved on. If she'd done so before he'd come back to Luna, it would have been easier. Probably. He'd not have woven through the stormy sea of their unresolved relationship only to come to the undeniable conclusion that he'd not gotten over her. He'd not have accepted the reality that he never would.

But no. Janie had waited until Hunter had dug beneath the layers of his own livid resentment and found that it'd been love turned wrong side out the whole time. She'd waited for him to see that she was it for him, forever. *Then* she'd decided to try dating again . . . with someone else.

Was she doing this on purpose? Was this calculated torment?

Not his Janie, the sweet girl who had given him comfort when he'd been barely a young man. Not the tender one who had come up to his *trash-can trailer* and took his side about the lodge, even when it meant crossing her best friend. Not the generous woman who had readily volunteered to cater his groundbreaking party only days before . . .

But maybe the woman he'd labeled *vampire* in his contact list last fall.

Rolling his fists, Hunter brought them to his forehead and groaned against the agony of this twisted mess.

"God, I'm a weak man. A broken man." His lips trembled as he whispered into the dark emptiness of his room. "I don't know how to handle this." With a shuddering breath, he lay his hands flat against his face. "I don't think I can. Not without being ugly."

He let that honest confession settle into the chill of the autumn mountain night. It felt desperate and hollow, and he yearned for the hope that had filled him when he'd asked Jesus to save him to pour back into the empty places.

"Please, God . . ." His hands slid from his face and rested on his chest. "Walk this hard path with me."

Not knowing if the King of everything would lower himself to such a unworthy request, Hunter let it lie there in the vacancy between this lonely Montana night and the kingdom of heaven.

Surprisingly, he drifted to sleep, the ache still there but the untethered recklessness abated.

Nineteen

Sitting at the back of the small church felt strange for several reasons. The first was that it'd been years since Hunter had done such a thing. The second, he sat alone in an old wooden pew near the far west stained-glass window located nearest the exit. When he had attended a service, it had always been in company with Mama B, Hazel, and Janie. Third pew, east side, near the aisle. That had been the standard seating arrangement.

That hadn't changed for the Truitts. There both women sat, Mama B at the end of the pew, her lovely grown daughter at her side.

Hunter swallowed, his eyes resting on that glossy dark hair. Thick tresses hung just past Janie's shoulders, curling at the ends. She rarely wore it down. Hunter's fingers twitched with the desire to feel the soft fullness. Once upon a time he'd owned the privilege to run his rough hands through the length of it. He used to love tugging her ponytail free. It didn't take much for him to remember the scent of sweet apples from her favorite shampoo. The smell of anything apple—from candles to cider—had since taken him back to her.

Inhaling, half expecting to pick up the scent of apples even though five pews and a three-foot aisle were between them, Hunter experienced a contradiction of relief and disappointment at the almond-vanilla that hit him instead. Likely that came from Jeremy's wife, Leslie, as the couple sat directly in front of him.

Man, he needed to move his mind away from Janie Truitt. He'd come to church to learn more about God. And truly, he knew a hunger for knowing more. It shouldn't be this hard to set his mind on the preacher at the front.

When reaching for discipline failed though, Hunter let his attention slide back to Janie and then onto the broad shoulders belonging to the man on her left.

Grady Briggs was a church man apparently. Or he came to impress Janie. Hunter didn't know the other man well enough to know which would be the likelier case, but the snide, ugly part of him wanted to assume the latter.

And why are you here?

Ah. That. The sharp thought finally did the job of redirecting Hunter's attention. Not to impress Janie. Not to stare at her and speculate about Grady. He'd come to worship the God who had brought salvation to his soul.

The man at the front adjusted his glasses, ran a finger along the page of his open Bible, and began to read. "'Trust in the Lord and do good; dwell in the land and enjoy safe pasture. Delight yourself in the Lord and he will give you the desires of your heart. Commit your way to the Lord; trust in him and he will do this: He will make your righteousness shine like the dawn, the justice of your cause like the noonday sun.'

"Hear the word of the Lord from Psalm 37. Let us set our minds on it, determine in our hearts that we will listen. Lord, let us hear Your voice." Pastor Dunham lifted his eyes from the page and scanned his small flock. The building would hold barely more than fifty, but the seats were full. This man had served tiny Luna as a spiritual guide for as long as Hunter could remember.

He wondered, when Pastor's slow gaze passed over Hunter, if the man knew who Hunter was. For some reason he hoped so.

"Sometimes it is easy to take the Word of God and make it say what we wish, don't you think?" Pastor tapped the page he'd read from, then chuckled. "This verse here, for example—'Delight yourself in the Lord, and he will grant the desires of your heart.'" He shook his head. "Ah, my friends, if you knew the way the younger version of your pastor had twisted that . . . you perhaps would not think much of him as a pastor! I used to think that meant that if I made sure I didn't swear while I played football, and I made sure I said that God gave me the athletic gift, then He'd make sure I was successful."

Taking both sides of the pulpit, Pastor leaned forward. "Guess what? I played one year at Montana State, and then I was cut. Lost my scholarship—which I was pretty sure was God's payment for my being such a good Christian athlete—to a guy who swore like a sailor and took all the credit for his playing skills for himself." He stepped back and folded his arms—which still held the bulk of an impressive lineman—and shook his head. "That didn't seem very fair of God at all. Nor did it match what I had made this verse out to be. And you know what? I was *mad* about it. Me and God, we had a pretty good standoff."

Amusement sparkled in his eyes as he leaned back toward his congregation. "Guess who won?" He laughed. "Here I am, so it shouldn't be much of a mystery.

"Here's the thing, my beloved friends. We have to take all of what God says, or none of it. So in this passage here, we need to hear the whole of it. Let's look at the verbs. *Trust. Do good. Delight. Commit. Trust*, again. Sounds like a little more like a lifestyle and not so much like a trade contract, doesn't it? And what does it say God will do? Look at the end of this list—He will make our righteousness shine. That's *His* endgame. He wants whatever we do, and whatever we go through—and make no mistake, He *allows* us to walk those paths, whether hard or easy—He wants the end of our stories to be the kind that bring Him glory because He makes us better people for His kingdom. That's a little different than I give a few nods to God and He gives me what I want, isn't it?"

Pastor rubbed his thinning hair and sighed. "To be honest, guys, sometimes I still wish He'd have let me be the all-star ballplayer I had wanted to be. But then I have to step back and take stock. If I had been, would I have ended up in a crisis of faith that eventually led me to deeper study, and that led me to seminary and then ministry? Would a path of football glory taken me here, to you?" He shook his head. "I don't know, but I can say that it wasn't in my game plan for God. See, He had something for me to do that I didn't understand. I couldn't have even imagined it. But standing here now, having been with you all for over twenty years, I can tell you honestly, I wouldn't change what I'm doing, the life I have now, and most importantly, the walk I enjoy with God.

"So what does that mean for you? I don't know—I'm not here to tell you to stop chasing your dreams and ambitions. I don't know if they are God's dreams for you or not—that's not for me to say. The only way you're going to know is to listen to Him. To do what He says here. Trust Him. Do good as you go. Delight in Him—just in being in His presence. Let it fill you with joy. Commit to following Him—whether He takes you to your dreams or a different way entirely. And trust Him to complete the good work He has started in you. To make you worthy of His kingdom, useful to His plans.

"A trophy of His grace.

"Trust in the Lord and do good. Seven words to live by. Sometimes they're easy. Sometimes they're really hard. Either way—good times or hard times—let us determine to say with the writer of

Psalm 119, 'You are good, and what you do is good; teach me your decrees.'"

Hunter's mind had moved fully to the sermon, and as Pastor closed, he flipped the Bible that John had sent as a gift to the front and pulled a pen from the slot in the pew in front of him. On the first blank page, next to the one where John had written *For my son in faith. May God bless you and keep you. May He make his face shine upon you and give you peace*, Hunter wrote *Psalm 37* and then *Psalm 119*, then *Teach me to trust You.*

The closing prayer had been spoken by the time Hunter was done writing. He closed his Bible, stood when the rest of the people did so, and slipped out the back door. As he moved, his passing glance grazed over Janie. His chest squeezed with pain, but even as his heart clenched, Hunter lifted those words he'd penned up to God.

Teach me to trust You.

Even if that meant letting her go?

Yes. Even then.

Janie took down the trio of large mixing bowls from her open shelf and lined them up next to her deep sink, where steaming water splashed from the faucet. Technically the bowls didn't need cleaned—the stainless steel gleamed with spotless cleanliness already. But she needed something to do with her hands while she waited for Hunter to arrive for their scheduled meeting.

It should be quick, this little get-together she'd arranged, because she had a plan all written out and ready to go, and that was thanks to back-to-back nights of little rest. First, the night Gemma stayed with her, and Janie couldn't sleep until she'd heard that Bennett, Hazel, and Nathan were safely back in Luna. Then last night. Every time Janie had willed herself to sleep, a new round of nagging questions had taken another lap through her mind.

NINETEEN

What had Hunter thought of church service? What had made him decide to go yesterday? Had he noticed that Grady had landed himself next to her—and did he assume that she'd asked him to?

After the fifth series of those disquieting queries had made it clear that she would not sleep last night, she'd taken up her legal notepad and recorded her ideas and set her mind on the planning for Hunter's groundbreaking.

Sloppy joes. Hunter loved the homemade sauce Mama B had taught her how to make. And he'd suggested Janie start making buns at the café . . .

It was a perfectly normal thing to want to make what would most please a client. Nothing questionable in her motives there at all.

Watermelon. She'd written that on Saturday night, then penciled a line through it last evening. *Hunter didn't love watermelon.* Plus, it was out of season. She'd replaced watermelon with fried apples. *Use brown sugar—he loves it that way.* Everyone who tasted her fried apples complimented the extra caramel-y flavor, which was a result of brown sugar. So it wasn't just Hunter.

Oven-fried potato wedges. Would he remember that she'd come up with her own seasoning combination? The secret was chipotle powder instead of paprika, a touch of brown sugar, and lightly spraying the wedges with apple cider vinegar before she baked them.

And caramel apple cheesecake bars. Hunter would love them. The thought had made her grin as she thought of how many times she'd tried different variations of the recipe until she hit perfection. He'd not had them yet, but she knew him well enough to be certain the shortbread crust, thick layer of rich cheesecake balanced with tart cinnamon apples, brown-sugar streusel topping, and gooey sauce would make him groan with appreciation.

Not that that had been what she'd been aiming for when she'd worked out the dish several years back. In fact, every time she'd imagine his reaction, she had scowled, named his memory a curse, and reminded herself there was a whole town of people to feed that did not include Hunter Wallace.

But he would like it. No, he would love it, and this was his party.

Janie's hands were buried in suds and hot water, working over the second of her large mixing bowls, when the back door to her kitchen creaked open. She glanced over her shoulder, banishing the heat that ruefully threatened her cheeks—certainly from the steamy dishwater and not at the thought of having been caught thinking of him before he walked in the door.

"Morning, Janie." His voice had that rough, hasn't-been-warmed-up-yet morning quality.

A tickle rushed down her spine. "Morning." She winced at the squeak that hung on her greeting. Rather than let her eyes drink in the sight of this full-grown, bearded, and oh-so manly version of the boy she once knew, Janie zeroed in on the work in her hands.

Hunter hung up his jacket, rolled his sleeves, and filled the spot beside her. "Here."

Her chin jerked upward as his body pressed to her side. "What are you doing?"

"Washing was always my job." He took the bowl from her dripping hands. "You dry."

He didn't allow his gaze to linger on her the way she stared at him. In fact, it seemed he worked hard not to meet her gaze as he cleared his throat. "Better yet, I'll wash and dry, and you tell me what you think should happen at this party Gemma has me doing."

Was he... pushing her away? That wasn't fair. After all, he'd been the one to move into her space. Literally. If he'd wanted to keep his distance, there was a whole twenty-by-twenty-foot kitchen. He hadn't needed to sidle up *right* next to her at the sink.

Janie crossed her arms. Hunter stayed focused on the sink.

After an extended moment, she sighed, let her arms fall, and went to the desk beside her pantry to retrieve her notes. "I worked on a plan."

"Good."

"Do you have anything specific you want, before I—"

"Nope. Hit me with the plan, and I'll let you get on with the day. I know you're busy."

His rushed words, chilled tone . . . Janie felt a sting zap her heart, and she had to duck her head to hide her wince. Not that he'd have seen it, with his stiff back to her. She cleared her throat, willing kindness into her voice though she wanted to throw something sharp and scathing at him with her words.

Or cry.

"I thought we'd go with rustic casual but filling and delicious."

"Sounds foodie."

Translation—he didn't know what she meant and wanted only to know what dishes she planned to make.

"Sloppy joes."

He stopped drying the bowl, his shoulders pulling straight. "Your homemade sauce?"

"Of course."

He held still. Then nodded.

Janie watched, waiting for him to turn around. To give her some hint that he wasn't going to keep a glacier between them forever.

Hunter slowly set the dry bowl on the counter and reached for the last one waiting by the sink. He plunged it into the water, working the dishcloth in the depths of suds. He didn't even glance her direction.

"Is that it?"

"Of course not." Janie concentrated on her list, naming her selections in rapid-fire sequence.

When she was done, Hunter was drying the final bowl. He set it on the counter, wiped his hands, and finally turned to look at her. "Thank you."

She swallowed. "Is it . . . Do you approve?"

He nodded. For a moment, those brown eyes warmed as he held his gaze on her. But in the next heartbeat, he stiffened and moved for the door. "Thanks. Let me know what it's going to cost, and I'll get you a check."

"Hunter." Janie paced three strides toward him.

Jacket half-applied, he froze. Then he turned.

Janie shivered at the chilled distance he placed between them with that hesitant look. Even so, she eased forward another step, maintaining a straight posture and lifted chin. "It's time to let the past go, don't you think?"

Lips pressed into a thin line, Hunter scowled.

Janie pressed on anyway. "Can't we be friends? I mean, Hazel is my best friend, and Luna is a small town, and we can't avoid each other. This war between us is exhausting, don't you think?"

His silent study revealed none of his thoughts. Well, not *none*. He wasn't approving, that was for sure. But he wasn't stomping out, angry and intimidating.

"Friends?" His low voice held zero certainty. "You think that's possible?"

"I hope so, Hunt. We used to be best friends."

Best friends who'd fallen in love. Who had promised forever. There was no going back to that, and she didn't expect it. But something a little more comfortable—and little warmer—than this?

Hunter finished putting on his jacket. He visibly swallowed and scratched his hair behind his right ear. "Okay, Janie."

She stared at him, not sure what was worse—his flat voice or the fact that he'd just lied to her face. But he didn't linger long enough to work that out. Instead, he mumbled "Thanks for working with me on this" and took himself out the way he'd come in.

Once again Janie didn't know if she wanted to cry or stomp in frustration.

Twenty

"Hunter Wallace, right?" Pastor Dunham stood beside the table at the café's big window, nearer to Bennett than to Hunter.

The friends had met at the café early on Wednesday to load up on coffee and carbs before the moving truck containing all the Crofton kids' belongings arrived later that morning. Once the truck was unloaded, they'd take both Bennett's Bronco and Hunter's truck, journey to Bozeman, stay the night in Bennett's house there, and load his things the next morning.

It was bound to be a long, busy forty-eight hours ahead, and they would need some fortitude. Janie's breakfast pies and cinnamon rolls seemed like the way to go.

Pushing back the chair, Hunter stood and held out his hand toward Pastor. "Yes, sir."

Pastor Dunham's smile was broad and genuine. "It's good to see you again. And nice to see you in church the other day."

Warmth infused Hunter's cheeks, though it wasn't from embarrassment. Rather, a solidifying sense of being seen and wanted was a gentle balm against his otherwise still-bruised heart. "It was good to be there. I've been thinking about the sermon, even these days later. I need to hear that my mission is to trust God and do good."

Nodding Pastor said, "Don't we all? I hear you are out of the navy?"

Hunter looked toward the table, then glanced up at Bennett, who gave him an encouraging tip of his head. "I am. I'm back at Elk Canyon now and hoping to carve a living out of a hunting lodge at the smaller pond. We break ground next week."

Hunter's mind flitted to that event and then retraced to the Monday morning past, when he'd met Janie at their agreed upon time. She'd been kind, and she'd asked for friendship from him. Frustration stirred in Hunter's gut. Though he didn't want the war they'd engaged in either, Hunter wasn't sure he could do friendship with Janie, even if he'd told God that he wanted to trust no matter what.

"Seems like that would be a good fit for you." A curious glance toward Bennett reminded Hunter that he'd not introduced his friend.

Hunter snapped out of his mental track involving Janie and God and disappointment. He gestured toward his friend. "Pastor Dunham, this is Bennett Crofton—an old college friend of mine. He's dating Hazel and has recently moved to Luna."

Pastor stepped back, Bennett stood, and they shook hands, exchanging *nice to meet you*. Then Pastor patted Hunter's shoulder again. "I'm very glad to see you, Hunter. You'll be back at church again, I hope?"

"Yes, sir."

"Very good." The man ended the conversation with another firm pat.

Hunter sat in the wake of Pastor's departure, and he met Bennett's waiting stare.

"You went to church?" Bennett asked.

"I did."

"With Janie?"

In spite of her being there. With Grady. "No. On my own."

Bennett grinned. "I like that. And I liked your pastor. Was it a good service?"

"It was. Gave me something to think about rather than continually brooding about Janie going out with Grady." A hard ask, that. Hunter couldn't seem to keep his train of thought from steering straight back to her every five seconds.

"That would definitely be an improvement then. Trust in the Lord and do good?"

"Yes. From Psalm 37."

Bennett nodded. "You going again this Sunday?"

"Planned on it."

"Mind some company?"

Full appreciation locked into place, along with some measure of relief. Hunter smiled. "That would be good. And since we're talking about church and God, I'm going to be honest with you. I really need prayer. And help. Janie keeps offering friendship, and I can't do it. There's just too much history, and I can't get past it."

"Yikes." Bennett offered a sympathetic grimace.

"Yeah. It makes me feel wretched. I'm pretty sure this isn't how God wants me to live—who He wants me to be. But I feel like Nathan must have felt that night when he got lost. Just out there alone in the dark . . ."

Bennett sipped his grape juice and then leaned both elbows on the table. "I have a buddy up in Bozeman who is a solid Christian. Maybe he could help?"

Hunter lifted his brows. "How so?"

"Like a prayer group or something?"

"You mean we get together?"

"Right. José would be willing to make the trip, I'd bet, if we only did it a couple times a month. I could ask. Either way, you'll meet him tomorrow—he's helping with the move."

Hunter nodded, surprised that he felt keen on the idea of a group study. Never in his life had he voluntarily exposed his soul to other men. Well, with John on occasion, when it had seemed like there was no other option unless madness was Hunter's ticket.

"There's John Brighton too." Sometimes insanity had seemed like a relieving option. Maybe then the pain would subside. Thank God for John. Hunter had been worse, mentally and emotionally, than he'd truly understood. "He's the one who has been teaching me about the Christian life. Maybe he'd FaceTime in or something?"

Bennett lifted his mug, took a long pull of his coffee, and nodded. "I think we should make it happen." His attention veered toward the counter, where Janie was certainly serving patrons saddled up on the high stools. One of them being Grady. "Grady offered to help today. You gonna be okay with that?"

Hunter swallowed. Nodded. "Muscle is muscle." As to his own muscles, they already bunched with tension. He was going to be one big cramp by the time these two days were done.

"I'm sorry, Hunt. I didn't know how to turn down his help."

Hunter shrugged. "He seems like a decent guy."

"Yeah." Bennett nodded. "He does. That almost makes it worse, doesn't it?"

Again Hunter shrugged. He didn't want to talk about it anymore. "How's Nathan doing with Mama B?"

"I'm sure you can guess. She's a got a way, you know?"

"Oh yeah, I know." Mama B could love fierce, in a way that made a young man want to be a good man. Back when Hunter had been a teenager, he'd thought she was just a really good mom—and she was. But he saw now that she leaned hard into God's love, and it spilled out of her. That was her secret sauce. "Your mom comes in tomorrow?"

Bennett nodded. "Should get here about the same time we get back to town. I hope." He blew out a breath. "Not a moment too soon either. I sure wish she'd been here when Nathan got hurt. Not that she could have set the bone, but it would have been nice to have her there reassuring me. I've never been so scared—or felt so out of my depth." His hands on his mug, resting on the table, Bennett eyed Hunter. "But also grateful. Thank you for finding him."

"You don't have to thank me. I was relieved. And to be honest, I'm pretty sure God led me to him. I was thinking about the whole thing again just last night—it dawned on me that I didn't need my inhaler. I should have—I ran from the ledge to where you were waiting, and I had him on my back the whole time—but my lungs didn't shut down on me. It was like for those minutes, I'd been restored to full health or something. That seems crazy."

Bennett's eyes widened. "Wow. I didn't realize . . ." He shook his head. "Wow. Still more to thank God for."

"Yeah. Things I'm better off putting my thoughts and energy toward." Hunter glanced back at the bar counter.

Grady reached across the pine counter, covered Janie's hand, and stood to leave.

With a sharp inhale, Hunter returned his attention to Bennett. "Hazel won't be down for the next few days."

Bennett nodded. "We talked."

"I'm sorry. Maybe I should have taken this client."

"She says she's better at it." Bennett lifted a curious brow.

"She's being honest. I never was the hunter she is, and I never cared to be." He chuckled, shaking his head. "I got the wrong name, I guess. I preferred being in town to roaming the trails. That, and me having been gone the last seven years means she's a more qualified guide. But I am sorry it takes her out of the picture when your life is so chaotic."

Bennett leaned back against his chair. "It's not like I didn't know what she does for a living."

"But it bothers you?"

He shrugged. "Only that she's up there alone with a couple of burly men."

"It's never been a problem. I think you know firsthand Hazel can handle herself. And I do vet these guys."

Bennett's nod was followed by a disapproving lift of his brow. "I also know firsthand how beautiful she is when she's out there in the wilderness being her mountain-lioness self." He leaned his forearms on the table. "I'm pretty sure I'm not the only man to notice."

Ugh. Hunter never thought of his sister that way—all beautiful in the first light of a mountain morning, when the October mist swirled over the lake. When the snow-capped peaks seeped golden sparkles and shadows crept away from the warmth of new day. He hoped never to think of her that way again. But suddenly he saw this scenario from Bennett's point of view and wasn't so comfortable with it.

"Maybe I shouldn't have asked her to continue guiding once the lodge is open."

Bennett shook his head. "You need her. And she needs you. I don't mind the hunts. The thing is, I'd hoped we'd . . ." He ran a hand along the back of his neck and then let it drop to his lap. "It is what it is. And it'll be better when you have the lodge open."

Hunter knew exactly what Bennett had been going to say—that he'd hoped they'd be married. Hazel would truly be his—by willing promise—and known to all the world. And he'd feel free to live up at Elk Canyon, by her side. Able to protect, should she need it.

Would Hazel ever understand? Would she ever yield to the idea of marriage—embrace it, even, as a gift? Didn't seem likely to Hunter. But for her sake, and for the man sitting across from him right then, Hunter prayed for a miracle.

Another lake shore miracle? There was Bennett. And there was Hunter.

God was a big God—it wasn't too much to ask.

Twenty-One

Snuggled in her bed, feet still chilly from a full day out with her two clients, both looking to bag an elk, Hazel read the text that Janie had sent late Thursday afternoon. The one Hazel didn't receive until she'd called it a night. Her heart strummed with anxious energy that threatened to turn into unreasonable anger.

Janie: *Have you met Bennett's friends?*

Beneath the typed text was a snapshot that had certainly been taken surreptitiously. There was Bennett, standing next to a man with short black hair with his arm around a petite lady whose long, thick hair matched the color of the man's. And on the other side of Bennett, another woman. A young beauty who grinned up at Bennett as if he was her favorite person to look at ever.

Names scrolled through Hazel's mind. José, who was married to Rosalina. And his younger sister, Isa. Who had given Bennett horseback riding lessons.

Scowling hard at her phone, she picked out exactly who was who in that snapshot. The blood in her veins raced with scalding heat.

She typed one word in response to Janie's question. *No.*

But come morning, that was going to change.

Janie tasted acrid guilt as she prepared the industrial-sized coffeemaker for morning. She shouldn't have sent Hazel that text. She'd known it even before she'd secretly taken that shot of Bennett standing with the Romeros.

Why had she done it?

Bracing herself with both palms against the counter, Janie shut her eyes and forced herself to examine the scrambled mess in her heart and mind. José and Rosalina were both wonderful, lovely people. If it had been only them to come down and help Bennett and Hunter yesterday, all would have been fine. She and Grady would have gone over, the group of them would have unloaded the vehicles, and Janie would have offered the large pot of turkey noodle soup she'd prepared without a hint of reservation.

But it hadn't been only José and Rosalina. There had been Isa.

Isa, who looked like Salma Hayek. Isa, who'd laughed at everything Hunter or Bennett had said, whether it was funny or not. Isa, who apparently had a PhD in flirting. Particularly with Hunter. But also with Bennett. Even sometimes with Grady.

Janie's stomach roiled.

Why had she sent a text she knew would upset Hazel? Because she'd wanted an ally. Someone who would, like herself, immediately dislike this beautiful young woman, even though she was friendly and funny and helpful.

Just standing there, picturing the girl's sugary smile and unending energy, made Janie want to howl.

The back door to the kitchen squeaked, and Janie jolted straight. Pushing off the counter, she strode into the dining room and stopped short at the sight of brown eyes shaded by the bill of a US NAVY hat.

"Hunter." Her whole body stiffened. "What are you doing here this early?"

He drew back, his eyes flickering with insult. "I thought maybe you could use a hand this morning. Since I stayed at Mama B's, and I was awake . . . and you said you wanted us to be friends . . ." He shook his head, then turned back toward the door.

"Wait."

He glanced over his shoulder.

"Sorry," she said. "I haven't had my coffee yet." Yeah, that was why she was snippy.

One brow cocked. But he said nothing. Then he slowly shed his black coat and hung it on a peg beside the door. "Will Grady mind?"

"Mind what?"

"If I'm here helping you before the sun is up."

Janie shrugged.

"I'm not up for stirring trouble."

"We've only gone out a couple of times."

Hunter grunted. It sounded like disapproval. Then he moved to the sink and washed his hands. "Do you have something I can do that I won't ruin?"

"I'm going to put the rolls in the glass display, and then the pans need washed."

He nodded. They worked, no exchange between them. When the rolls were in their proper place for the morning, and the aroma of coffee filled the whole café, Janie filled two mugs and set one on the counter beside Hunter.

She sipped hers while she studied his profile. His jaw was tight, lips pressed firm, brow creased. Everything about him screamed tension. And yet he'd come. Why?

Janie cleared her throat. "Isa is . . . pretty." That was what she wanted to open the day talking about?

Hunter stabbed her with an irritated glance. "Sure."

"You didn't notice?"

"I'm a man. Yes, I noticed the pretty girl."

"She seemed nice."

He dropped the pan he'd been washing, letting it clatter to the bottom of the sink. Then he shook the suds off his hands, snagged the towel near Janie's hip, and turned to her while he dried his hands. "What are you doing?"

Her pulse raged with something hot and intensely uncomfortable. She had no idea what she was doing. Words were just pouring from her mouth, unbidden, unthought, and most certainly unwelcome.

"I just . . ." What? What on earth was she *just* doing? "Thought maybe you liked her."

"Would that be convenient for you?"

No, it absolutely would not be convenient for her. Though she didn't want to look at the selfishness that drove her sense of distinct *inconvenience*.

"You'd feel better about dating Grady if I found someone else?"

Huh. Maybe that was what this was. Janie ignored the *liar, liar, liar* buzzing in the back of her mind. She shrugged, working hard at mere friendly interest. "I thought I saw a spark."

Also not true. She'd seen Isa's full appreciation for Hunter's manly, military build, his good-looking face, and his heart-jolting smile. That wasn't a spark—it'd been a glowing blaze on the young woman's part.

Hunter's part? Had there been a spark?

Come to think of it, he hadn't seemed to mind Isa's touchy ways. Hadn't tried to carve distance so the girl couldn't graze her fingertips along his arm. He'd laughed at her stories.

Maybe there *had* been a spark.

Janie grasped at the friendship thing she'd determined to have with Hunter, which required she doused the fire of... whatever the burning thing was in her belly.

Hunter clenched his jaw, scratched the spot behind his right ear, and turned back to the sink full of suds.

"You're not going to answer?"

"No."

"Because you don't want to say?"

"Because this is a stupid conversation for you and me to have."

"Why?"

He glared at her. "We aren't that kind of friends. You want to date Grady, go ahead and date him. But don't try to make it okay by assuming every pretty girl who crosses my path somehow turns my head. They don't." He took a small step toward her. "They haven't." The gap between them narrowed to a mere breath. Brown eyes blazed with a strong concoction of anger and determination. "They won't."

Janie's heart thundered at his proclamation, at his electrifying nearness. The allusion of his words were both heady and frustrating. Hunter's heart had never wavered...

Who could believe that? Years had passed before he'd come back—and even that had been forced by a medical discharge. And in that space of time? The only thing she'd ever had from him had been resentful texts and disapproving glares when he'd actually been there in person.

Love? No, that wasn't love. That was a man scorned and eternally mad about it. And yet there she stood, swooning at the idea that he still held her in his heart.

Foolish.

She chose to ignore her flighty reaction and focus on his implied insult. "I don't need to make dating Grady okay." She steadied her breath, demanded her pulse settle back into something closer to normal. "It *is* okay." Her chin lifted, and she crossed her arms. "It's better than okay."

Who was she trying to convince?

"Great. That's terrific." He pulled back, wiped his hands on the towel, crumpled it into a ball, and then launched it at the wall. Without another word, he stalked to the door, ripped his coat off the peg, and stormed out into the semidarkness of the just-breaking day.

The door clapped shut. Loudly. Janie startled at the bang. Then she scowled at it, willing her heated anger to penetrate clean through the solid metal door and into Hunter's back.

Twenty-Two

The food was as he'd expected—delicious and exactly right for this event. The party had been exactly what Gemma had stated—precisely what his lodge needed to start with.

Using a bottle of cheap champagne, they'd christened the newly drilled footings as the Lake Shore Splendor. Then John and Victoria Brighton, who had generously made the trip all the way from Nevada specifically for this event, quietly gifted Hunter with a much nicer bottle of wine.

"Don't drink it alone," John had warned.

Hunter understood his concern, as John knew Hunter's family history. "I won't. I'll save it to open when you come next. Perhaps when the Splendor is open in the spring?"

John exchanged a look with his wife, who smiled in her lovely and approving way, and he nodded. "You can count on it."

It all should have made Hunter swell with pride and happiness. As it was, though, Hunter couldn't keep his focus on the excitement of a dream in the works or even on how kind it had been for all of these people to come up the mountain on a cold October evening, through the blanket of fresh snow, and to an outdoor celebration. His mind repeatedly veered instead to the dark-haired, blue-eyed beauty who had catered his party.

Janie hadn't let him down. At least, not with her catering. But there was the issue of her plus-one.

Hunter's attention clamped onto the stocky dark-haired man who had accompanied her. Grady was quietly accommodating. Attentive. Respectful. And Janie rewarded him with sweet smiles, lingering looks, and her hand tucked through his arm. Which all seemed over the top from where Hunter was standing.

Hadn't she said they'd only gone on a few dates? Hadn't she implied that it wasn't serious at this point?

Then what was with this show?

Hunter stood near the bonfire, brooding in the few moments that he'd been left to himself. As it had at least a hundred times already that evening, his gaze sought the woman who possessed his thoughts. Wasn't hard to find her, as her hearty laugh drew his attention as easily as it gripped his heart. There, near the southern footings, Janie stood with Grady, engaged in some story with Jeremy and Leslie Yates. By Grady's expression, whatever tale had been told had been mildly amusing but not laugh-out-loud funny, as Janie's reaction had been. She was putting on a show. For Grady or for Hunter?

Janie turned her head, and her eyes met Hunter's stare. She held still for a breath, then turned her face back toward Grady.

A clear message if he'd ever seen one.

"Did you want a moment alone, or have you been rudely abandoned?" A smooth feminine voice filled the space behind him.

Hunter turned toward the unfamiliar voice, then managed a tight grin at the petite young woman it belonged to. "Hi, Isa. You're enjoying the evening, I hope?"

"Of course." She eased to his side, her expression sweet. Such a pretty girl . . . and not a shy one at all. Up until Janie's comment about seeing a spark, Hunter had enjoyed the young woman's company.

Now he was as comfortable with it as he would be with a rattler in his boots.

"You look like you might be exhausted though." One small, gloved hand landed on his arm. "Bennett says Hazel gets worn out by people. Is that a family trait?"

Why had Bennett shared that about Hazel with this girl? Hunter doubted Hazel would appreciate being discussed. Especially with Isa, as Hazel had given the distinct impression of dislike for this girl when she'd come to help Bennett and the kids move into the Elliot house.

Bennett had better be cautious with this one.

"Hazel and I aren't a whole lot alike." Although in truth, yes, people could be wearing to him in certain circumstances. This one—where Janie hung on Grady's arm, rubbing it in Hunter's face—being a prime example.

The smile Isa allowed was nothing short of triumphant. "Ah. So you're not a hermit."

He bristled at the condescending tone referencing his sister. Even if Hazel was, for the most part, a hermit. She was also a woman with feelings, and his little sister. And Hunter wasn't in the mood to be accommodating anymore. As the moments passed, in fact, he felt his ire cock and was ready to fire.

"No."

"No offense." Isa sighed as she looked toward the fire ring. "I'm sorry. I didn't think about how that would sound." Wide brown eyes lifted to his with sincere remorse. "Sometimes I say dumb things."

Ah. A sweet girl who wasn't easily offended or ready to spar with him at the first opportunity.

"Don't we all." Hunter let his shoulders loosen. Man, had he been this tense all night? By the ache in his back, he'd have thought he'd done two hundred pushups that day.

Tipping her head, Isa's expression turned warmly appreciative. "How about I get you a cup of apple cider? Then I'll come back, and maybe we can start over?"

"That's sounds like a good deal."

With a pat on his arm, Isa nodded and moved out of the ring of firelight and toward the long tables that had been placed where the great room of the lodge would take shape. Hunter followed her with his gaze—she was easy to track with that red wool hat. His vision collided with Janie and Grady yet again.

Janie watched him, her smile having vanished. When Hunter's eyes met hers, she raised a brow. Then she pivoted her attention back to Grady, said something to which he nodded, and arm in arm they made their way to the bonfire.

Awesome.

Janie and Grady stopped a few strides from him, and Isa arrived with two cups of cider a few beats later. Hunter accepted her offer with a grin that felt as plastic as a GI Joe.

"It's a good party." Grady broke the tension. "Thank you for including me."

Hunter hadn't included him. Janie had. Even so, he nodded, then lifted his cider for a long sip.

Isa slipped closer. "When will you open?"

"Hopefully, in May, if all goes well." Hunter shoved his free hand into his pocket. "That way we can catch the end of turkey season and have a soft start before the fall season hits."

"Are there many turkey this way?" Grady sounded skeptical.

"No. Not a ton. But we have a lowland draw that's fairly shrubby. Hazel says there's a consistent flock in there, and she's been careful to let the numbers grow over the last few years."

Grady nodded. "Smart of her."

"Bennett says there's no one who knows these hills better than Hazel," Isa said.

Appreciation mixed with more concern as Hunter glanced down at the woman nearest him. Isa met his look, hers completely guileless. Was that an act, or was this girl truly unaware of her flirtatious tendencies? Hunter preferred to think of her as sweet and innocent.

"That's the truth," he said. "There's no one like Zel when it comes to Elk Canyon."

"You're lucky to have her, then." Isa dipped a firm nod. "And I hear she likes horses too."

"She does."

"Will you include trail rides in your stay packages?"

Hunter rubbed his bearded chin. "I haven't thought that far. I doubt Hazel would be up for guiding those."

"You're not good with the horses?"

"Not awesome, no."

Isa made a disapproving face. "What is with these men who don't like horses?"

Hunter chuckled. "I take it *you* like horses."

Isa grinned, sipping her cider.

"Are you any good with them?"

"I've been giving Bennett riding lessons."

She was? How did Hazel feel about that? Hunter brushed away the nagging concern. He had enough of his own trouble to sort through. And right now, Isa offered a nice respite from it. "Maybe I should have you come here as a wrangler then."

"Little soon to start expanding, don't you think?" Janie's sharp disapproval drew Hunter away from those sweet brown eyes smiling up at him.

Repocketing his hand, Hunter shrugged. "It's good to think ahead. Plan ahead."

"Since when did you do that?"

"Since always." Hunter scowled.

"Seems a little risky, to make expansion plans when you haven't even started with the basics."

Hunter shifted his stance, as if he had to physically brace himself against Janie's attack. "I'd rather make plans and move forward than to stay stuck and afraid."

Janie glared at him. "Is that a rebuke?"

"No." He drained the rest of his cider. "Just a fact."

Grady cleared his throat. "I've got an adventure coming up myself."

He did? Did anyone there care?

Janie plastered on her fake-sweet grin and looked up at her date. "What's that?"

"A monthlong trek at some of the southern national parks in Utah. Arches. Bryce Canyon. Zion. A group of my college friends and I are going to backpack them until Thanksgiving."

Janie stared at him. "You haven't said anything..."

Grady rubbed the back of his neck. "I was going to talk to you about it the next time we went out."

"Oh." She turned toward the fire, and several long moments drew out in tense silence.

So. They weren't serious, else Grady would have mentioned this trek before this moment. And Janie wouldn't be standing there looking more put out than truly hurt by his failure to disclose his plans.

As the moment scraped by, and contrary to his frustration with the woman, Hunter felt bad for Janie's flustered silence. "Don't park rangers have to stay at their assigned posts?"

Grady shrugged. "A week of this adventure is actually a paid assignment. One of the rangers in Bryce is taking time off, and I'm going to fill in for him. The rest, I've saved up PTO, and the fall season is a little slower. Once I start my study on the spotted skunks, I'll have to stay put. It all just came together, and there are four of us who have always wanted to take this sort of trip, so we're going for it."

Janie recovered, straightening her posture. "It sounds amazing. Like an adventure of a lifetime."

"Yeah?" Grady's tone lightened with something hopeful.

"For sure."

"I was... well, I wanted to talk to you about it later, but..."

Hunter's heart froze. He knew exactly where this was going, and he suddenly wanted to be sick. And to smash something. "Come on, Janie. An adventure of a lifetime?"

Grady stopped his stammering, and both he and Janie looked at him.

"Yes." Janie crossed her arms. "That's exactly what it sounds like."

"This from a girl who has *never* left Luna."

A shocked Grady looked at Janie. "Never?"

"Not yet," Janie said.

"Not because she lacked the opportunity."

Lips pressed tight, she shook her head. "Maybe just not the *right* opportunity."

Hunter's mind nearly exploded. The right opportunity? How could leaving to go with the man you said you loved *not* be the right opportunity?

"You wouldn't," Hunter seethed.

She merely arched a brow.

He shook his head. "You wouldn't last the month. You wouldn't last five days."

"No?" She stepped closer. "You've never believed in me, so I don't know why your doubt surprises me. But know this, Hunter Wallace—you've underestimated me for too long."

"Does that mean you want to come?" Grady's timid voice sounded hopeful and fearful at the same time.

Janie whipped around. "Am I invited?"

"Yes." Grady cleared his voice, then looked around Janie and right at Hunter. "I mean, it would be totally on the up and up. Nothing sketchy. There's another woman in our group—and it'd be the five of us, and we would all have solo tents. Nothing... I mean..." He swallowed. "It'd be..."

"Hunter doesn't need to know all the details. I'm not beholden to him."

Of course she wasn't. She'd only promised to marry him, was all.

"Bet." Hunter spat the word out like he'd just bit into a bitter wild rose hip.

"What?"

"You won't last the month. You won't last half of it." He crossed his arms and stepped toward her. "I'll bet on that."

Janie fixed a hard look on him and then drew her brows together. For a moment he thought she'd back down, but then her stare flickered toward the woman at Hunter's side. Fire and fury blazed from her eyes when she set them back on him. "Fine. What shall we wager?"

"The café." He went for the last thing she'd risk.

"What?"

An anchor tethered his wild, out-of-control storm. She wouldn't. Not her café. Not the thing she'd put her heart and soul into for the past several years.

Janie wouldn't risk that for some stupid bet she knew she wouldn't win.

"The café. That's the wager. You lose, you leave the café and come and work for the lodge instead."

"Have you lost your mind?"

"No." Hunter leaned nearer, lowering his voice. "I know you, Janie Truitt."

Her glare went as hard and cold as the Black Gulch. "You arrogant—" She seamed her lips before the rest of that not-so-nice phrase escaped. Then she stepped back, slipped her left hand into Grady's, and held her right hand out toward Hunter. "Fine. The café."

The world stopped turning. An icy pain sank through Hunter's chest. She wouldn't . . . she couldn't actually mean . . . "F-fine?"

"When I win, and I will win, you'll owe me."

Hunter blinked. She was doing this? She . . . she couldn't. She just couldn't.

"What will he owe you?" Isa asked from behind Hunter.

"I've been looking into a full marketing package—one I can't afford."

"You think I can?"

TWENTY-TWO

She shrugged. "That's the wager. My café or your marketing budget. Either way, one of us loses our business. Sounds fair, right?"

"Sounds awful," Isa muttered. "Maybe you two should work this out some other way."

Hunter's core trembled. But as he stared at Janie, the full force of his anger kept him from backing down.

This woman made him crazy. And he always ended up doing something he'd come to regret.

Even so he stuck his hand out to meet hers. They shook. The deal was done.

And even as he sealed the bet, he knew the truth. He'd just lost what had mattered most.

Twenty-Three

Bennett found Hazel's cabin empty, which was a disappointment but not really a surprise. She had a client for the next two days. More than likely they'd been up at sunrise and on the trail not long after.

But as was expected, her front door was not locked. With a gentle push, he opened it and stood back. "Head on in, Nathan. I doubt the hike over the ridge will be very fun for you."

Nathan hobbled past him and into the cabin. But then he pivoted to face Bennett. "What am I going to do here by myself?"

A good question. Hopefully, not mess up Hazel's home. Bennett didn't truly think Nathan would do that, but he'd brought him up the hill with him to keep him out of trouble at home. Especially since Bennett's mom was there, and that seemed to irk Nathan, making him even more unpleasant.

Bennett adjusted his stocking cap. "I don't know, Nathan. You're kind of putting me in a hard spot here. I can't trust you on your own—you wander off. I can't leave you with my mom because you're determined to make her miserable even though she's done absolutely nothing to you. But you seem to like Hazel, so I guess I'm hoping I can trust you not to mess up her cabin."

"Hazel doesn't treat me like an unwanted kid."

Sharp pain drove through Bennett's chest. Did he treat Nathan like an unwanted kid? He didn't think so. He got frustrated with him for acting like a punk, but that wasn't the same thing. For several moments Bennett examined the past few weeks with his younger siblings. He was out of his element, admittedly. But *unwanted*?

He honestly didn't feel that way about them. Truthfully, Bennett didn't see his actions communicating that.

Their father, however . . . Yeah. This could easily be a projection of how their dad treated Nathan. And Bennett got that. Deep in his soul, he understood.

Sighing, he shoved his hands into his pockets and leveled his gaze back on Nathan. "What do you want to do?"

"I could try, you know."

An unexpected response. It dawned on Bennett that maybe there was something up here in this wild, nearly untouched place that called to Nathan. Perhaps that was why Hazel seemed to have some undefined connection with the boy.

And there was Hazel's statement after Nathan's accident. The thing about a boy needing to prove something to himself.

Bennett nodded. "If you want to. Let's do it."

Nathan's expression remained stoic, but he crutched his way back to the door, past Bennett, and out the cabin.

The short hike between the upper lake and the pond took longer than the typical eight minutes, but Nathan managed just fine—and without complaint. Did he hold his head a little higher? He certainly hadn't speared Bennett with a glare of resentment every ten seconds. That seemed a marked improvement.

Hazel had been onto something.

As they descended the slight hill that led into the meadow where Hunter's lodge was taking shape, the sound of metal whacking wood cracked with rhythmic clarity. *Whack, whack, whack,* then a *shrrk*—the sound of wood tearing apart. Bennett followed the sound around Hunter's trailer and into a cove tucked among aspens. There, Hunter wielded a small axe as he set up another section of pine to split.

Whack, whack, whack . . . shrrk.

One round piece of wood cleaved into two wedges. Hunter nudged the half that hadn't tumbled to the ground off his splitting base.

"Time out," Bennett called, catching Hunter before he set up the next hunk of wood to be split.

Hunter turned halfway, his look unsmiling but not necessarily unwelcoming. Then he went back to the pile of unsplit logs, picked up another candidate, and set it up on the base.

Bennett wasn't sure if Hunter was ignoring him or just preparing for when this visit ended. Either way he continued toward his friend. Hunter pivoted again to face his guests, rolled his head toward one shoulder, then the other, and adjusted his hold on the handle of the sharp hatchet. "I wondered if I'd see you today."

"That would explain your lack of surprise."

Gesturing with axe in hand toward Nathan, Hunter attempted a grin. "Surprised to see this guy. Made the hike hobbled?"

"It wasn't so bad." Nathan seemed to stand straighter.

"Good man." Hunter strode toward them, stopping a couple of feet short of their spot. "Know how to start a fire?"

Nathan visibly swallowed. "Hazel showed me the other day."

"How about you go work that skill a minute." Hunter nodded toward the trailer. "Keep it small and in the fire ring."

Nathan nodded, then moved toward the trailer.

Bennett appreciated Hunter's efforts, even if it seemed precarious. "Hopefully, he doesn't set the forest on fire."

"Fresh snow on the ground should make that a hard task." Hunter switched the hatchet from one hand to the other. "I assume you're here to talk about the other night."

"Intuitive."

Hunter rubbed the back of his head. "Janie... she makes me crazy sometimes. One minute she says she wants to be friends, and the next minute she's hanging all over Grady, rubbing my face in it. I just... lost it."

None of that came as a surprise. Bennett had even felt a slight edge of disapproval toward Janie the night of the party. She *had* been a little showy with Grady. Maybe it had been the natural progression of their budding relationship—Bennett couldn't say. But he could see where Hunter was coming from.

Even so...

"If winning her back was your plan, you took a wrong turn." Bennett reached across the space between the two of them and gripped the handle of Hunter's hatchet. Just to be safe. "This isn't going to get it done."

Releasing the handle easily enough, Hunter's shoulders collapsed into rounded defeat. "I know."

"What are you going to do?"

"I've been up here arguing with myself about it."

"And?" Bennett set the hatchet on a downed pine that hadn't been cut into sections yet.

A puff of white escaped his mouth as he sighed deeply. "I'm going to have to reach for some humility and go talk to her. Call it off."

Bennett nodded. Tough call but the right one. "Think she'll change her mind?"

Hunter shrugged. "I don't know. She's as stubborn as Hazel." He smirked with a side-eyed glance. "But she also doesn't like to leave home. I meant it when I said I didn't think she'd make five days. I shouldn't have said it, but it is the truth. Janie never wanted to leave Luna. Not for a week, a month . . . definitely not for a lifetime."

Ah. The past was becoming clear. "Is that why you broke up?"

Face toward the ground, Hunter nodded. "I couldn't stay and she couldn't leave, and neither one of us were willing to budge." He moved to grab the puffer vest he'd shed sometime during his wood splitting. After zipping it into place, he folded his arms. "I guess that makes us both stupidly stubborn."

"Admitting it is the first step."

Hunter rubbed the wool on his face. "Janie is pretty mad."

There was that. "Pretty sure she thought you were flirting with Isa, so that might have had something to do with the whole thing."

Hunter shook his head. "Isa was just there. She's a nice girl—maybe too nice. But I don't think she means anything. Think I should tell Janie that?"

Bennett snorted. "I think unless Janie brings it up, you'd best leave Isa out of it."

A long stretch of thoughtful silence extended. Bennett moved to check on Nathan's fire-building progress. A slim orange flame danced in the middle of a wood teepee, constructed exactly how Hazel had showed Nathan.

A well of pride deepened, and appreciation ran into it. "Nathan has a fire started." Bennett took a step toward Hunter's camp, but Hunter grabbed his arm.

"I'm not too proud to beg, if it would do any good."

Man, Hunter was in deep. Every bit as much as Bennett was with Hazel. Sure seemed like one of them should come out with a whole heart and a happy ending.

"If I can keep my temper in check."

Yeah, there was that too. They were but men, after all. And the women they loved seemed to have a special knack for pulling the crazy from them.

Bennett clapped Hunter's shoulder. "I'll pray for you, then."

His hand was met by muscles so tightly bunched that Bennett feared they might tear at his touch. As they came near enough to the campfire where Nathan waited, Hunter shook his head. "Maybe you should pray for Janie."

Bennett eyed Hunter, the shift in his friend's tone marked. No longer was he the desperate man willing to grovel. Now irritation stamped every word.

Oh boy. Just thinking about Janie had obviously summoned the crazy in Hunter.

Nathan watched Hunter as he picked up a rock and tossed it into the lake. "Maybe this trip is exactly what she needs."

His implication was clear: Janie would come home, head bowed in humiliation.

"You don't mean that, Hunt." It would tear Hunter's heart up even more to see Janie defeated. Of that, Bennett felt certain.

Hunter tipped his head back and growled. Then he looked at Nathan. "Don't ever fall in love. You'll never think straight again."

Nathan laughed.

Bennett shook his head and chuckled. "At least you can finally admit it."

Janie flipped through her legal pad of notes. Her eyes felt gritty, and her head pounded with exhaustion, but even so, she nodded at the plan.

It would work. She hoped. Now, if only Ms. Crofton would agree . . .

After several minutes during which she splashed her splotched face with cool water, applied some makeup hoping that it would disguise the blue under her eyes, Janie descended the stairs from her living quarters, entered the café's kitchen, and left through the back door.

The walk across town was brisk, and the evening stirred with a hint of snow as the sky rested in silence. Starlight and moonlight would be snuffed out by the thick blanket of clouds that had smothered the sky since late afternoon. Her visit should be brief, or her walk back home would be through inky blackness.

She rehearsed the lines she'd settled on while she'd pieced together her plan. Now if she could deliver them with convincing optimism . . .

As tired and emotionally strung out as she was, that felt like a herculean task. But Janie drew on the late dose of caffeine and the lingering swell of fury that had propelled her through the night before as she approached the old Elliot house, lifted her hand, and knocked on the door.

Gemma answered, her hair gathered up in a messy bun on the top of her head and her copper eyes bright. "Hi, Janie!"

"Good evening, Gemma. How was school?"

"I joined the cheer squad today. So that's happy." Her smile held the power of the Energizer Bunny. Even so, its brightness was false.

"I'm glad."

Her shoulders drooped. Just a touch. "It's small. And the school won't allow tumbling or pyramids—something about insurance."

"Oh." Janie reached for her shoulder. "I'm sorry."

Gemma shook off her threatening gloom. "Want to come in?"

Janie nodded and followed the girl into the house. Rather than being assaulted by obnoxious colors and ugly carpet, she stepped into a comfortable, welcoming home. Newly finished pinewood floors gleamed. The walls had been painted a subdued gray, and the upper portion above the chair-rail panels had been papered with a subtle willow-leaf pattern. It felt calm and inviting.

"You all have done good work," Janie said.

Gemma smiled. This time the expression seemed genuine. "It feels better in here, doesn't it?"

"Bennett has a talent for this, it seems."

"He says it's only because he's worked with designers so much over the years, and he has access to what's trending now." Gemma shrugged. "Don't go into Nathan's room though." She shook herself, as if horrified. "It's still the same as it was when we first came to look at the house."

Janie chuckled. "Got it. I was wondering if Bennett's mom was here? My mom said she thought she'd come to help make supper?"

"Oh! Yep. She's in the kitchen." Janie pointed to the wide arched opening that led into the dining room. The kitchen was separated from the rest of the house by a doorway off the left side of the dining room. Janie nodded. "It's good to see you, Gemma. Thanks for your help with Hunter's party—I think it went really well."

Her stomach burned as she referenced that event. She'd have preferred to leave it out of her thoughts—but that would negate the whole reason she'd come to talk to Ms. Crofton. And it would be rude not to thank Gemma—the girl had been a tremendous help.

Gemma grinned wide. "It was fun. I hope I can help you again sometime."

"I'll count on you for that." With that, Janie made her way toward the back of the house. Once at the kitchen door, she knocked and poked her head in.

Ms. Crofton stood at the gas stove, stirring a pot. With a slight startle, she turned and then welcomed Janie with a grin. "Hi there, Janie. I was lost in my head and didn't hear you come in."

"That happens." Janie hugged her notebook as she stepped toward the counter. The kitchen was laid out galley-style, and there wasn't much of a walkway down the stretch of workspace. She found a spot in the far corner and tucked herself out of the way.

"What brings you to us tonight?"

Janie cleared her throat and reached for her prescribed speech. "I've come to beg help from you."

"Me?" Ms. Crofton's surprise was understandable. They weren't close, having only met the day Bennett moved into the Elliot house. Even so, Ms. Crofton had been staying with Janie's mom this last week and a half while she looked for something suitable for herself. There was a connection there, even if it was new.

"Yes. Well, you see I'm going on a trip, and I'll be gone for several weeks." Her heart raced as she plowed into her speech. "I don't want to close the café for that long, and though I know you'd like to establish a clinic of sorts here, I thought perhaps, while you're still finding your feet in Luna, that maybe you would help me out."

Ms. Crofton blinked. "With the café?"

"Right."

"You want me to run your café while you're backpacking?"

Oh. So even Ms. Crofton knew about that. Janie should have guessed that she would, as Bennett had been a witness to that whole humiliating scene, and Ms. Crofton had been somewhere at the party as well.

So much for hoping this would be a quiet wager. At this rate, the whole town was likely betting on it. Likely, against her.

A billow of indignation puffed up, causing Janie to stiffen her shoulders. "Only in the mornings, and I will make all of the rolls and casseroles ahead of time and freeze them. I have detailed notes . . ." She held out her notebook "And it might be a good way for you to get to know people in Luna. Everyone comes to the café. When it's time to open your clinic, you'll have already made connections."

The back door thwapped shut, and Nathan crutched his way into the kitchen before Bennett ducked into the room behind him. "Oh. Hi, Janie. What brings you here?"

"She wants me to run her café while she's gone."

Nathan smirked. "This move is way more entertaining than I'd thought it would be."

Bennett's brows folded. "Homework, Nathan."

The boy on crutches shrugged. "I'm betting on you, Janie." He winked and then hobbled his way out of the kitchen.

You and no one else, kid. "Thanks, Nathan."

After a short groan, Bennett held a long look on his mom, then turned to Janie. "You're really going to do it?"

"Why shouldn't I?"

Pressing his lips closed, he looked toward his feet and rubbed one arm. "Maybe you and Hunter should—"

"Don't," Janie snapped.

Bennett's head jerked up.

Janie fastened a hand on her hip. "Don't take his side."

"I'm not. It was a stupid thing for him to do, and I don't think that he meant—"

"It doesn't matter what he meant or didn't mean. I'm going." Her heart throbbed in her chest, and Janie huffed. "Never mind. I should have known better than to ask."

"Don't say that," Ms. Crofton said. "I only hesitate because I have no experience running a business like yours. But if you have instructions and you need help, I'm here and available."

A rush of emotion nearly brought a surge of tears. Finally. Someone who wasn't going to tell her how dumb this whole thing was. More than she'd found from anyone else—including her own mother.

"Janie, this is ridiculous. You can't bet your whole livelihood on you doing something you know you won't enjoy because you're too mad at a man to have a real conversation with him!"

"He made the bet, Mother."

"And you took it. What were you thinking?"

She'd been furious, that was what. There Hunter had been, all handsome mountain man standing beside the fire, sidled next to that pretty little friend of Bennett's, looking condescendingly down at Janie. There wasn't a whole lot of thinking—only reacting. And now it was done, and she wasn't going to give Hunter the satisfaction of victory—especially when it would only confirm what he'd thought of her. That she was a coward and she wasn't capable.

Even as steam billowed through her veins, Janie focused on the hope Ms. Crofton had tossed her way. "You'll do it?"

Ms. Crofton glanced at Bennett, who stared at her with stern disapproval. Then, with a small lift of her chin, she turned back to Janie. "Yes. I'm happy to help. Maybe I can get Gemma to help me after school and on the weekends. It might be good experience for her."

Bennett jammed a hand through his hair, shook his head, and walked through the kitchen. "You two need to be locked together in a single room cabin during a weeklong blizzard."

That was a weird thing to say. Why would she need to be locked in a cabin with Bennett's mom?

Throwing both hands up, Bennett continued through the kitchen and turned toward the dining room. "Leave us out of the middle."

Us? Us who? What was he ranting about? Janie looked back at his mom, who watched her son with disapproval. When she looked at Janie, she shook her head. "Don't worry. He's gone up to try to talk sense into Hunter. By the looks of it, that was a failed venture."

Oh. Hunter . . .

Locked in a cabin with Hunter? As mad as she was with the man right then, he'd not last a day.

Twenty-Four

Hunter turned on his cot for the hundredth time, or so it seemed. Sleep refused to offer its relief, despite his physical exhaustion. Landing on his back, Hunter growled into the darkness. The muscles in his neck, shoulders, and back screamed in protest against his second full day of wood splitting. Obviously, it had not been enough though. He still couldn't sleep.

What else could he do? Squeezing his eyes shut, he willed himself to enter rest. Rather than drifting into numb, black relief, his mind replayed the whole encounter again. Janie hanging on Grady's arm.

Janie gazing up at Grady as if everything he said was amazing. Janie pinning Hunter with a loathing look.

Maybe just not the right opportunity.

She knew exactly how sharp that spike was and how deep she'd driven it. Even now, several days later, Hunter could barely breathe through the pain.

He sat up, his thick, rated-negative-twenty-degree sleeping bag slipping off his frame. The frigid night bit at his exposed skin as he braced his elbows against his legs and buried his face in his hands.

"Help," he groaned.

What was he supposed to do? Every time he thought he should go down and call off this whole stupid bet, reaching for that humility he'd told Bennett he needed to put on, his emotions tumbled straight through that willingness to beg and landed right back in anger. He didn't want to risk that response when he faced Janie again.

Hadn't God asked him to trust Him? Hunter was an outstanding failure.

Putting off talking to Janie wasn't doing him any good. Every day he resolved to apologize, and then he didn't do it, because it might spark yet another round of bickering. Every night he went to bed miserable and exhausted, only to toss and turn and agonize and replay the whole thing all over again.

Ugh! This needed to end. Now.

He tossed the covers aside, stood, and snapped on the overhead light. Jerking his clothes from the chair where he'd tossed them, he jammed his legs into the jeans, his arms into the sweatshirt, then smashed the stocking cap onto his head. Grabbing a stick of gum from a cabinet, which he slammed shut, he then snagged his coat as he stomped toward the narrow door and shoved his arms into it as he marched to his truck.

Snowflakes drifted silently around him, falling from the starless night sky. It wasn't heavy, but up here it could turn so quickly. Didn't matter—Hunter was going.

TWENTY-FOUR

The truck engine started on the second turn, and he didn't wait for it to warm up before he crammed the gear into drive. His mind was made up, and they would have this out now.

Luna held in quiet peace when he parked in the alley behind Janie's Café. He tested the back kitchen door and found it opened freely. He scowled—shouldn't a woman be more cautious about her business and her home? She had a dang key, for goodness' sake. Even if Luna was isolated and a town of merely six hundred souls, all of whom Janie knew, she should lock up. It was a sensible thing to do.

Hunter tucked that away to discuss later as he jogged up the back stairway that led to her loft. At the closed door to her apartment, he raised his fist and pounded.

Nothing.

Might have something to do with the fact that it was sometime after one in the morning. Even so, Hunter knocked again. "Janie!"

He tested the door and was relieved to find that at least she'd secured that.

Yet again he pounded and called her name.

And then the door jerked open. Blue eyes, fierce and sheened with sleep, met him from the other side.

"What are you doing?" she scowled.

"We need to talk."

"It's after midnight. Go home."

"No." He stepped inside her apartment.

"Are you drunk?"

"Not even a little." Though there had been that temptation.

Janie tugged on the blanket she'd wrapped around herself. Her hair hung free from its normal ponytail, a glorious dark mess that spilled over the edges of her shoulders and onto the cream softness of that blanket.

Man, she was beautiful. Hunter rolled his fingers into his palms. He stared down at this stunning creature who held the power to drive him mad.

No. No madness tonight, no matter what the hour was. He focused on what he'd intended to do two days ago. "I'm calling this off."

"What?"

"The bet. It's off." He edged closer. A waft of her deliciously feminine scent—a hint of apples and vanilla and something that was all Janie—teased his senses.

Those gorgeous blue eyes widened. Was there relief in them?

Hunter leaned nearer. The breath he drew was all her, and as his pulse charged, a delightful fog overcame the exhaustion of his mind. Janie alone had the capacity to put him a little tipsy, no alcohol required.

"Janie." Her name slipped from his lips in a rough whisper, and the longing that came with it had him reaching to finger the wild mess of her unbound hair. So soft. One touch was not enough. "You don't need to prove anything."

Her stare softened and warmed. And then she blinked. Blue ice replaced that tender look, and she wrapped his wrist in a firm grip to push his intruding hand back to his chest. "Who says I need to prove anything?"

"You did." Hunter fought to plug the drain of fuzzy warmth her chilled response pulled. He was so tired of feeling frustrated with this woman. Especially when she'd just muddled his senses like too much sweet strawberry wine.

Squeezing his eyes shut, he shook his head and willed clear thought back into his mind. "You said I've underestimated you for a long time." He shook his head. "For the record, I've never underestimated you."

Janie stepped forward, her body as stiff and straight as a fence post. "That is a lie, and you know it."

"How do you figure that?"

"You're mad that I made the café work. That's why you want me to lose it."

"Where do you get these insane ideas? Why on earth would I be mad that you've done well?" He stared down at her, feeling his careful hold on annoyance slip. "I'm proud of you, Janie."

She winced. The blanket slipped from her shoulder, and when she fumbled unsuccessfully trying to reposition it, Hunter reached to tuck the fold back around her.

Her glare hit him like a slap as she shrugged away his touch. "I don't need your help. And I don't need you to rescue me. I'm going on this trip, and nothing you say is going to change my mind."

"You hate traveling."

"We've both changed."

"Not that much."

"You're certainly not the man I thought I knew." She jutted her chin up. "You were the one to send Bennett here under false pretenses, intending to take away your own sister's home. The Hunter I thought I knew wouldn't have ever done that."

Gone was the warm buzz she'd summoned moments before. Cold anger seeped into his heart. "That was low, Janie. You know I had my reasons."

She flinched and then swallowed. "For all I know, you'll go around telling everyone I was the one to come to you in the middle of the night, groveling. Why should I trust anything you say?"

Hunter rolled his fists, barely holding back the rise of his temper. He leaned closer, caught in the fierce storm that swirled between them. Heart throbbing, he held frozen in place. "I wasn't the one who broke the promises."

She stood unmoving too, holding his stare with that blue gaze. Teasing his emotions. Owning his heart.

One step and the gap between them would vanish. One draw of his arm and he'd know the euphoria of the way she felt against him. One dip of his mouth and he'd drink in the intoxicating sweetness of her lips.

Lost in the force of all that sizzled between them, temptation was nearly the victor.

Suddenly she stepped back and looked down. It took every ounce of his military-learned discipline not to reach for her, dare her to look him in the eye and say she didn't feel what he'd just felt.

"Go home, Hunter."

"I don't have a home." He hadn't since the day she'd given him back his ring.

Pain creased her brow, as if she knew exactly what he'd thought and understood the meaning behind it. She shook her head, and with a gentle hand, she nudged him back toward the door. "What's done is done."

After he stumbled past the threshold, she eased the door closed.

Hunter shut his eyes as he slumped against the wall. The chill around him sank clean through. He resented its familiarity. This was life without her.

Not the life he wanted.

Hazel wandered the trail that connected her cabin with Hunter's place, her pack of dogs yipping as they wove in and out of the aspens. This path had become wider and well-worn in the months since Hunter's return.

The thought provoked a grin—and then the wonder that she would be happy about such a revelation stirred her heart. Bennett had spoken of God's miracles a few times. The miracle of his life changing directions. Of finding love where he'd least expected. And of Hunter's return. As much as Hazel had shied away from Bennett's God talk, she had to own that he had a point.

Those things did seem magical. Was that the same as a miracle? And if it was, what had suddenly stirred God to act at Elk Lake when for so long it had seemed He'd not cared?

An intruding *beep, beep, beep* . . . broke into her deep thoughts, rending the peaceful mountain forest with its mechanical blare. The three dogs who had made this trek with her all stopped, their muscled bodies tight and ready to defend against whatever that unnatural sound was.

"It's okay, guys." Hazel sighed. "It's just the workers for the lodge."

Hunter had said the groundwork should be done and the foundation poured within the week. That seemed fast for such a large project, but Hazel knew only relief at the speed. Large machinery did not belong at Elk Canyon, and the sooner they could do their jobs and be gone, the better.

Hazel motioned for the animals to continue on. "Stay close and be good."

Another few minutes and she rounded to the clearing that had been christened Lake Shore Splendor. Seemed a good name, though at the moment, the scraping of earth and the scattering of ugly orange and yellow equipment marred the scene.

Not forever.

Interesting, that the ugly mess before her nudged a bit of sentiment in her mind. She and Hunter, they'd been a mess. And things seemed to have hit an ugly rock bottom before they'd gotten better.

But they had gotten better. So much better.

Miracle?

God, are You real?

That seemed a rhetorical question. Hazel had spent her life soaking in the wonder of the world around her. She couldn't believe that all the beauty, the complexity, the majesty of nature had just randomly come together by accident. And more, this intense thing between her and Bennett—this deep love that stirred her soul? How did that just randomly evolve from heartless, emotionless organisms into the powerful driving force that it was in people?

In Hazel's estimation, it just couldn't happen. There just had to be a cause. That left her with a knowledge of God from a distance. But she'd assumed that would remain that way. Distant. Impersonal. And maybe . . . a bit resentful. Resentful because if God could stir the winds and hold the earth and design every living thing, couldn't

He make life less painful? If He endowed man with a soul that longed for love and wholeness, why did He remain aloof and far off?

Why didn't He care?

Maybe He did?

Hazel wasn't sure she was ready to go that far. Such thoughts were too deep, too big, and too scary to really ponder for long. So if Bennett talked of miracles, Hazel turned her attention to the dogs, or to fishing, or to anything else that she could feel and touch and understand. When Hunter brought up his new faith and talked of being saved, she would shrug and say that was nice for him.

She was content with the lake and life as it was.

But it wasn't true. Not entirely. There were these moments when she was alone. The depths stirred in her own heart, a deep discontentment that yawned in her soul, and there was nothing to distract herself with. Nothing to push away the longing for more. It was like her soul had been stirred, and now it was hungry . . .

Standing at the edge of the tree line, Hazel indulged in a rare moment of surrender, and the question tumbled from her mind, through her heart, and took flight toward the heavens.

God, do You care?

A presence settled at her feet, and the warmth nudged her palm. Scout. The faithful pup—who wasn't truly a pup anymore—had pushed her soft head beneath Hazel's hand. Though a mild disappointment wove through her heart—had she expected an answer from heaven?—Hazel grinned down at her companion.

"You're something, you know that, girl?"

The dog looked up, and her tongue lolled to one side as she panted through a doggy smile. *Here for you.*

Yep, Scout always was.

"Hazel." Hunter emerged from the other side of the moving equipment, a hard hat on his head and his right hand lifted in greeting.

Not interested in donning a hat like his, or meeting the men who crewed his excavation team, Hazel waited at the edge of the clearing.

When he closed the space enough not to have to shout, he spoke again. "What do you think?" Turning, he motioned to the work.

"It's a mess right now."

"Won't take too long. The forecast looks good, and Evan says this is his most efficient team."

Adjusting her stocking cap—the orange one Bennett had brought up over a year ago—she studied the emerging footprint and nodded. "You were right. It will fit well right there."

"You didn't believe me?"

"I thought it would be too big." She shrugged. "It's a whole lot bigger than the cabin."

Hunter nodded. "The clearing over here is triple what you have at the big lake. I imagine that years ago, the big lake was a much deeper bowl of water and this one was much wider." He pocketed his hands in his coat.

The machines clanged and beeped as they scraped the earth to bedrock and leveled the space where the lodge would take shape. Ice and Cream scurried between tractors, then jogged to the water's edge for a drink before bounding back to where Hazel and Hunter stood.

The stretch of stillness grew heavy. Perhaps that was just for Hazel—she'd had a lot on her mind when it came to Hunter for the past several days. Ever since his groundbreaking celebration.

"Hunter, I promised Janie that I wouldn't let you come between her and my friendship."

"Okay . . ." He angled his body to face her. "I don't want to come between you."

Hazel nodded. That wasn't exactly what made her nervous about this conversation she didn't really want to have but felt like she should. "The thing is, I don't want things between you and me to fall apart either. I mean, now that . . ."

"Now that we're no longer enemies?"

A small chuckle slipped from her mouth, and Hunter nudged her with his elbow.

"I'm a big boy. Sometimes I even act like it." His mouth twisted to one side. "Though I know I still do some really dumb things."

Speaking of . . . "That bet—"

"Was really dumb." He looked toward the construction, his brow furrowed. "I know."

"Can't you call it off? Janie really doesn't like going places. Almost as much as I don't. And her café—Hunter, she's worked hard to make it what it is now."

Hunter nodded. "I know that, Zel. I tried to call it off night before last. She says she's going and that's the end of it. And that she doesn't need me to rescue her. And that I underestimate her." He turned a tormented scowl toward Hazel. "Is that true? Do I underestimate Janie?"

Hazel shrugged. "I think Janie gets mixed up about some things sometimes. Every once in a while, she would say something like 'Hunter didn't think I could make this work.'"

"She did?"

"Yeah. Not very often. I didn't know why she would say that. I just figured she was mad at you for leaving, and maybe you guys had argued about her taking over the café from her aunt."

"Never. I don't remember talking much about it at all, to be honest. But maybe I wasn't listening. Maybe I was too busy planning a way out of Elk County. I don't know . . . but I never thought that she couldn't do it."

A deep rumble shook the ground as a large vehicle climbed the widened access road toward the construction site.

"That will be the concrete." Hunter glanced toward the direction of the road.

Hazel nodded. "I'll get out of your way. But—"

She wasn't sure what she wanted to say. She only knew that she understood Hunter's desperation and that with her whole heart, she hoped he wouldn't lose. And she didn't mean the bet.

Impulsively, she took a step and wrapped his arm with both of hers.

Hunter tucked her into his side and flexed. "Thanks, sis."

She pressed her head into his shoulder, then pulled away. Turning, she summoned her dogs, and they made their way back to the cabin. Once there Hazel saddled Mr. Big. It was time she and Janie had a talk.

"We leave in four days." Janie summoned what she hoped was a thrilled expression as she rolled out the last of the dough for the twelve dozen cinnamon rolls she'd been working on. Next she'd spread the butter, sprinkle on the filling, and then she'd roll it all into a spiral that she could cut and freeze. Three more days at this pace and she should have her freezer stocked and ready for Ms. Crofton to take over.

Her stomach burned. Likely at the thought of things going wrong while she was gone. Or at the thought of going, period. She worked to ignore the nervous sparks that shot painfully from her gut to her chest.

"Janie, that's about the most forced excitement I've ever seen. Well, maybe with the exception of Bennett, when he first came claiming he wanted to hunt."

Janie turned away. "No it's not."

"Look at me and tell me you really want to go backpacking with four strangers."

"Grady's not a stranger."

"He's not much more than one."

Dusting flour from her hands, Janie spun around and planted her palms against her aproned hips. "You hike with strangers all the time."

"I always have the advantage of knowing exactly where I am and how to get out of a sticky situation if I need to." Hazel leaned forward against the counter. "But that's not relevant. We're talking about you going off to do something you don't even like doing with people you don't know."

"I told you, Grady isn't a stranger." Janie wiped her fingers with a dishrag and tossed it into the sink. "I like him. He's a good man. A gentleman. And he's assured me this isn't . . . he doesn't expect . . ." Her face burned.

"Great. Good for him. What about his friends?"

"One of them is female."

Hazel shook her head. "Hunter says he begged you to forget this."

"Yeah. So he can win."

"He called off the bet."

"Right."

"Why are you doing this?" Hazel smacked the stainless-steel counter. "You hate traveling. You hate sleeping on the ground in a sleeping bag. You don't like to be cold. All reasons you've given for not staying at the cabin. Not to mention this." Hazel spread her arms wide, encompassing the café.

"Ms. Crofton and Gemma are stepping in to help. It's all arranged. It will be fine. Everything is going to be just fine. I'm going to have fun, and Grady is great. It's all perfect." She was babbling.

Hazel tipped her head, a knowing arch in her brow. Janie only babbled when she was flustered. "What does Mama B say?"

"I'm a grown woman." Resentment charged through her veins. Why did everyone have to be against her? Even Zel! How was that fair? "Maybe there's something to this leaving thing."

"What does that mean?"

Janie glared at her best friend. "It means that maybe it's time I make new friends. Time I find out how life looks outside of Luna. After all, Hunter did. My dad did. Who knows what I've been missing?" Her heart cracked even as she said the words, opening old wounds and oozing bitterness.

Hazel didn't flinch, though the mossy green of her eyes lost their fire. She shook her head. "You don't mean that."

Blinking, Janie looked away. "Maybe I do."

The kitchen settled into merely the humming of the refrigerator and the quiet drip of the leaky faucet into the sink. She needed to get that fixed before she left.

Dread gaped wide in her gut. Which was silly. *It's only a couple of weeks.*

What if it wasn't? What if it turned out to be more—what if she left and didn't come back?

Was that what she wanted? In the past few weeks—months even—it seemed like she'd lost her footing here. Everything had become too complicated. Too awkward. Maybe, after all these years of clinging to home, it was time to let go.

How ironic would that be—the moment Hunter came back, Janie decided to leave?

A long sigh whispered into the silence as Hazel took a step closer. "Promise you'll call me?"

Through a storm of anxiety and confusion, Janie lifted her head and looked back at her friend. "You want me to?"

"Every day, I hope."

Relief tumbled through Janie as she stepped forward and hugged Hazel. "You're still on my side?"

"I don't think there's a side in this, Janie. You and Hunter—" Hazel cut off whatever she was going to say as she stepped back, gripping Janie's arm. "You've always been my friend. I'm always going to be yours. No matter what."

Janie nodded. "No matter what."

At least she still had that. As Hazel left through the back kitchen door, Janie tried to inflate her enthusiasm with that consolation.

It fell flat.

Maybe everyone was right. This was foolish and silly. Did she really have something to prove?

The memory of Hunter standing across the bonfire, holding her with a contemptuous stare surfaced in her mind. The fire in her belly flared, and her spine stiffened. She didn't want to live like that anymore.

Hunter saw her as a coward.

She did, in fact, have something to prove.

Twenty-Five

Grady passed a steaming tin mug of coffee to her, concern etched in his folded brow. "You okay?"

With a forced grin, Janie nodded her head. "I'll be fine. We're here for the night, right?"

"Yes." He rubbed the back of his neck, then lowered onto the chilly ground beside her. "Tomorrow's hike is going to be intense."

Janie clenched her jaw. Three days and her body screamed for her to stop. Though the scenery had been extraordinary—red sculpted sandstone, vivid painted skies, deeply carved ravines, and crystal clear streams—all Janie could think in that moment was how much she wanted her warm, soft bed. A mug of her homemade apple cider. A hot shower.

She wanted to go home.

You wouldn't last five days.

Frustration knotted in her belly. Why was Hunter always there, clinging to the fringes of her mind, making her miserable?

Unbidden, a visceral memory of his fingers twined in hers, his nose feathering down her skin, and his lips brushing across hers surged into her exhausted homesickness. Squeezing her eyes shut, she rolled her fists as longing pressed hard into her chest.

How could she want that more than all the other comforts on her mental list? As if *he* was the call beckoning her heart. He was the cause of her homesickness.

She was mad at him!

You miss him.

This was his fault.

You didn't have any part of it?

He made her crazy.

True. And happy. And whole.

Where were these thoughts coming from?

"Janie?"

The gentle masculine voice at her side startled her, and Janie fluttered her eyes open. "Sorry. I was . . ." Missing home. Missing Hunter.

"Maybe this was a bad idea." Grady's shoulders slumped as he leaned his forearm on a his propped-up knee. "If you want to go back, I'll—"

Stubborn determination had her lifting her chin. "I'm just tired this evening. And sore. If I can stay at camp tomorrow, I think the next day will be fine."

Grady didn't answer.

"Were you planning to camp here again, or was there another plan?"

He cleared his throat. "Well . . ."

TWENTY-FIVE

"Oh." Janie lowered her gaze to her dusty hiking shoes.

"It's okay. I'll come back this way."

Tears stung her eyes, but she shook her head, trusting that the dusk provided her weakness with cover. "No. I can do it." She sipped the coffee Grady had given her. It was acrid and finished with a lingering burnt taste. As had the coffee every day since they'd started. And the food? MREs were not real food, no matter what mountain men and military people claimed.

Oy. She missed her kitchen. The smell of yeasty bread. The mouthwatering taste of apple pie. And a properly brewed cup of joe.

Janie swept away the image of all of that and pinned happiness on her exhausted face. "Maybe I'll just call it a night early."

Grady studied her. He was a nice man. He'd been patient with her as she'd lagged behind the group. Worked to include her when they sat around their evening campfires, exchanging stories of their backcountry jobs or shared memories of their school days. But as he rubbed her aching shoulders right then, that was all there was.

Grady was a nice man.

No thrill at his touch. No heart fluttering at his good-looking grin.

And it seemed, as they spent more time together, his evaluation of her had gone in the same direction.

Janie was a nice girl. Not an adventurer who could keep up with him. Not a woman who could spark passion in his eyes—either by way of irritation or of desire. Just . . . a nice girl.

They'd had a nice time. It was all . . . nice. And that was all.

His thumb pressed several circles into the tender muscles in her back, and then Grady stood. "You'll be okay?"

"Yep." Janie lifted her mug. "I'll finish this and crawl into my tent."

He nodded. "I'll be at the fire, if you need anything." He pointed toward the stone ring in which a carefully controlled flame danced orange in the darkening valley.

Janie lifted her mug by way of dismissal, and he wandered the twenty feet toward the rest of the group.

With the disappearance of the sun, the air turned chilly fast. Janie sat swimming in her misery until the mug in her hand grew cold. Dumping what remained of the nearly full cup, she gathered her shoes, crept to her solo tent, and crawled into the rated-thirty-below sleeping bag. She snuggled in and pulled out her phone.

Three bars.

More than she'd had since they'd started. With her thumb, she scrolled to Hazel's name in her contacts and hit Send.

Hazel picked up on the third ring. "I was getting worried."

"I haven't had service." A lump swelled in Janie's throat. So silly. It'd only been a couple of days. But she was so tired. So sore.

"You doing okay?"

Yes, everything is great. Grady is great. Her mind scripted that tall tale. "It's really pretty here" was what came out of her mouth. Which was true. And not something that shouldn't have made her voice crack or pricked tears out of the corners of her eyes.

"You don't sound okay."

Janie bit her lip. She hauled in a deep gulp of air and then let the truth come forth. "I'm not built for this."

For a long pause, Hazel didn't answer. There was only the sound of her shuffling something in the background.

Then, "I told you before you left. The bet is off. Just come home."

Janie froze. "I wasn't talking to you, Hunter." Anger exploded in her mind. How could Hazel do that to her? "Put your sister back on the phone."

"Janie, you sound miserable, and you don't have to do this."

"Yes I do."

"Why?" Patience became a vapor in his tone, replaced by a strong, familiar tone of frustration.

Why? She huffed. Because he would never respect her if she quit now. And she would always be mad at him for revealing her weakness.

Was she always going to be mad at him either way? And where had this starving need for his respect come from anyway?

You were the one to call it off.

That . . . that was true. *She'd* called it off.

If Hunter wasn't on the other end of the phone, she might have crumpled into a sobbing heap as that series of thoughts pierced through all her messy feelings about him.

She'd broken the promises.

She'd been the coward who wouldn't go with him.

How could he possibly respect her after that?

"Janie . . ." He whispered her name, wrapped it in tenderness. Delivered with a hint of longing. It seeped past the anger and resentment and shame, calling to her heart. *Come home.*

Even so, a hardness remained lodged in her chest. "I'm not a quitter."

"No, you're not."

"Then quit trying to make me one."

Hunter's silence met her harsh tone. Then, "I'm sorry I pushed you into this."

He was sorry?

He wasn't allowed to be repentant! He was supposed to be a bully so she could continue being mad at him, and that would fuel her to the end of this stupid bet!

Janie gripped that surge of anger, even as she knew it was irrational. "Well, I'm in it. And I'm finishing it." She pulled the phone from her ear and smashed End.

And as she let tears trickle down the side of her face, the sense of her own foolishness filled in where anger had left a void.

Pray, daughter . . .

Mama's prescription from weeks before crept into her self-induced misery. Maybe it was about time she took the medicine.

Hunter stared at the skeleton of his vision coming to life. Evan had told him they'd have the lodge completely dried in by the end of the week. It was happening so fast. He should be floating on the helium of success. And part of him was thrilled.

But there was the other part that acted as a lead weight to his euphoria. The part that plunged deeper into hopelessness for every day that Janie had been gone. Eleven, as of 9:22 that morning. If one kept strict accounts.

Usually, Hunter didn't. Only when it came to Janie. And then . . .

Then he'd kept track of everything, whether he wanted to or not.

The day he'd first dared to hold her hand—a whole fifteen days after he'd hauled her close and whispered that he'd needed her. They'd wandered together down the trail from the cabin one summer afternoon, and he'd slid his fingers along her palm, then woven them with hers. Hazel had been somewhere else—Hunter didn't remember where or why—but it'd been an exhilarating moment snagged with only Janie. His heart had floated on a rush of pure, intoxicating adrenaline.

From that moment to the first time he'd touched his lips to hers—thirty-eight tension-filled, longing-drenched days. For a sixteen-year-old kid, that had seemed like an agonizing length of time. From that first kiss to when he'd given her a ring and a promise to come back—just over two years.

And from the day she'd given him back that ring . . .

That last one, Hunter didn't like to keep count. Only that every day since had been tinged with anger, disappointment, and heartache.

Which brought him to the eleven days of torture since Janie had gone off on her adventure with Grady, the Game and Parks guy. Eleven days of Hunter living in the depressing fear of the pair of them falling in love. Eleven days of Hunter's imagination tormenting him with visions of moonlit kisses and promises whispered in the vast beauty of a red rock canyon and a vivid painted sky.

Those were supposed to be his kisses. Those promises had already been given—to him!

As defeat threatened to give way to another spasm of resentment, Hunter turned his mind toward God. *How do I deal with this?*

As soon as the query lifted from his heart to heaven, *Trust the Lord with all your heart; do not depend on your own understanding* scrolled through his mind.

He'd forgotten about that.

But would God make it all turn out the way he wanted?

Hunter pondered the journey in Job that the men's group had been taking. Because of a cosmic battle unknown to the man, Job's life became a whirlwind of disaster. And yet he found the strength to say, *Should we take the good from God's hand and not the bad?* And at the end of the story, after all the questioning, and arguing, and railing, and lamenting, God revealed Himself and restored the man.

Why did bad things happen? Sometimes, this side of heaven, man would never know.

Would Hunter's plea for Janie's heart to come back to him be approved? Maybe, maybe not. But faith in God, the kind of trust that says *Your will be done* would lead him to say *You are good, and You do good.*

Did Hunter yet have that kind of weighty faith?

He squeezed his eyes shut. "Your will be done." It was a weak whisper. Only a seedling in his heart. But it was there, reaching toward the life of the Son. "Your will be done."

The second time came stronger.

Hunter reached for his phone, sitting on the overturned log he used as a side table. Pulling up Janie's name, he started a new text.

You are capable, Janie. You can do this.

Send.

He tipped his face so that he had a full view of the stars shimmering in brilliant light. So close he might reach out and finger the sparkle of each diamond.

Can You bring forth the constellations?

No, Hunter could not. God was God and he was not. With an intentional yielding of his heart, Hunter left Janie in the hands that held all of heaven and earth. And he prayed that she would win.

"Your will be done."

Twenty-Six

She wasn't going to make it.

Janie wrapped her flannel-clad arms around her legs and laid her head against her knees. Her back tinged with sharp ache, and her shoulders blazed with tight heat. The pounding in her head throbbed—this headache worse than it'd been the night before.

Three more days...

Just three more days of hiking, backpacking. Three more nights of sleeping on the cold, hard ground.

She could do three more days.

No. I can't. And I don't want to.

That was the raw truth of it. She wasn't this girl. She wasn't Hazel Wallace or even Grady's college friend, Emma. She was just Janie. The girl who liked a good mattress and a warm comforter. The girl who thrived in a kitchen, not a canyon.

Maybe that made her a wimp. Right then, as her body sagged with exhaustion and muscles spasmed with pain, she didn't care. Much.

The scuffling sound of rocks beneath shoes alerted her to someone coming from behind her. Janie couldn't summon the energy to look back, but she felt fairly certain it would be Grady. He had consistently been the first one awake in camp, and by the smell of burnt coffee, she guessed he'd made her a cup.

"Morning." And that masculine voice, quiet against the breaking morning stillness, confirmed it.

Janie pulled in a draw of chilly arid air. And forced herself to turn. "Good morning."

She winced as she attempted to move. Grady held a staying hand, finished his walk toward her, then lowered onto the ground at her side. He passed her that steaming mug and settled his gaze on the eastern horizon.

A ball of golden-orange fire flickered above the rim of plateaued earth in the far distance, spilling its wealth of brilliant-yellow light into the canyon of hoodoos—an impressive gathering of spires—dialing up the natural pale orange and pinks of the sandstone to the richest orange red. Patches of snow and small areas of evergreens contrasted against the bowl of earthen fire. The breathtaking view was worthy of silent awe.

Light crawled up the canyon, and as the sun fingered her limbs, welcome warmth seeped into her tired muscles. Janie sipped the coffee Grady had brought her, grateful for the heat in her belly. She drew in a long breath and released it as a sigh of relief.

"You're tired." Grady reached to massage her neck with one hand. Rarely did he touch her—a hand here and there when there was a steeper section of trail. Fingers brushed her shoulders when he helped her relieve the burden of her pack. But something more personal? More tender?

Not really. Even this . . . His fingers were firm and kind, but the sensation behind it was friendly concern.

Janie released another sigh. "I am. This is . . . I've never done anything like this."

From the corner of her eye, she saw him nod. Then he rubbed his palm along the width of her shoulders. "Don't take this wrong, Janie." He paused, pulling his touch away. "I'm not trying to be cruel, but I think you need to go home."

His tone had been anything but mean, but tears pricked Janie's eyes just the same. She adjusted so that she faced him. "I'm holding you guys back."

He shook his head and then met her eyes. "That's not a worry—we're not in a race here. And no one is upset, so don't let your mind go there. The thing is . . ." He rubbed the back of his neck, his gaze drifting back to the spectacle of the canyon below. Then he looked back at her. "The thing is, I know you don't really want to be here. And I'm not sure that you'll make the Under-the-Rim Trail. If we'd done it first, maybe . . ." He shook his head. "I don't think it's wise for you to attempt it at this point."

Janie looked at the mug in her hand, studying the muddied contents within. She nodded. "I'm sorry, Grady."

"I know." He shook his head, then took her hand. "Janie, whatever compelled you to take this dare, I don't think it's worth it. And I think that whatever it was doesn't really have anything to do with backpacking or you leaving Luna."

She dared to peek at him. "I'm sorry I mixed you up in this."

A compassionate grin tipped his mouth, then he drew her knuckles to his lips. "Go home, Janie. Fix things with Hunter."

Shock had her eyes widening. Then heat flooded her face. "Grady, I didn't mean . . ."

"I know." He squeezed her hand. "Don't worry about me. I'm a big boy." He shifted to face the canyon again, letting go of her hand only to gently squeeze her neck again. "It was worth a shot, hmm?"

Relieved by his kindness, Janie chuckled. "If you think so, then you're nicer than most men. I think."

"Don't know about that." Grady stood, then motioned to her tent. "When you're ready, I'll help you pack up. There's a shuttle service at the next checkpoint. I'll call ahead and make sure one is running this late in the season, and if it's not, I'll make other arrangements for you."

Janie worked up the gumption to scramble to her feet. Grady lent her a hand, and she groaned as she stretched to full height. "I have never been this sore in my life."

"For the record, I'm impressed. First backpacking trip and you went more than ten days? That's remarkable."

"Thanks." She leaned back, attempting to loosen the clenching of her spine. Didn't help. "You're coming back to Luna, right?"

Grady chuckled, then he pulled her into a hug. "I'll be back, and I'll come looking for pie."

"If I still have a café."

"You will." He stepped back and squeezed her arm. "I have no doubt. You will." With a nod, he stepped away.

Janie sagged, part with relief, part with the weight of guilt. Mama had told her not to put Grady in the middle of her battle with Hunter. She wished she'd listened. It was only luck—or grace—that Grady had kept this situation from exploding.

Thinking of Mama, and home, she should let someone know she was heading back. Reaching into her coat pocket, Janie retrieved her phone.

Dead.

Of course it was. She hadn't charged it when they'd stopped at the last checkpoint. She'd been so tired that she'd found a rock to lean against and gone immediately to sleep. All the way until Grady had nudged her awake and regretfully told her they had to get going if they were going to make camp by sundown.

No matter. She'd find somewhere to charge it along the way. For now, she was going home. Even the dread of facing Hunter couldn't squelch the relief in that.

Twenty-Seven

Janie pressed her head against the window of the vehicle, glad she was alone in the backseat. Grady had made quick arrangements, and though she was once against thrust into traveling with strangers, she was too tired to care. She'd sleep all the way back to Montana.

The phone in her hand vibrated. Squinting one eye open, she expected that it was simply a battery alert.

But there was a new text. From Hunter.

You are capable, Janie. You can do this.

No, she couldn't. But the joy of going home offset the defeat. Even so, the need to sob nearly outweighed her body's demand for sleep. In fact, if she'd been alone, she would have done both—cried herself to sleep.

Go home... Fix things with Hunter. Grady's instructions pressed into the fuzziness of her emotions, and she smiled. She planned to do just that. In about ten hours, give or take.

Hopefully, by the time she got there, she could think straight.

Janie's silence was worse than her sparring. Especially when he'd laid aside everything that tangled him up into the mess he'd been and tried to encourage her in that text the night before, and she'd ignored him.

For a whole stinking day, Janie hadn't responded.

Hunter grabbed a broom and swept the subfloor that would soon be covered with dark stained hardwood. The roof had gone up, and the interior was dried in. That day—a sunny one—the roofers had laid shingles while the electrician had run the wiring.

Everything was progressing nicely. And Janie had nearly made the two-week mark.

How could he be so angry with her and proud of her at the same time?

With energy equal to the eight-hundred-meter races he used to run in high school, Hunter made the bristles of that tool swish-swash across the already clean surface until he came to the framing for the wide window that overlooked the pond.

It was the perfect view, just like he'd envisioned. And on this evening, with the lowering sun catching the iridescent light of the snow dusting the trees across the ice-covered water, it would be spectacular.

It should be spectacular.

TWENTY-SEVEN

But Hunter's damaged lungs were burning, and his shortness of breath wasn't due to the view, even if the gold-gilded sparkles were perfect. With the broom in his left hand, he propped the tool vertical against the floor and leaned against it. The wheezing from his lungs hummed into the air between his spot and the window a mere foot away.

So many mistakes.

Hunter squeezed his eyes shut, the pain in his chest more than the spasming of his damaged lungs. A series of recent replays scrolled through his mind.

You wouldn't last five days.

Such a stupid, cold, arrogant thing to say.

If winning her back was your plan, you took a wrong turn. This isn't going to get it done.

Bennett's blunt words hadn't been news, but their sharp accuracy sure did pierce like an arrow.

Come home.

Plain demand. One more reason Janie would never allow her heart to turn back to his. Why would a beautiful, successful, kind woman want a man who did and said such stupid, condescending things? He despised himself for them—there was no reason to think she wouldn't as well.

Opening his eyes, he caught the last layer of golden light fade from the shoreline across the pond as the sun sank behind the hills at his back. Darkness would fall fast, as it always did, leaving the canyon in a lightless chill that felt very much like the valley Hunter found his heart in.

And he had no one to blame but himself. "God, I can't seem to let this go." Every time he thought he had surrender down, another willful surge would roll.

If only he'd never made such an impetuous bet. If only he'd been successful in talking Janie out of it.

If only God would hurry up and make him the better man he longed to be.

Shadows enveloped the pond, the unfinished lodge, and Hunter himself, folding him in another lonely night. So much majesty and beauty surrounded him, but standing there alone, he felt only the vastness of emptiness. The plans for the Splendor that he'd made were moving forward with efficiency. The future seeming promising. But to go into it alone . . .

A shuddering breath left his lungs. Defeat pressed hard against him.

God, how can I live like this?

This plan he'd forged hadn't been for himself. Not from the beginning. Yes, he wanted a life that was purposeful and fulfilling. But this lodge wasn't intended to be all about him. He'd thought carefully about how he could provide for his sister with this. How they could someday pass on a better legacy.

And in his mind, he wouldn't be going forward with his hands empty. In his mind, there was Janie. Beside him, her hand in his, facing the future together as they'd promised so long ago. This lodge was for her. For all of them.

A chilled draft stirred at his back, followed by the sound of a door shutting.

Likely Hazel, or maybe Bennett. Hunter remained unmoving, staring at the nearly frozen pond while he labored to tuck away his broken heart.

"You win."

Hunter's spine snapped straight. Breath caught. Slowly he turned, letting the broom clatter to the floor.

A tear trickled from those beautiful blue eyes. When she tried to speak again, her lips trembled.

Hunter's heart fell to pieces all over again. He'd thought the last thing he'd wanted was to witness Janie walking into happiness on the arm of another man. Not so. As he watched this beautiful woman fight against tears of defeat, truth became very clear: *This* was the last thing he wanted.

With two cautious steps, he moved nearer. "I . . . what?"

Janie blinked, and another fat tear dropped from her eyelash. She swiped it away. "You won." Her jaw clenched as she swallowed, then she narrowed the space until a mere two-foot gap of chilly space remained between them. "I couldn't last two weeks, just like you said."

"You only had two days left."

She wrapped her arms tight around her middle. "I couldn't do it."

A surge of liquid heat blurred his vision. "Janie..." Hunter shook his head. "I didn't win anything."

Swiping another tear, Janie sniffed. "You don't want to claim your victory? You'd have my café and your hired cook."

Hunter motioned between them with two fingers. "This isn't what I wanted."

"Then why did you make the bet?" She stepped closer, her voice a hoarse whisper.

Hunter dared to trace the length of her arm with his fingertips. "I called it off. I don't want you as my hired help. I don't want you to lose the café."

That stubborn chin lifted. "Then what do you want, Hunter Wallace?"

"I want us to both stop losing." He stepped closer still.

Janie moved backward. "That's not how a bet works."

"I'm not talking about a bet." Reclaiming the proximity she'd pried open, he clasped her arm in a gentle hold. "I'm talking about you and me and this ongoing war. I want it to stop."

She trembled in his grasp but didn't retreat. Instead, she nodded. "How do you suggest that happen?" she whispered.

Hunter held her gaze, feeling himself pulled to her as a surge of warmth bloomed between them. Raising his left hand, he found he trembled as he slowly grazed his fingers up the length of her bare neck. His heart galloped when her eyes slipped closed at his touch.

He swallowed, desperately hoping he didn't screw this up. "Maybe we could start with me being honest."

Janie visibly swallowed. "Honest about what?"

"About why I keep acting like a jerk with you." He lowered his head, grazing her temple with his lips. "And telling you that I'm sorry for it."

Janie moved only enough to recapture his gaze. "I tried to be your friend, Hunter."

"I know, and it made me crazy."

"Why?"

"Because that's not what I want. It's not all that I want, and I don't know how to be a casual friend with the woman I'm still in love with." There. He'd said it. And meant it with every torn corner of his heart.

Janie stared up at him, a blend of disbelief and tenderness in her look. "You still . . ." She closed her lips and rolled them tight while her brow furrowed.

How could she not know? Hunter slipped both palms along her jawline to hold her face. "I never stopped, Janie. Even when I tried, I couldn't stop loving you."

A stream of tears rolled next to her nose. "You left," she cried.

A leftover ache rolled through his chest. Would they never recover from that? Hunter nodded. "You stayed." He felt the warm trail of his own tear cut a path toward his beard.

Dizziness swam through his head as Janie reached to smudge that wet trail with the pad of her thumb. "I'm sorry for it, Hunt."

Her touch was thrilling and comforting at once, and Hunter couldn't suppress the longing to feel the loveliness of her mouth any longer. She met his tentative kiss with equal hesitation.

"I wanted to hate you for hurting me," she whispered.

"I know," Hunter choked out.

A cry shuddered through her, and she gripped his shirtfront. "I was sure you hated me."

Pressing his forehead to hers, he closed his eyes. "I was angry. Disappointed. Hurt. But never hate. I can't, Janie." Opening his eyes, he let himself take in the beauty of her face. Was this, at last, the redemption of all that had been wasted between them? "I know it's come out all wrong, but the truth is that I can't stop loving you.

I'm sorry for all the ways I broke your heart." With a rattling inhale, Hunter took the final plunge. "Please tell me we can start again . . ."

Tears ran like spring rain down her soft face. Rather than answering, she pressed into his chest, slipping her arms around him. Hunter gathered her close, still uncertain about what her silence meant. But wanting more than his own reassurances for her heart's healing. Clearly she needed it.

They both did.

After several long minutes, her shoulders calmed their quaking, her hold around him loosened, and she slid her hands back to his chest. Leaning back only enough to look up at him, she sniffed. "It's been such a waste. These years of anger and bitterness."

So much of Hunter wanted to agree and to turn away from those ugly memories. Dark years of loneliness. Of resentment and ugliness. He deeply regretted all of that. But the study he and John and Bennett and José had been doing gave him pause. Slowly he shook his head. "Nothing is wasted by God. Isn't that something we can learn from Joseph, in Genesis?"

Those blue eyes widened, then Janie shook her head. "If I had been braver, we would have married. We could have been together this whole time, sharing happy memories rather than a seven-year war between us. Maybe we would have a couple of little ones by now, and . . ."

Her cheeks pinked, and he wondered why that embarrassed her. Hunter thrilled at the idea of raising a family with her. Right here in Luna, on the land of his inheritance at Lake Shore Splendor. He couldn't think of anything that would speak redemption more clearly than that.

But that would keep for later.

Smoothing her hair away from her wet face, he silently prayed for right thinking. "What if I had never changed, because I got exactly what I wanted and didn't feel the deep need of my soul? Maybe I wouldn't have met the Brightons, and John wouldn't have told me about Jesus."

Janie's furrowed brow smoothed.

Hunter let his hands drift down to hers, and then he clasped them. "And surely had we been together, you would have stopped me from sending Bennett to Elk Lake."

At that, her lips parted. "I would have."

Everything that was good and on the path to real healing now would never have sparked. Hazel wouldn't have Bennett. Hunter and Hazel would never have had some of those hard, honest conversations, and they would still be at silent odds with each other. Their childhood would still be in the murky shadows of misunderstanding and resentment. And Bennett wouldn't have woken from his own path of destruction via temporary amnesia and might still be the selfish, ungodly man he'd been before.

And those two precious teenage kids in Bennett's care? They'd not be there in Luna with them, that was for certain.

Was it all worth the heartache between Hunter and Janie?

Don't trust your own understanding... It was true! Hunter would never have understood any of that—even until this moment. But there it was—God had worked the bad for so much good!

Janie released a quavering breath. "I still regret hurting you, Hunter. I wish it had gone differently."

Oh... the sweet ache those words provoked. Streams of healing ribboned around his heart, flowing into a river of renewed love. Stronger, deeper than it had ever been before. Now infused with the pure love that came from knowing and walking with God, who was the author of true romance.

That last thought gave Hunter pause. *The author of true romance.* .. He could trust that. It seemed like such a simple thing—that God wrote his story, guided his steps, and redeemed his missteps. And yet, wow!

God had miraculously penetrated his stubborn, arrogant heart. He'd shown him real love—the kind that took a rebellious man, an orphan, and loved him anyway. Renewed him. Gave him a fresh life, new hope.

And now this?

Hunter didn't deserve it. Even when he'd tried to let Janie go, if that was what was best for her, he'd been ugly. And yet somehow here she was. Tucked against his chest, filling his arms. Drenching his heart.

"We're different now." Hunter secured her firmly against him. "I'm different now—and praise God for that. I'm still learning how to walk this new life. How to love better."

Janie reached to slide her palm along the side of his face. "Maybe we can learn together?"

The miracle of her offer exploded in his mind, sent his heart leaping, and provoked a laugh-cry that seemed embarrassingly unmanly. Even so, he leaned to brush a kiss across her lips. "With all my heart, Janie. That's what I want."

As he retreated, she curled her fists into his shirt and pulled him back. Her kisses were sweet and lingering. Tender. Then passionate. When he thought his chest might explode, Hunter slowed their kisses until they cooled back to gentle tokens of promise.

"I'm glad I couldn't do it," Janie whispered.

"Do what?"

She searched his face, her study delaying on his eyes. Man, he could drown in those pools of blue, soft with love, warm with wonder. Then she traced the edge of his bottom lip with the pad of her thumb. A sweet torture that made him hungry for her soft kisses all over again.

"Stop loving you," Janie responded.

Hunter chuckled and pulled her tight against him again. "If there must be one thing you're not capable of, Janie, I'm glad that is it." Hopefully... surely by now she knew he'd never doubted her ability to do well in whatever she set her mind to. To be certain of it, Hunter resolved in that moment to spend the rest of his days making sure she thoroughly knew his respect.

"Me too."

As she snuggled in deeper, Hunter felt the release of anxiety ease the tension in his neck and shoulders. He could spend the rest of his life like this—tangled in Janie's warm embrace. This time, he'd love her better. By God's grace, from this point forward, he would do life better.

And please, God, let it be a life with her.

Twenty-Eight

Though it wasn't anything she'd have dreamed up herself, Hazel took in the scene before her with a heart full of appreciation.

The Splendor was really something, even in this partially finished state. Beautiful, majestic, but somehow it beckoned one to marvel at the natural beauty of its surroundings. In fact, in the shadow of the mountain rising in layers all around it, and the shimmering water of the minor lake, that grand lodge seemed somehow understated.

Like it was meant to point out the majesty around it rather than to claim such glory for itself.

That evening as she approached the lodge from the ridge trail, Hazel smiled. Hunter had spent the day before stringing lights along the front deck and the roofline, preparing for this evening's gathering. The first, he'd said, of many Thanksgivings at the Splendor.

A year ago Hazel wouldn't have believed the amount of joy that filled her as she strode toward that scene. She wouldn't have imagined the scene at all.

As she passed the tree line, the sound of a vehicle approaching from the road gave her pause. She waited while Bennett's Bronco passed by, the passengers within all waving at her. Bennett, his mom—who'd insisted Hazel call her Tara—Gemma, and Nathan. Even Nathan wore a mildly pleasant expression.

She liked that. Surprisingly, she really liked Nathan. It was like she got him—she knew what he was thinking and why he acted the way he did. And he seemed to recognize that about her, and felt seen.

The Bronco parked, and the four people who now filled so much of her existence popped out. Huh. From just herself to now this . . .

Miracle?

That question kept resurfacing. And more and more, she felt the keen answer—yes.

Hazel jogged down the trail and met Bennett, who held out a hand for her. She gladly slipped hers in his, and he leaned down to snatch a quick kiss.

"Hi there, mountain lioness."

She grinned. "Happy Thanksgiving, city boy."

"It certainly is." He squeezed her hand, and then they followed the crew, who were already making their way toward the front of the lodge. "Nathan will get to move into a boot next week."

"That's good news."

"A relief for all of us."

Hazel chuckled. It was no secret that Nathan was getting more than sick of the crutches, and it brought out his worst self—which, to be honest, didn't take much.

"We'll have to think of some way to celebrate."

TWENTY-EIGHT

At her comment, Bennett stopped, tugging her to a halt beside him. For a long moment, he simply stared at her in the dimming evening light. Then he smiled—the sort of heart-melting grin that made her wonder how on earth she'd snagged him.

He could be with anyone . . .

But he chose her. Her heart stirred with sweet warmth.

He chose to be with her.

Miracle?

Yes.

"You keep surprising me, Hazel Wallace."

"What?"

Bennett shook his head, then lifted her hand to kiss the back of it. "You heard me." He winked, and they moved to join the party.

And it was a party. A celebration of Thanksgiving like none Hazel had remembered. Possibly because the holiday was often celebrated quietly in her cabin. Alone. Sometimes she'd made it to town, and then it was a small affair with Mama B and Janie.

This year they had all gathered at the recently dried in and powered Lake Shore Splendor. Hunter and Janie had invited—enthusiastically—them all to a dinner they would make.

Together.

Something giddy danced within as Hazel thought of her brother and her best friend finally reconciled. Together at long last.

The evening plunged forward. Dinner was as expected—delicious and more than enough, thanks to Janie's culinary efforts—along with some assistance from not only Mama B but Gemma and Tara as well. As darkness enfolded the lake and the lodge, the gathering made their way onto the front deck. The lights twinkled happily against the night, their reflections yellow gold against the black water of the lake.

Splendor indeed. Hunter certainly had a vision.

"Guys, will you give me just a minute?" Hunter spoke from alongside the railing, his arm draped over Janie and the twinkle lights just bright enough to reveal his wide smile.

"Congratulations on the lodge, my friend!" José lifted his mug of cinnamon cider. "It is awesome."

"Thanks." Hunter gripped his friend's shoulder, then he ran a hand down his bearded face. "But that's not the reason I want you to raise your cider mugs." His grin stretched as wide as the Montana sky. "My friends, let's raise a toast to the woman who prepared this amazing Thanksgiving meal for us. To Janie—the love of my life."

Mugs lifted, and a smattering of chuckles sounded through the group as everyone said "to Janie!" with heartfelt enthusiasm.

Janie beamed, though she ducked her head and waved off the praise. "I had help, and you all know it."

"I just need one more minute." Hunter turned to face Janie at his side, securing her hand in his.

"One more minute for what?"

Hunter knelt on the snow-dusted deck, and everyone drew in a collective breath. "One more minute to step into a life I've been yearning for. Janie Elizabeth Truitt, I've loved you since I was fifteen. I swear I'm going to love you until they put me in my grave. Will you marry me already?"

Janie stared at him, stunned. Then a tiny grin grew into full joy that mixed laughter and tears into one animated nod. She swiped her cheek, sniffed, and sputtered a "Yes!"

And in a half a breath, Hunter was on both feet and had her swept into his arms.

Hazel watched her brother and her best friend as they spun around in utter happiness. How could her heart feel so full and yet hollow at the same time? Biting her bottom lip, she clapped along with the rest of the gathering. And she dared to glance at Bennett, who stood near the railing opposite her.

His gaze had already locked on her. So much love there. But the hope? It wasn't in that long-held look. Instead, in the depths of those beautiful blue eyes was an ache. She felt it in that hollow corner of her heart.

The corner that wouldn't budge, wouldn't be filled, and wouldn't be ignored.

TWENTY-EIGHT

Hazel lowered her eyes, finding her fur-lined mukluks, and released a quiet, shuddering breath. How could she be this broken? Squeezing her eyes shut, the question settled heavy in her heart.

Bennett had found healing.

Hunter had found healing.

Janie had found it too.

Suddenly Hazel felt lonelier and more isolated than she ever had in all of her years living up at Elk Lake alone.

She was broken. And she wanted healing, the kind the people she loved had found.

But maybe it wasn't available for her.

Bennett held Hazel's hand as they walked toward the shadowy outline of her cabin. The soft crunch of snow beneath their feet and the occasional whisper of a breeze were the only sounds. Since passing through the cover of trees, neither had spoken a word.

In the silence, Bennett attempted to organize his thoughts. The evening had been perfect—and a beautiful celebration of life and hope and gratitude, capped by Hunter and Janie's engagement.

Shortly after the proposal, Bennett had clapped Hunter's shoulders and tugged him into a hug. "That was fast." He laughed.

"Over a decade in the making." Hunter had stepped back, his full smile locked in place. "We've wasted enough time. It's time to get on with life."

Bennett had nodded, shaking Hunter's hand and then wrapping Janie in a hug. "I'm happy for you."

"Thanks." Janie had patted his arm, then glanced behind him.

Bennett hadn't, but he guessed Janie was looking at Hazel, because when she'd shifted her eyes back to him, there was a hint of pity.

That only stirred the ache in his chest more.

An ache that refused to subside as he and Hazel neared the cabin.

"You've been really helpful with the kids, Zel." He felt inane as he spoke, but the long silence had become unbearable. He didn't want to dwell in it a moment longer. "Especially with Nathan. Thank you."

Stopping at the bottom of the deck steps, Hazel turned and looked up. "You don't have to thank me."

They were good together—worked together well. She made his life easier—better. And he'd seen so much growth in her over the past several months.

And he loved her. Man, how he loved her.

Tonight, love hurt. Like a giant hole in his chest, filled with a longing that seemed would never be quenched.

Hazel bit her lip, raised one hand to his chest. "Bennett..."

He could feel the strain in her voice and knew exactly what she was going to say. *Let's not change anything*... And he resolved to say okay. Kiss her good night and walk back toward the lodge alone.

"We could try..." Hazel's whisper blindsided him.

Brows furrowing, Bennett lifted his look from their joined hands to her eyes. "Try?"

She swallowed. "You... we..." She wet her lips. "We could live together."

His gut clenched, as if she'd kicked him. He wanted to cry—because this was his fault. He'd led her to believe that that sort of arrangement would be good enough. He wanted to be angry, because how could she think, after the conversations they'd had over the summer, that it would be good enough?

But that night, as he felt her heart's brokenness as much as he felt his own, Bennett shook his head and covered the small hand that rested on his chest. "It's been a good night. Let's not ruin it."

Hazel looked toward her cabin, rolling her lips together. Then she nodded. Finally in what seemed like a forced move, she met his gaze again. "I do love you, Bennett."

His lips quivered. He bent and brushed a kiss across her mouth. Then he turned, releasing her hand, and strode into the dark wilderness.

Midway back to the lodge, Bennett stopped. If he looked at just the right angle, he could see Hazel's lake, the black water catching the light of the rising moon.

Tears seeped onto his cheeks as he thought about the story in Genesis he'd recently read. Esau had sold his blessing for a bowl of soup, trading the future of blessing for a moment of satisfaction.

Bennett had done the same thing.

"God, I'm sorry..."

His shoulders quaked as he lowered onto the snow-covered earth. There he sat, hands covering his face.

How many times could he fail before God would give up on him?

That was not the last time you saw Esau...

The whisper nestled into his tumultuous mind. Bennett's knowledge of the Bible was limited, but he'd read enough to know that when Esau and Jacob had finally met again, years after their dramatic fallout, the older brother was not the vengeful man one would have expected. Though Jacob approached his estranged brother with well-deserved fear, Esau greeted Jacob with open arms.

Something had happened in Esau that enabled him to live well—even if he was not the chosen brother. Even if he'd traded his birthright for a moment of fleshly satisfaction.

There was mystery in that. And in that hard, desperate moment, a glimmer of hope.

Bennett's thoughts moved from the Old Testament to the New, to a teaching of Jesus in Matthew. As he wiped his eyes and raised his face toward the starry night, he repeated the simple prayer of the tax collector in Jesus's parable. "God, have mercy on me, a sinner."

That was all he could ask or do. He couldn't change Hazel. He couldn't make this pain go away. But he could cast himself upon the mercy of God.

No, that wasn't all. That was everything.

THE END

(for now...)

I HOPE YOU ENJOYED this return to Luna, Montana! Isn't it exciting to see Hunter and Janie figure out their tangled relationship? Yay for their engagement—we have a Lake Shore Splendor wedding in our future! But Bennett and Hazel... oh boy. They're still on a rough road, aren't they? Will they be able to find themselves on something more stable? And will Hazel ever bend her stubborn heart toward God?

Rest assured, we have more to discover at Elk Lake Canyon! Hunter and Janie, Bennett and Hazel . . . their stories aren't done, not to mention Gemma and Nathan and Tara Crofton.

And, hmmm . . . Isa . . . what's going on with her?

Keep watching for the release of those stories in the next few months. Be on the lookout for Lake Shore Awakening, book 4 in the Redemption Shores Saga—coming to you in the spring of 2024 (I'm aiming at late March)!

I hope you've enjoyed this third book in Redemption Shores. Would you please leave an honest review to let other readers know what you think? Thank you!

Printed in Great Britain
by Amazon